Stepping STONE

THE STONE SERIES: BOOK TWO

DAKOTA WILLINK

AWARD-WINNING AND INTERNATIONAL BESTSELLING AUTHOR

PRAISE FOR THE STONE SERIES

"There's a new billionaire in town! Fans of Fifty Shades and Crossfire will devour this series!"
— **After Fifty Shades Book Blog**

"It's complex. It's dirty. And I relished every single detail. This series is going to my TBR again and again!"
— **Not Your Moms Romance Blog**

"This read demanded to be heard. It screamed escape from the everyday and gave me that something extra I was looking for."
— **The Book Junkie Reads**

"Hang on to your kindles! It's a wild ride!"
— **Once Upon An Alpha**

"A definite page turner with enticing romance scenes that will make you sweat even during those cold winter nights!"
— **Redz World**

"Alexander and Krystina are an absolute must read!"
— **Tracie's Book Review**

DAKOTA WILLINK, LLC

This book is an original publication of Dakota Willink, LLC

Copyright © 2016 by Dakota Willink
ALL RIGHTS RESERVED.
IN ORDINANCE WITH THE U.S. COPYRIGHT ACT OF 1976, NO PART OF THIS BOOK
MAY BE REPRODUCED IN ANY FORM OR BY ANY ELECTRONIC OR MECHANICAL MEANS
WITHOUT WRITTEN PERMISSION FROM THE AUTHOR. PLEASE DO NOT PARTICIPATE
IN OR ENCOURAGE UNLAWFUL PIRACY OF THE AUTHOR'S INTELLECTUAL PROPERTY.

Library of Congress Cataloging-in-Publication Data
ISBN-10: 0997160330
ISBN-13: 978-0997160338
ISBN-13: 978-1-954817-11-1
Stepping Stone | Copyright © 2016 by Dakota Willink
Cover art by BookCoverMasterClass.com Copyright © 2017

BOOKS BY DAKOTA WILLINK

The Stone Series
(Billionaire Romantic Suspense)
Heart of Stone
Stepping Stone
Set In Stone
Wishing Stone
Breaking Stone

The Fade Into You Series
Untouched (New Adult Romance)
Defined (Second Chance Romance)
Endurance (Sports Romance)

Take Me Trilogy
(Billionaire Romantic Suspense)
Take Me Under
Take Me Darkly
Take Me Forever

Standalone Titles

The Sound of Silence
(Dark Romantic Thriller)

Please visit www.dakotawillink.com for more information.

STEPPING STONE

THE STONE SERIES: BOOK 2

DAKOTA WILLINK

DRAGONFLY INK PUBLISHING

To my husband...
My heart and the greatest man I've ever known.

Krystina

The wind whipped around me, causing my hair to slap me across the face. I impatiently shoved it out of my eyes and fumbled with the credit card reader prompts at the gas pump.

No, I do not want a car wash. No, I do not want a receipt.

The only thing I wanted was to fill my tank and get out of the rain. It had been a long day. The drive that morning to Stamford, Connecticut from my apartment in Greenwich Village took longer than expected. Traffic out of the city had been a complete bear, and I had hoped to make it back in time to miss the rush-hour commuters.

"Card read error. Please see attendant," said a computerized voice from the speaker on the gas pump.

"Dammit," I swore. Hastily shoving my credit card into the pocket of my suit jacket, I hurried towards the main building of the gas station.

Once inside, I brushed the rain droplets from my sleeves and was grateful to see there wasn't a line at the checkout counter.

"How can I help you, Miss?" asked the elderly gentleman working behind the counter.

"The pump wouldn't read my card. I was told to come inside to pay."

"I'm sorry about that. That one's been acting up all day. Are you looking to fill her up?"

"Yes, please. Thirty dollars should do it."

"Okay. Let me see here..." he trailed off in concentration, pulling his glasses down the bridge of his nose to peer at the computer screen before him. Taking my credit card, he began inputting my purchase into the register's computer at a painstakingly slow pace.

I tapped my foot, trying to ward off the impatience I felt. Using the merchandise displayed at the register as a distraction, I scanned over the assortment of candy bars, beef jerky, and chewing tobacco. A pack of Big Red chewing gum caught my eye and caused me to smile wistfully in remembrance of an innocent flirtatious gesture.

Almost instantly, pain lanced at my chest, and I pushed the thought away.

Don't think about it.

Acting on impulse, I grabbed the pack of cinnamon-flavored gum and tossed it on the counter.

"I'll take this, too," I told the gray-haired cashier.

After what seemed like forever, the man handed my credit card back to me.

"You are all set, Ms. Cole. Have a lovely evening," he told me, taking me by surprise. Living in today's plastic society, I didn't think people paid much attention to the names on credit cards anymore.

I thanked the gentleman in return, pocketed my card and the gum, then headed back outside to fill my tank.

When the gas pump came to a halt, I screwed the gas cap back onto the prehistoric old Ford and hurried to get back into the car. After fastening my seatbelt, I leaned my head back against the seat, dreading the long drive home.

Do I really want to do this commute every day?

I knew the answer, but I didn't have much choice. Marketing jobs in New York City were proving to be almost nonexistent. When I received the call yesterday for a job interview in Stamford, I didn't think twice about it. I woke up bright and early today, risked my life on the I-95, and completely aced the interview with LD Marketing Solutions. I was offered a job on the spot.

The only thing left to do was accept the position.

As if on cue, my cell pinged with an email notification. It was from the lead coordinator at LD. I opened the email and quickly scanned the contents. It was a thank you letter with a formal job proposal attached. I didn't have to open the attachment to know what it said. They already quoted me the starting salary and benefits package. It was a sweet deal.

Frustrated, I tossed my cell phone into my purse.

"I just don't know what to do," I said aloud to the empty car.

The reason for not immediately taking the offer from LD Marketing nagged at me as I shifted the car into drive and headed towards the interstate. Deep down, I knew I was still undecided about the job opportunity with Turning Stone

Advertising. However, the solution to that should have been obvious.

If I wanted to avoid seeing Alexander Stone, there was no way I could actually work at a company he owned.

Don't think about him. Separate it and focus on the job possibilities.

But despite the numerous lectures I gave to myself, it was hard not to have the two coincide. While the offer from LD Marketing was a good one, the opportunity at Turning Stone was even better. I went from having zero job prospects to having two practically overnight. The problem was the job with Turning Stone came with a major string attached to it.

Alexander.

Crossing his path would be inevitable, and I wasn't sure if I had the strength to withstand him. In fact, I *knew* I didn't have the strength. Our short-lived relationship was proof of it.

He was like a drug to me—toxic and unhealthy and so undeniably addictive.

During the few short weeks Alexander and I spent together, something shifted inside of me. But I had yet to determine if it was for the good or the bad. He uncovered parts of me I hadn't known existed, revealing dark desires I hadn't been aware of. Nevertheless, I was confused over my newfound passion. I didn't know if it was real or if it was just something messed up in my psyche.

But how am I supposed to know? It's not like I have a ton of experience.

My history with men was a short list, but it was a tainted one. The only long-term relationship I'd had to date was with Trevor Hamilton, the controlling, abusive asshole who had beaten and raped me.

I shuddered as the memories threatened to resurface.

I had stayed away from men altogether after that disaster, and I had been happy.

But was I really?

I thought I was until Alexander Stone came into the picture. Our chance meeting had changed everything for me. I had been drawn to him from the moment I saw him. There was no refuting the carnal need burning between us. With only one look from him, the air in the room would hiss and crackle, like the wick of a time bomb waiting to explode. So, I decided to take a chance.

However, Alexander turned out to be more than I bargained for. Even then, I was willing to give it more time— to give *us* more time. But then Alexander took me to the BDSM nightclub. I received a slap in the face from my ugly past that night, sparking a knee-jerk reaction. I wasn't sure if that night was a blessing or a curse.

I mean, really? I hadn't seen Trevor in two years. What were the odds of seeing him there, of all places?

No matter what the odds were, in an instant, my past and present collided. The lines became blurry, and I no longer knew who I was. So, I did the only thing I could do to survive. I said goodbye to it all.

Including Alexander.

Until I could sort things out, I had to put some distance between us.

Distance?

I snorted out loud at the term.

I pretty much ran from Alexander that night at Club O.

In the days that followed, I considered going back to my shrink but decided against it. I thought about talking to Allyson, my roommate, but there was too much she didn't know. I eventually came to the conclusion I didn't need anyone else to tell me what was wrong. I already knew. My past was interfering with my ability to be in a healthy relationship. I was the only one who could work that out. If it meant being alone for a little while longer, so be it.

The thought of being alone again tore at my heart, and a feeling of melancholy settled around me.

Snap out of it, Cole. It's in the past.

The check engine light for the car flickered on. I tapped the dashboard to see if it would go off. Usually, that worked, but for some reason, it wasn't this time. I pursed my lips in annoyance.

I really need to get this car in to see what's going on.

The only reason I hadn't yet was because I rarely drove the thing. Public transportation was easier and cheaper in the city, so there hadn't been a need. However, if I decided to take the job in Connecticut, I would have to look into getting a more reliable set of wheels sooner rather than later.

I continued the drive in silence. I didn't dare turn on the radio, as every song I heard seemed to remind me of Alexander in some way or another. Quiet was better, as I could use the time to simply think.

Not about the past, but my future.

2

Alexander

I drummed my fingers on the desktop, anticipating the video footage that should be arriving in my inbox momentarily. I had been waiting to receive it for a full solid week. But now that I knew it was finally being sent, edginess was beginning to get the best of me.

Why I was so hell-bent on seeing it was beyond me. I already convinced myself that what happened was for the best. I knew Krystina Cole and I were not cut out for one another. We were incompatible in more ways than I could count—she was nothing but a ball of sass, and I was the man who failed to dominate her. But I also knew I had to have answers for why she so suddenly took off on me.

You're an idiot, Stone. Just let it go.

I spun in my office chair and stared through the glass wall at the Manhattan skyline. I wanted to let it go, to let *her* go. But even after two weeks, she was still at the forefront of my mind. It was making me restless. Irritable.

But worse—I felt empty.

I have always been so sure of who I was and what I wanted out of life. But now, here I sat, not knowing a damn thing. I didn't know how I had let some woman fuck it all up.

Because she wasn't just another woman.

She was Krystina Cole.

My angel.

A stab of regret sliced at my heart, annoying me beyond all belief. Regret was a sign of weakness and failure.

That's not who I am.

My inbox finally pinged with the arrival of the much-anticipated email and broke me away from my thoughts. Turning back to the computer, I clicked on the link that would take me to the video feed.

Convincing the owner of Club O to give me the video from the night I took Krystina to the exclusive nightclub had required some major finagling. For the privacy concerns of the other members, he had been reluctant to give it up. I had to call in more than just a few favors in order to obtain it.

Thankfully the footage wasn't that long, as we had only been in the club for about two hours that night. The hard part was going to be locating Krystina amidst the crowd of hundreds.

I scanned the grainy black and white video and took note of the time stamp.

21:43. That was around the time we entered The Dungeon.

I fast-forwarded the feed to thirty minutes later, knowing exactly where we had been at that time. We were on the platform, watching a staged BDSM scene unfold below us on the dance floor. Within seconds, I was able to point out Krystina. She was leaning back against my chest, her lush curls rippling over her shoulders as she took in everything happening below.

I watched her face, mesmerized by her beauty, and I felt my heart constrict. I reached out and touched her face on the computer monitor.

Fuck me. I miss her so much.

Despite the poor quality of the video, I was still able to make out her facial expressions. She went from curious to astounded in the blink of an eye, her conflict causing me to feel another pain of regret.

I shouldn't have brought her there. It was too much for her.

I shook my head, dismissing the thought I had been repeating for two weeks.

What's done is done. There's no changing it.

I advanced the video a little more, bringing it to the time when I walked away from her to use the restroom. This was the part that interested me most. For when I returned, Krystina had changed. Something had happened during the time I stepped away. I was sure of it.

I watched her sip her drink and tap her foot to what I assumed to be the beat of the music that could not be heard in the silent video. After a few moments, a man stepped up behind her. She glanced over her shoulder at him, but when she turned back, her face was panicked.

I hit pause and zoomed in as much as I could without distorting his facial features. He was the man Krystina, and I had run into as we were exiting the club.

The asshole.

Who the hell is this guy to her?

I resumed playing the video and watched when Krystina turned back to him. From this angle, I could no longer see her face. However, I could see his smug expression as plain as day, and it pissed me off.

He reached out to touch her, and she jerked away, causing her drink to fall out of her hand and splash all over the floor. She didn't even seem to notice it as her arms waved about angrily.

And he—he was obviously laughing at her.

What did he say to her?

I slammed my fist onto the desk, angry I hadn't been there to help her—angry she didn't tell me who this guy was when I asked her.

And angry because she had walked away from me.

Why?

A knock at my office door interrupted me. Bryan, my accountant, popped his head in.

"What's up, Bryan?" I snapped, annoyed at the disruption.

"I just finished running the last two weeks of expense reports. It isn't pretty, Alex," he told me.

I sighed and shook my head. As much as I wanted to tell him to get lost and I didn't give a flying shit about the expense reports, I knew I needed a diversion from the video before I started a full-out manhunt for this stranger who upset Krystina. I was ready to snap and forced myself to take a calming breath before speaking again.

"You're such a miser. You never think it's pretty." I turned back to my computer, paused the video, and switched off the monitor. "Come in, and let's get this over with."

Bryan laughed.

"That's why you pay me the big bucks. Somebody has to keep an eye on you," he joked, claiming the seat in front of my desk.

"Say what you want, wise guy. But I managed just fine before taking in your sorry ass," I told him.

My accountant and longtime friend was brilliant with numbers. If the truth were told, he was better with them than I was. I had the business head, but he was the one to keep the many financial pieces in place. Hiring him was one of the best decisions I ever made.

"The design consulting fee came in from Kimberly Melbourne," Bryan began. "It's insane. I don't know why you use her."

"You know why I do," I quipped.

"I know, I know—because she's the best. But even so, this is just for the consultation. You haven't even gotten the final bill yet."

I waved him off, not caring about the damn bill. Making sure the offices for Turning Stone Advertising were top-notch was the concern, even if I didn't have Krystina to lead the team.

At least for the moment.

"You've made your point. What's next?" I asked, ready to move on.

"The property in Westchester. What's your interest in it?"

"I haven't decided yet, but the price was good."

"You do know it's zoned residential, right?"

"Of course, I do," I snapped.

"Just checking," he said, hands held up in mock surrender. "I know you had Laura working on obtaining the details for it. I just wanted to make sure she didn't miss that one key fact. Lately, your focus has been on commercial properties only."

"Laura wouldn't miss something that important."

Bryan looked pointedly at me and leaned back in his chair.

"Hey, man. Look, let me stop being your accountant for five minutes. You've been in a foul mood for over a week now. What's up?"

"Nothing. I'm fine."

"That's a load of bullshit. Matteo mentioned you were seeing someone. Is she the reason you're so wound up?"

I narrowed my eyes at him, warning him to back off.

"Matt has a big fucking mouth. I said I'm fine. Besides, I'm not seeing her anymore. Just drop it," I added with finality.

He looked at me skeptically but picked up his file again and didn't push it further. He thumbed through a few papers and resumed where we left off.

Thirty minutes later, we finished going through the rest of the reports.

"I hesitate to bring up this last thing."

"Just get it out, Bryan. As you pointed out, I'm already in a foul mood, so it can't get much worse."

"I know this is important to you, but the money you're shelling out for Stone Arena is making me nervous. And before you go off half-cocked, allow me to clarify. It's not the investment that concerns me. It's the hefty price tag for the naming rights."

"We've been through this at least a hundred times," I said, pursing my lips in irritation. If Bryan wasn't my friend, I might have fired him for the sole reason of bringing the subject up *again*.

"I get it. Seeing European football become mainstream in the States was your grandfather's dream. You've told me all the reasons why the soccer arena is important to you. But I wouldn't be doing my job if I didn't advise you against it one last time."

I glared at him.

"I've heard you—loud and clear many times. I'm not budging on this one," I asserted.

"Okay, okay. It's your money," he conceded as he stood up to leave. "Oh, and one more thing. There is a discrepancy in one of the reports. Not with the business, but with your personal expenses. You were double charged for the Mandarin Day Spa. For some reason, it hit Justine's expense account and your personal expense account."

"Justine?"

"Yeah. I'm assuming your sister went there last week."

So did Krystina.

"Yes," I replied absently, not sure what to think about the coincidence of Krystina and Justine going to the same spa. "Justine said something about planning a spa day with Suzanne."

"It's no big deal. I'll just have Laura call the Mandarin and straighten it out."

"Do you know what day Justine was there?" I asked, even though I was fairly certain of the answer.

Bryan began riffling through his spreadsheets.

"She was there on Saturday. Two weeks ago. Why?"

"The charges are correct. Krystina was also there that day, and her expenses were charged to my account."

Bryan raised his eyebrows in surprise.

"Krystina? Is that the name of the girl you were seeing? I didn't realize it was that serious."

"It wasn't. And when you pass by Laura, please tell her to come in here," I added dismissively.

I was suddenly in a rush to get him out of my office. A few pieces to the puzzle were starting to fit together, and I was overwhelmed with a sense of urgency to put them all together.

A few minutes later, my PA knocked on the office door.

"Mr. Stone, Bryan said you wanted to see me?"

"Yes, Laura. Two things. I want an update on the Westchester deal emailed to me by the end of the day tomorrow. Also, find the phone number for Allyson Ramsey. She works for Ethan DeJames, so it shouldn't be too difficult to track her down. Once you have it, send it to my phone."

"Yes, sir. Anything else?"

"No. That's it. I'll be leaving here shortly, and I might be tied up for the rest of the night. Route anything of importance through Hale, and he'll get in touch with me if it needs my immediate attention."

"Will do. Enjoy the night, Mr. Stone."

"Thank you, Laura."

Once she was gone, I turned back to my computer and the video feed I had been watching. I backed up the footage by a few minutes and took a screenshot of the man who was harassing Krystina at Club O. After sending the image to my cell phone, I powered down the computer, grabbed my suit jacket, and made my way to the parking garage attached to my building.

Climbing into the Tesla, I reached for my phone and was

happy to see Laura was able to obtain Allyson's number so quickly.

Here goes nothing.

I dialed the number and hoped my instincts were correct.

"This is Ally. How can I help you?" she answered.

"Allyson, it's Alexander Stone."

There was silence on the other end of the line for a moment before she spoke again.

"I'm at work, Alexander."

"I figured. We need to talk. Alone."

"About what? I mean, other than the fact Krys has been acting weird."

"Weird? In what way?"

"She's just not herself. Krys tells me everything, but she's been really tight-lipped. Then this morning, she took off for a job interview in Stamford, and I was like—whoa! What happened to Turning Stone? What's going on with you two, Alex?"

"We had a bit of a..." I trailed off, feeling somewhat shocked that Allyson knew nothing about Krystina and me splitting. I tried to think of the best way to summarize things. "It's a long story. And honestly, I don't really know what happened."

"Okay, buddy. Now you've got me worried. What did you do to her?" she accused.

Why is it always the guy's fault?

I glanced at the clock. It was going on four.

"I can be to you by four-thirty. I might be able to shed some light on a few things. Maybe together, we can figure out what's going on in that stubborn brain of hers."

"Oh, so now she's stubborn? You listen to me, Sto—,"

"Allyson, please," I cut her off. "Trust me on this."

I could sense her hesitation, but fortunately, she agreed before I had to do something more drastic.

"Make it five o'clock. I still have a few things to wrap up here," she informed me.

"Fine. See you then."

————

I SAT DOUBLE-PARKED in front of Ethan DeJames. Horns blared at me in frustration, but I didn't give a rat's ass. It was ten minutes after five. Allyson was late. I was usually a patient man, but I found my patience running thin at that moment. I tapped my thumb on the steering wheel in irritation.

When she finally came out of the building fifteen minutes later, it was all I could do to not lose my mind on her when she climbed into the passenger seat.

"Sorry. I was dealing with a temperamental model," Allyson apologized as she climbed into the passenger seat. "They always think they know best. Geez, it's freezing outside!"

She ran her hands up and down her arms to ward off the chill.

"Here. Take my coat," I offered, shrugging out of my suit jacket.

"Thanks," she said, not hesitating to take the jacket from me. "It was warmer this morning. I didn't know the temperature would drop so much, or else I would have worn a coat today."

"No problem. We've been spoiled with the warm weather up until now," I said casually, trying to ease into a conversation with a bit of small talk. "I appreciate you taking the time to meet with me."

Suddenly all business, Allyson turned and looked incisively at me.

"Cut the BS, Alex. What's going on?"

A straight shooter. Good. I don't want to pussyfoot around any more than you do, sweetheart.

I went right to it and showed her the screenshot from the Club O video feed. Her face instantly paled, and I felt my stomach drop. The man in the picture was probably exactly who I feared it was, but I had to ask nonetheless.

"Who is this?" I asked.

"Where did you get this?" she returned rather than answer me.

"It's a screenshot of the video feed from a club I took Krystina to."

"I don't know who it is. You'll have to ask Krys."

She pressed her lips together into a stubborn line, stared out the windshield, and wouldn't say more.

"Don't play games with me. I have a master's degree in psychology, and you're a terrible liar. I can tell by your face. You know who it is."

Allyson's head whipped around so fast that I would be surprised if she didn't strain a muscle.

"Don't try to psychoanalyze me, Stone," she bit out. "I say you should ask Krys because this isn't my story to tell. If you want answers? Ask her."

"I believe I already know the answer," I replied calmly. "I just need you to confirm."

"You don't know anything."

"Actually, I do. Krystina filled me in on her past and how she was raped."

"She told you that?"

Her eyes flashed with hurt, and I instantly realized my mistake. Krystina told me she never shared the details of her horrific experience with anyone else. And that included Allyson. I had been the only one she told.

"Yes. It was difficult for her, but she did eventually tell me. Don't look so hurt over it, though. There's a reason why she did."

"Really? Because I can't think of why she would confide in you, someone who is practically a stranger," she spat out accusingly.

She turned to look out the windshield again and crossed her arms. Whether it was in anger or because she felt wounded, I couldn't be sure. I only knew I didn't have time to worry about her ego just then.

"Allyson, look at me," I ordered. When she turned back, I was as blunt as possible to make her understand. "She told me because she was afraid she couldn't give me what I wanted—her submission."

She raised one eyebrow at me, looking as if I had sprouted antlers. At the very least, her surprise told me Krystina never divulged anything to Allyson about what we did behind closed doors.

She shook her head in disbelief.

"This is a flipping joke, right?"

"No, it's not a joke. I'm a Dominant."

"Oh, well, doesn't this just get better and better!" she

exclaimed, tossing her hands up in the air. "How in the hell did Krys get herself mixed up with you? I can't believe I didn't know! Wait—I did know! But then she backtracked on what she said and... Either way, I dismissed it all. I wasn't paying close enough attention to her. This is bad. I'm a terrible friend! To go from not dating anyone for years to messing around with a Dominant! I'm sure she had no idea what she was getting herself into!"

Interrupting the mini-rant she was having with herself, I held the phone out for her to see the screenshot again.

"Allyson, chill out. Krystina is a big girl, and she can make decisions without consulting you first," I said dryly. "I didn't force her to do anything she didn't want to do. But now, I'm really worried about her. Especially since I now know she didn't talk to you about the night we went to Club O. Is the name of the man in this picture Trevor?"

She stared at the picture for a few moments before seeming to come to a decision.

"Yes. That's him. Trevor Hamilton," she finally said. "Now, are you going to tell me why he was in the same place as you and Krystina?"

I exhaled the breath I hadn't realized I was holding. I had hoped my suspicions were wrong about who the guy was in the picture, and I was overwhelmed with guilt over leaving Krystina alone to deal with that monster. I wanted nothing more than to get to her. To hold her. To tell her everything would be okay.

I closed my eyes and leaned my head back against the seat, not wanting to get into the long, sordid tale of how Krystina was driven to walk away from me.

"It's too long of a story, Allyson," I tried to dismiss.

"Well, it's about a twenty-minute drive back to my place. You can tell me about it on the way."

I admired her tenacity, even if it was grating on my nerves. Knowing I wasn't going to put off this incorrigible woman, I didn't hesitate with my response.

"You'll get the abbreviated version. Deal?"

"Deal."

Putting the car in drive, I merged into traffic and began giving her a brief synopsis about my relationship with Krystina and how we came to be at Club O.

By the time we pulled up to the apartment building Krystina and Allyson shared, I had come to the end of the story. Somehow, I managed to tell the tale without revealing the complication of my mother and father. I wasn't going to get into that with her, especially since Krystina didn't know the whole truth.

Once I had successfully squeezed the Tesla in between two cars on the curbside, I turned to face Allyson. She had been silent the entire time I was speaking, but her expression was thoughtful. It was as if she were trying to piece it all together, just like I had been.

"After we argued for a few minutes, she got out of the car and walked away. I haven't heard from her since," I finished.

"That's it? I mean, you didn't go after her?"

"It was a difficult moment. She said things, and I wasn't thinking straight."

"Have you spoken to her at all since that night?"

"No. Our only communication was a few texts I sent her about the job at Turning Stone. I wanted to let her know it was still on the table, but she never replied to me," I said and pursed my lips in annoyance. Krystina's lack of response had infuriated me. "Either way, it doesn't matter. I know I made a mistake. I shouldn't have let her walk away in the first place."

"Yeah, dumbass. You can say that again," she said, but there was no real heat in her words—only sadness.

"I'm going to get her back, Allyson."

"I like you, Alex. I don't know why," she said with a frown. "You're nothing but one giant sack of bad news for Krys. But I can tell you really care for her. Your eyes soften when you talk about her. She won't be easy to win over again. She's stubborn as a mule."

I laughed at that.

"Trust me, I know it!"

"Wishing you luck won't make a damn bit of—" The ringing of her cell phone cut her off. "Well, speak of the devil."

"Krystina is calling you?" I asked quickly.

"Yeah. So?"

"Don't tell her I'm with you. I haven't decided how I'm going to play this yet."

She threw a strange look at me before pulling her phone out of her purse.

"Hey, doll," she said into the receiver. After a few minutes, she spoke again. "Time for you to dump that hunk of junk, Krys. But yeah, I'll be there as soon as I can."

She ended the call and tossed the phone back into her purse.

"What was that about?" I asked.

"Her piece of crap car broke down on I-95. I have to go and get her."

Instantly, the play I had been looking for fell onto my lap. I seized the opportunity.

"Let me go to get her."

"Hell, no! Are you nuts? Talk about an ambush!" she exclaimed and shook her head back and forth rapidly.

"Allyson, I need time with her."

"She'll want to kill me!"

"Then she'll get over it. Trust me."

"Do you use that line on her? 'Trust me' with that smooth voice of yours?"

I smirked at her mocking tone, and for some reason, she found it humorous.

"Are you laughing at me?"

"Yes, Stone. I think I am. But you're right. You and Krystina need to figure this thing out. I'm worried about her. She hasn't been acting like herself for a while now. Go get her, and I'll deal with the fallout later."

I smiled then, happy I managed to convince her of my way of thinking. I knew winning back Krystina's affection would take some work, but Allyson may prove to be an asset to me.

"I'll try to soften the blow for you," I said with a wink.

She opened the door to climb out of the car. But before she shut it, she leaned back down, her face becoming serious.

"Take my advice, Alex. Go slow. Baby steps. As strong as Krys can be, she's also fragile. You'll have to tread carefully on the stepping stones to her heart."

3

Krystina

Through my review mirror, I saw headlights approach and pull off to the side of the road. However, even though it was dark outside, and the rain had slowed to a drizzle, I could tell it was not Allyson's Jeep behind me. The headlights were too low to the ground. I started to get nervous when I saw a shadow of a man exit the car and head towards me. I quickly fished around in my purse for my can of pepper spray.

When I turned back, I was shocked to see Alexander Stone's astonishing blue eyes peering at me through the glass. My heart crashed against my chest. I sat there, completely stunned, staring back at him. Seeing him again turned me into an unresponsive, trembling mess.

What is he doing here?

He needed to shave, which was uncharacteristic of him. And although the stubble was unusual, it did nothing to mask the handsome features underneath. That perfectly chiseled face, square jaw, and those intensely bright blue eyes—he was just as devastating as ever.

He must have recently come from work because he was still wearing a shirt and tie. However, his sleeves were rolled to his elbows, and his blue tie was loosened at the neck. It was damp and chilly outside today, and I absently wondered why he didn't have his suit jacket on.

He made a motion for me to roll down the window, bringing me back to reality. I was relieved there wasn't a serial killer standing outside of my car, but I was still stunned to see it was Alexander. I had to remember to keep my wits about me, as just the sight of him threatened every molecule of intelligence I possessed to abandon me.

Don't bend, don't bend. Hold your ground. You can do it.

I gave myself a pep talk as I waited for the window to roll down.

"Why don't you have a coat on? It's cold outside," I scolded.

"Starting a fight with me already, Miss Cole."

"Well, er...no," I faltered. "I-I was only making an observation."

He flashed me a crooked smile, and I just about melted into a puddle.

"Oh, angel. How I've missed you."

I felt my heart flutter from his words. We stayed staring at each other, still and silent, his face remarkably impassive as he studied me.

"What are you doing here?" I asked in an attempt to break the silence. "Where's Ally?"

"I'm assuming she's at home, as that's where I dropped her off."

"Wait, what? You were with Ally? Why?"

"Always so many questions," he chuckled. "I'll explain it later. What seems to be wrong with your car?"

"I don't know. But it doesn't matter. I'll figure it out. I don't need you to help me."

"And just as stubborn as ever," he laughed.

"Don't mock me, Alex."

"I would never," he admonished, his eyes alight with humor. "So, are you going to tell me what's wrong with your car? Or do I have to stand out here in the rain until you let go of your pigheadedness?"

I narrowed my eyes at him, annoyed he was right. I was in a bind and was left little choice in the matter, thanks to Allyson. She had some major explaining to do.

"The stupid check engine light has been coming on now and again, but it usually goes off after a bit, so I didn't worry about it. But then it started making this weird grinding sound, and smoke started to come out from under the hood. That's when I pulled over and called Ally. So you can imagine my surprise when I saw it was you coming to my rescue," I finished dryly.

"Hmm," he mused. "Hop out of the car. Let me see if I can figure out what's going on."

I opened the car door to climb out, but my arm got caught in the seatbelt and caused me to stumble. When Alexander grabbed hold of my elbow to steady me, an electric current lit me on fire.

I looked up into his eyes. They were scorching, searing

right through me and fanning the flames flickering in my belly.

Oh, no...

"Don't do that," I told him.

"Do what?"

"That thing with your eyes. You're trying to eye-sex me."

He flashed me another crooked smile, and a low chuckle reverberated through him.

"Is it working?"

Um, maybe. Yes!

But I couldn't speak the words as Alexander leaned in closer to me. His mouth was mere inches away. Even though I knew what was coming, I was unable to stop it. It was as if my brain had shut down, and my body took over.

Suddenly, a tractor-trailer whizzed by, pulling on its horn. The sound was deafening, and I jumped, the interruption startling me out of my trance and back to reality.

"I-I can't..." I trailed off, at a complete loss for words, feeling pissed for being so weak. Even after everything I had been telling myself, I couldn't last more than two seconds around him.

How does he do this to me all the time?

"You can't what, Krystina?"

"I can't kiss you. You can't kiss me. We aren't the same as we were before. I don't want you to think there's something still between us."

"Think? I don't have to *think* anything, angel. I know what's between us."

I wanted to deny him more than ever, knowing I wouldn't be able to keep up the fight for much longer with him standing so close to me. I summoned all the courage I could muster and tried to ignore the sexy way a damp lock of hair fell over his brow.

"There's nothing," I tried to deny.

The rain started to come down, the slow drizzle replaced by large droplets splattering on my cheeks. I was about to mention we should probably get out of the rain before it started coming down any harder when Alexander placed his hand over my heart. The feel of his warm hand on my chest stunned me into silence as my heart beat rapidly against his palm.

"Are you going to deny you feel it?" he asked quietly. His voice had become low and raspy, the sound of it resonating through me.

"You imagine things," I said, swatting his hand away.

His eyes flashed dangerously, and in one swift motion, he cupped the back of my neck and pulled me towards him. Then, without warning, he crushed his mouth to mine.

It happened so fast that my breath was literally sucked out of me as I tried to free myself from his grasp.

It's wrong. I can't do THIS!

I could not accept his kiss. If I did, walking away again would be that much harder and the hurt even more unbearable. So I kept my lips sealed in a firm tight line, refusing to give in.

Alexander fought me and continued to crush his mouth down against mine. He ran his tongue over my bottom lip, testing me for a weakness as I continued to deny him access. But I could feel the will slipping slowly away, my resistance now only halfhearted.

"Don't fight me, Krystina," he murmured against my lips. "It's been too long since I've last tasted you."

Lightning flashed in the distance, and a low rumble of thunder sounded. I moaned, losing all willpower to hold him off any longer. My body involuntarily gave away, prompting my hands to fly up and grip the back of his neck. Alexander growled his approval and deepened the kiss, pulling my body tighter against his. Our tongues lapped and danced together at an urgent pace. It was so good—*too* good. When his mouth began to work over my jawline, I resigned myself to being lost to him and hummed with pleasure.

After a moment, he inched back slightly, our lips hovering over each other's and our breaths mingling with every pant.

"Do you still want to say this is just a figment of my imagination?" he breathed.

Dammit!

I pulled back and looked away.

"You don't understand, Alex. I can't be with you right now."

"You're right. I don't understand. But I think I've given you an ample amount of time to figure things out. Now, we talk."

"There's nothing to say."

"Actually, there was a lot left unsaid. For starters, I need to apologize. I'm sorry I brought you to Club O. It was a mistake. And I know who you saw that night. I'm sorry I wasn't there for you, leaving you all alone when you had to face *him*," he said, biting out the last word with disgust. "I should have protected you. It's no wonder why you ran from me."

"How could you know—" I started. But then I realized how he knew almost immediately. "Ally."

Even though I never told her about what happened that night, I was fairly confident the two of them managed to piece together the details. My brow creased in a scowl, feeling even more betrayed and angry with my friend for scheming with Alexander behind my back.

"She is worried about you. Don't be upset with her."

"Either way, it doesn't matter what you know or what you think you know. What's done is done. We can't change it now."

"Maybe not, but we can try to make it right. Together. You gave me your trust once before. I need you to trust me one more time."

My eyes that had been absently staring at the pebbles on the asphalt snapped up to look at him.

Trust! I did trust you, and look where it got me?

I wanted to scream the words, suddenly remembering all the reasons why I had left him in the first place.

"No, Alex. It's not just about what happened at Club O. I trusted you, and you lied to me about your parents."

"What if I tell you about my parents? About everything? No more secrets, Krystina."

My stomach dropped, and the rain started to come down even harder, drenching us with each passing minute. Goosebumps traveled up my arms, but I didn't know if it was from the cold rain or Alexander's truce offering.

No more secrets.

I didn't know if I could trust it—trust him—again. I looked searchingly into his eyes, desperately wanting to give in.

Will the truth change anything?

I wasn't naïve. I knew the truth behind Alexander's parents would not fix all of our problems. And it certainly wasn't going to fix my personal issues with being in a normal relationship. But it was hard not to cling to a sliver of hope. I could not deny that when I was with Alexander, I had seen the shadow of the white picket fence. Maybe, just maybe, I didn't have to work things out by myself. Perhaps Alexander and I could do it together. I desperately wanted to believe that, but I also didn't want to face the pain if things didn't work out.

Not again.

"Why are you changing your mind so suddenly?" I asked cautiously.

He ran a hand through his dark waves, all mussed up from the rain and wind whipping around us. He looked out into the night sky as if he were searching for the right words. When he turned back to me, his beautiful blues were full of torment.

"These past two weeks have been hell for me. We're not over, angel. I'm not letting go of you."

There was a fierce determination in his eyes, and his purpose made me suddenly realize something. I could not continue to run from him. He will never accept the word no. I had to face this one way or another. If I was completely honest with myself, I knew I couldn't fight back if I tried. My heart wouldn't let me. Deep down, I never really wanted us to be over in the first place.

However, I couldn't let him know that. Not yet, at least. First, I needed an explanation before giving him a chance. I needed to understand why he had let two weeks pass before seeking me out. The text messages about the job didn't count. If what he was saying was true, I wanted to know why he didn't fight for us. He wasn't the only one to suffer while we were apart, and the ache I had felt during his absence was tremendous.

"If you don't want us to be over, then why did you let me walk away?" I demanded.

He winced and rubbed his temples with both hands. His eyes were pained when he spoke.

"It was the comment you made comparing me to my father. It was a low blow and very unexpected. I didn't know how to react."

"How was I supposed to know that?" I tried to defend. "I mean, it's not like you were forthcoming about your past."

My defense was weak, and guilt flooded through me. I was so confused that night, my emotions one big jumbled mess. I knew I wasn't thinking clearly, but I hadn't meant to hurt him.

"I know, and that's why I'm here. I meant what I said. We are not over, not by a long shot. If working through our issues means I have to tell you everything, so be it."

His expression held a certain amount of sadness mixed with resolve. But there was also a longing I had never seen before.

Why am I hesitating?

The truth is what I had been asking for. It was what I needed to cut down the barriers between us so that I could trust him.

"I'm not going to make any promises, Alex. We'll talk, but nothing more," I agreed quietly.

He wrapped his arms around me and pressed his lips to

the top of my head. I held my breath, not wanting my judgment clouded by his intoxicating smell.

We are just going to talk. That's all.

"Thank you, angel. Go have a seat inside the Tesla where it's warm," he said as he pulled away. "I'm going to make a quick sweep of your car to remove anything of value, then call Hale to have him arrange a tow for this jalopy."

"Hey! I like my car!" I defended.

"Krystina, just go to my car," he said, taking hold of my elbow and coaxing me in the direction of where he was parked. "We've been standing on the side of the highway for long enough. It's pouring rain, and it isn't safe."

Just as he finished his sentence, another truck flew by, blaring its horn and throwing a wet mist in its wake. Conceding to Alexander's point about safety, I allowed him to lead me to his car. Once I was seated inside, he closed the door behind me and made the call to his security detail about having my car towed.

A minute later, Alexander climbed into the driver's seat next to me.

"Nothing between us, huh? I found this in the middle console of your car. I thought you might want it," he stated casually before tossing the pack of Big Red chewing gum onto my lap.

I blushed ten different shades of pink before mumbling some nonsense about liking cinnamon. He made no comment but simply handed over my purse, cell phone, and credit card he had retrieved from my car.

When Alexander started the Tesla, music blared from the speakers, and I jumped. He hurried to adjust the volume to a barely audible level.

"Sorry. There was a song on that I liked right before I pulled up behind you."

"What was it?"

He looked at me strangely for a moment.

"I don't know the name of it," he said somewhat indifferently.

I wanted to point out that the elaborate touch screen of his ridiculously expensive electric blue Tesla displayed the artist and song title but thought it best not to provoke him with a snide remark about his lavish tastes.

Instead, I focused on the song currently playing. It was an oldie by Frank Sinatra that I knew well and always liked.

"Can you turn it up a little? I would, but I don't know how to work this thing," I admitted, motioning with my finger to the computer screen on the dash.

"Sure, angel."

Instead of pressing anything on the screen, he simply started talking to an imaginary person in the dash. The volume magically increased.

Show off.

I hummed quietly to Frank singing about getting back up from the unfortunate things life throws at you, trying desperately not to relate the song to my own life.

Stop having a pity party, Cole. It's just a song.

We rode in silence, the only sound coming from the radio and the blowing of the heat vents pushing out much-needed warmth. After a few minutes, the song changed to an X Ambassador tune.

"Talk about a jump in the music genre. Interesting playlist you have, Alex," I observed.

"It's streaming from an app, and it's supposed to be

filtered by what I listen to the most. The mix isn't usually this eclectic, though," he explained and pursed his lips. "I can change it if you want. Put on more of Frank?"

"No, this is fine." Leaning my head back against the seat, I listened to the current tune. However, after about thirty seconds, I began to hate the song. Too many of the lyrics were hitting home. "Actually, turn the radio off. I don't feel like listening to music."

He didn't turn it off but only lowered the volume.

"What's wrong, angel?"

Music.

My one solace, my only escape, had been failing me.

"Nothing," I lied. I snapped out the word rather quickly, making the fib obvious.

"Krystina," he said in a troubled voice. I turned to look at him. "I want you to know I'm here. For you. For what you went through. And for us. When you feel like you're falling, I want you to trust I'll be here to catch you."

"Alex, please don't," my voice cracked.

"I've got you, angel. You need to accept that."

I turned my head to stare out the window. Tears pricked my eyes. He didn't know how bad I wanted to do exactly as he suggested—to fall completely into him. Staying away was one of the hardest things I ever had to do. And now that he was here, I was having trouble remembering why I ran in the first place.

4

Alexander

When we arrived at my intended destination, I saw Hale waiting for us in front of the Bell 407GXP. The four blades of the helicopter were already in motion, signaling the pilot was ready for takeoff.

Perfect timing.

I glanced over at Krystina. Her head rested against the passenger door window, and her eyes were closed. She looked so peaceful, and I hated to wake her.

"Angel," I said, gently nudging her on the shoulder.

Her eyes fluttered open, and she jumped from being startled awake.

"I'm sorry. I had an early morning, but I can't believe I dozed off..." she trailed off, taking stock of her surroundings for the first time. "Alexander, where are we?"

"Air Pegasus. Come on. Hale is waiting for us," I

informed her. I climbed out of the car and left her sputtering after me.

"Air what? Hale is waiting for us why? Alex, wait up!"

I smiled to myself as I made my way to the main heliport with a confused Krystina in my wake. I would heed Allyson's advice about taking things slow. I knew Krystina was fragile. I would give her whatever it was she needed to move on from her past. However, I also knew a few hours of conversation wouldn't get us very far. I needed to have more time, and my window of opportunity to pin her down was limited. The faster I moved, the better. For I knew, if I gave her too much room to think, all bets were off.

"Hale, thanks for arranging this on such short notice," I said once I reached my security detail.

"It was no trouble at all, Mr. Stone. Luckily the storm has passed, so the flight should be a smooth one. Everything you requested is already on board. We are ready when you are."

"Ready for *what*, dammit!" I heard Krystina exclaim from behind me.

When I turned around to face her, she was flushed scarlet. Her lush brown curls whipped around wildly from the wind tunnel created by the blades of the helicopter. I could practically see the steam coming from her ears, but I wasn't the least bit rattled by the imminent temper tantrum. In fact, I had fully expected her to act this way.

"We're going for a ride," I calmly informed her.

"I am *not* going anywhere in that thing. I agreed to talk, Alex. You never said anything about—"

"Yes, you are."

In one swift motion, I silenced whatever argument she

may have had by hauling her up off of her feet and slinging her over my shoulder.

She beat at my back angrily with her fists, her legs kicking as she struggled to get free.

"Alex, what the hell are you doing? Put me down! Now!" Teetering precariously on the edge of my shoulder, she grabbed hold of my hips to keep steady. I would never let her fall but letting her think I might drop her made her stop writhing as she attempted to stay balanced.

Hoisting us both up into the helicopter, I dropped her into one of the passenger seats. Then, pinning her arms to the chair, I leveled my eyes with hers.

"It's about damn time you stopped trying to top from the bottom. Are we clear?"

"You're acting like a Neanderthal," she spat out, eyes flashing angrily.

Mother of God, you're beautiful.

As much as she was pissing me off, I felt my cock twitch. There was just something about a feisty Krystina that got my blood going. It took all the restraint I could manage not to bite that pouty lower lip of hers.

"Neanderthal? I kind of like that," I said with a cocky grin as I proceeded to fasten her in. Once she was securely buckled, I took the seat next to hers.

"Is this how you plan on fixing us, Alex? By ordering me around again?"

"Actually, yes. It's what I should have done in the first place. If I did, perhaps we wouldn't even be in this situation."

"Oh, yeah? Well, I don't think so."

She began to fumble with the complex harness strapping

her to the seat. I was about to stop her when Hale climbed aboard the helicopter and closed the door behind him.

Too late, angel. You aren't going anywhere now.

I motioned to the pilot, signaling we were ready for takeoff. Krystina, still hell-bent on figuring out how to unfasten herself, didn't seem to notice what was happening around her.

"I would leave the seat restraint secured if I were you. We are about to take off," I told her.

"What?" her head snapped up to look around, only to discover we had begun to ascend. She glared at me and folded her arms across her chest. She was seething.

"Simmer down, angel," I laughed.

"At least tell me where we are going," she said through gritted teeth.

"East Hampton."

"You're insane! I can't go all the way to East Hampton! Besides, my clothes are still damp from standing in the rain earlier. I need to change."

"Hale packed you a change of clothes. Don't worry about that."

"And how would Hale have gotten my clothes?" she demanded, sounding completely dumbfounded.

"You have an entire wardrobe at the penthouse. Remember?"

She gaped like a fish, seeming at a loss for words for a moment, before puffing out an exasperated sigh. When she spoke again about ten minutes later, she seemed resigned to the inevitable and was considerably calmer.

"What's in East Hampton?"

I smiled to myself, satisfied I had won this round.

"Lake Montauk. It's where my boat is docked."

"It's a little cold for a boat ride, don't you think," she remarked dryly.

"We're not going to take her out. I just thought it would be a quiet place for us to talk. Besides, it's the last weekend to use her. She'll be going to dry dock for the winter, and I wanted you to see her before then."

"I don't know why you had to go to such extreme measures. We could have talked someplace closer to home," she muttered, her words barely loud enough to hear over the noise of the helicopter.

"It's my story to tell this time, Krystina. So, therefore, we are going to do this my way."

Privately. Someplace where I know I won't be overheard.

We soared over the city, a silence settling between us. A pit formed in my stomach when I thought about what I was about to do. I was going to bare all by telling Krystina the truth about my parents and about who I really was. It was essential we were not overheard by anyone, and bringing her to my boat was the only neutral place I could think of on short notice.

However, if I were completely honest with myself, it wasn't just that I wanted privacy for our conversation. I wanted Krystina to be in a place she couldn't run from so easily. Because after she heard what I had to say, she would learn everything was a lie. And I didn't know if she would run or if she would stay.

Krystina

To say I was furious would be an understatement. My temper had been quietly simmering on the flight over. I was about ready to erupt like Mount Saint Helens when I climbed down from the helicopter.

I followed Alexander to a black Mercedes-Benz waiting to take us the remainder of the way to Lake Montauk. I didn't argue about getting into the vehicle, as I didn't want to be humiliated again by being thrown over Alexander's shoulder like a sack of potatoes.

Just the memory of his actions flared my temper even further.

Ugh! The assuming, arrogant jackass!

The man had no boundaries. I knew that about him, and I should not have been surprised by what he had done. There were no limits to the lengths he would take to get what he wanted—even if it meant kidnapping me.

Hale claimed the driver's seat while Alexander and I rode in the backseat in utter silence. The air was wrought with tension. I could feel Alexander's eyes on me, but I refused to look at him because I was afraid I might snap. The only thing stopping me from blowing my top was pure curiosity about finally hearing his story.

When the car came to a halt in a near-empty parking lot, Hale got out to open the car door for us. Alexander climbed out first and held his hand out to me.

"Come on, angel. It's time for you to meet Lucy," he said.

Not bothering to ask who Lucy was, I ignored his outstretched hand and got out of the car on my own. I knew I was acting like a brat, but I couldn't help but feel a little smug over the stunned expression of rejection on his face.

"Alexander, surely you don't expect me to play nice," I

said, flashing him an overly sweet smile. "I agreed to talk. I don't recall kidnapping being a part of the agreement."

Without warning, Alexander's hands came crashing down on top of the car, boxing me in between his muscular forearms. I nearly jumped out of my skin as the noise of his palms hitting the medal was deafening in the quiet parking lot.

"Enough!" he growled, his face mere inches from mine.

"Or what?" I challenged in return. I tilted my chin up stubbornly.

"So, help me, Krystina," he warned, shaking his head in aggravation. "I'm not going a round with you. Not now. And if it means I have to toss you over my shoulder again, I will."

"You wouldn't."

"Don't test me, angel. I've felt like a madman these past few weeks, and you have no idea what I'm capable of."

His expression was menacing, and I glanced around nervously for Hale. He was pulling duffle bags from the Mercedes trunk, conspicuously ignoring the confrontation going on at the side of the car.

Alexander backed away from me but took hold of my hand. His grip was firm as he practically dragged me towards the main gate of the marina.

"Alex, let go of my hand!" I said, trying to pull free of his grasp.

He spun to face me, pulling me against his hard torso.

"Why? So you can fucking run?" His words were harsh and angry, but his expression was pleading. "It was a mistake to let you go the last time. You won't be running from me again. I will not allow it."

"You can't control me!"

"This isn't about control. Why can't you see that? This is about you and me. It's about our..." he trailed off as if trying to find the right words. When he spoke again, his voice was thick with emotion. "It's our connection. I can't ignore it anymore. I need you, angel. I've been numb without you. And now that I finally have you with me again, all you want to do is fight. I can't decide if I want to take you over my knee or give you a good sense fuck."

"A sense fu—" I started to say, but the words caught in my throat, silenced by the finger Alexander held up to my lips.

"Stop talking, Krystina."

That was all he said before leaning in to seal his mouth over mine.

As angry as I was, my body betrayed me almost instantly. I didn't want to be kissing him, yet I wanted it more than anything else at the same time. It was as if my lips had a mind of their own, and I returned his kiss with a fever that rocked me to the core.

Within seconds, the heavy ache that had been in my heart for the past two weeks shifted, and I found myself giving in without restraint. Alexander was right about our connection. I had been numb without him, too.

I ran my hands up the lengths of his hard biceps, gripping his shoulders like I was hanging on for dear life. And in a way, that's exactly what I was doing—fighting to keep hold of our fragile, messed up relationship in any way I could.

I was fueled by so many feelings—anger, betrayal, desire, and longing. I threw my body and entire mind into the kiss. Pushing my tongue past Alexander's lips, I took and fiercely gave everything I could. I drew from the overflowing well of emotions to silently tell him I wasn't going to run again. Not this time. Because even after everything we had been through, I knew I didn't want to spend another day without him.

Alexander moaned and pulled me tighter against him. He knew what I was trying to tell him. I could feel it in the way he held me in his arms and from the transition of our passion-filled kiss. Our lips locked in frantic need. It was as if we were trying to make up for the two weeks of being apart. The feeling of urgency was unlike any other we ever shared. It wasn't driven by lust or pure carnal desire but more from unexplainable desperation.

He kissed along my cheeks and jawline, then pressed his forehead against mine. He cupped my face with both hands and looked down at me. When my eyes locked on his, I saw his gorgeous blues filled with relief.

"Welcome back, angel," he whispered.

I gave him a small smile before resting my head against his chest. I breathed in deep, finally allowing his intoxicating smell to invade my senses.

God, how I missed this.

The distant echo of people laughing some ways away brought me back to reality. The sound reminded me we were not alone, and Hale was somewhere nearby. I pulled back and looked around awkwardly. A blush crept up into my cheeks when I saw Hale standing by the car just a short distance away from us. Thankfully, he had the tact to be looking in the opposite direction.

One minute I'm throwing a fit, and the next, I'm lip-locked with my captor. He must think I'm crazier than Alex.

And speaking of crazy...

I turned my attention back to Alexander.

"You should not have hauled me over your shoulder like that," I told him, careful to keep my tone neutral and not argumentative. He merely raised an eyebrow at me.

"Would you have gotten into the helicopter any other way?"

"Probably not," I admitted.

"Well, then I'm not going to apologize for doing it."

He flashed me a cocky smile. I could only sigh and shake my head as Alexander took hold of my hand again.

"Who is Lucy?" I asked after we began to walk.

"You'll see."

I looked at him curiously, but he didn't elaborate.

Mr. Cryptic, as usual.

Alexander led me up a stone pathway towards an intricately designed wrought iron pedestrian gate. He swiped his access card through an electronic card reader, and the gate automatically swung slowly open. Buildings flanked either side of the path we were walking on, obstructing any view I may have had of the waterfront. I was sure the marina was deliberately designed that way to maintain the privacy of its members. I could already tell the place reeked of exclusivity.

When we reached the building's edge, we rounded the corner, and I stopped dead in my tracks. I was awed by the display before me.

"Wow! This place is nothing at all like the marinas back home. This is more like a miniature resort town than anything else!"

"I guess it is in a way," Alexander said indifferently, coaxing me to keep walking.

"Wait—stop. I want to look around for a minute."

Even in the dark, I could see the impeccably maintained landscape. The building to my left housed at least fifty golf carts, which I assumed were used to take guests to various locations around the massive marina. Little boutiques and cafes followed the long winding pathway to my right, the twinkling light from their windows dotting the shoreline and reflecting off the water. White gazebos lined the water's edge, inviting one just to sit and take in the sights. In the middle of it all, a grand lighthouse with an extravagant building sat off to the right side. It looked more like a mansion than a boathouse, and I assumed it to be the marinas main clubhouse. A banner was hung from the front porch, thanking members for a fun-filled season.

The entire setting was picturesque and had a magical sort of feeling reminiscent of the works of Thomas Kinkade. If I had any kind of artistic abilities, I would want to sit down and paint it.

"Where is everyone?" I asked in a whisper. I felt silly over my hushed tone, but I was afraid to disturb the peacefulness of our surroundings.

"It's quiet down here this time of the year. During peak season, it's fairly busy. Now, most of the club members have either stored their boats for the winter or gone south. They all scatter as soon as the leaves start to change," Alexander told me with a shrug. "Personally, I prefer the marina when it's less crowded. That's why I'm one of the last to keep my boat in the water this late."

Only a few people meandered about on the docks, and I

guessed that they were the last of the diehards trying to hang on to what little was left of the season. I looked out over the water to see how many boats were still there and widened my eyes in surprise. The boats in the water were not *boats*. They looked like miniature cruise ships. And just as Alexander said, there were very few left. However, the rows of slips seemed unending. I could imagine the marina being a pretty hopping place during mid-summer.

"Are you ready, angel?" Alexander asked, tugging at my hand to keep walking.

"Yeah. Let's go," I agreed absently, still feeling awed as I continued to take in everything around me. I thought about Frank's fishing boat and how lost it would be in a place like this. I smiled to myself.

I'm definitely not in Kansas anymore.

We made our way down towards the docks and through another security gate requiring a key card. We walked a little way before coming up on a boat named *The Lucy*. It was then that I realized who Lucy was. Lucy wasn't a who but a what. And Lucy was huge.

"This is your boat?" I asked incredulously. "It's enormous!"

"She's not that big, angel," Alexander laughed. "The yacht is relatively small by comparison. It's only one hundred sixty-five feet. Some of the other boats in the marina are as big as two hundred twenty-five. I thought about upgrading her a few years back, but I'm not sure if I can maneuver a boat much larger than this."

"You drive this thing?"

"Not often, but I can. I have my Captain's License, but I

have a crew with me when I take her out. Let's go in, and I'll give you the tour."

I followed Alexander up the gangplank, across a large open deck, through double glass doors, and into the salon. It felt good to be inside where it was warm. With all the chaos during the past hour, I hadn't realized how damp and chilly I still felt from being out in the rain.

I was about to ask if I could change my clothes before taking a tour but stopped when Alexander called out for Hale.

"Yes, sir," Hale said, appearing out of nowhere.

The man is like a shadow.

"Where did you leave our bags?"

"I put them in the master suite, Mr. Stone."

"Perfect. Krystina and I are all set for now. I've instructed Laura to come to you with anything that might need immediate attention. Other than that, you're free to take the rest of the night off," Alexander instructed.

"Very good, sir. Thank you," Hale said. He nodded his head to Alexander, then tossed me a very discreet wink that caught me off guard. I couldn't help but think that Hale wouldn't be very far away despite being told to take the night off.

The entire exchange somewhat amused me.

"Who is Hale to you?" I asked Alexander after Hale walked away.

"What do you mean?"

"I mean, he plays chauffeur, security, and gopher to you all at once. What's his title?"

"He doesn't have an official title," he said dismissively. "Come on now. Let's go change out these damp clothes."

Alexander turned to lead me out of the room, but I wasn't going to let him off the hook so quickly. I knew him well enough to know when he was trying to evade a topic. There was definitely a story there.

He continued to walk ahead, leaving me to follow behind with a barrage of questions.

"When did you two meet?"

"A long time ago."

Evade, evade, evade.

"He has a military air about him. Did he ever serve?"

"You'll have to ask him."

"Thanks, Alex. This was a really good talk," I said, my voice laden with sarcasm.

Alexander stopped, turned back to me, and frowned. Then, seeming to come to a decision, he took a deep breath.

"Hale's mother was my grandmother's childhood best friend. That's how I know him. I've known him my entire life, and he has been in my employment for over ten years. Outside of my grandparents, he is the only person I've ever trusted completely."

Alexander's reference to a piece of his history caused me to come up short for words momentarily.

"Oh, I see," was all I said. I wanted more details, but he must have known his admission was going to raise questions. He shook his head and held up his hand to signal I should bite my tongue for the time being.

"I will tell you about my parents, Krystina. I'll put all the cards on the table and tell you every single ugly detail. I promised you I would, and I never go back on my word. However, I'm not in a huge hurry to rehash it all. I want to enjoy tonight for just a little while longer."

I nodded my consent, not sure of what else I could do other than accept. He looked sad. But there was something else in his expression, too, as if telling me his story would somehow break him. I had seen many emotions swirl in the depths of his sapphire eyes—anger and determination to passion and lust. But never once had I seen fear.

I was suddenly very afraid of what Alexander had to tell me. And for the first time, I wondered if it might be better to keep Pandora's box closed.

5

Alexander

I opened the doors for the master suite and gestured Krystina inside. She glanced up at me curiously, her expression full of questions before she quickly looked away. I knew she wanted answers, but I had to hold her off for a little while longer.

Just have patience, angel.

I brought her here, quite literally kicking and screaming, and I had to make sure she was in the right frame of mind before I opened up. It was imperative the stage was appropriately set.

Walking over to the settee in the corner of the room, I unzipped the black duffle bag holding Krystina's clothes. I removed a pair of jeans, a cream-colored wool sweater, and fresh undergarments. I laid everything out neatly on the bed.

"This should keep you warm enough, but there is

another sweatshirt in the bag if you think you'll be needing it."

She stepped up to the bed and ran her hands over the jeans contemplatively.

"No. This should be fine," she murmured. She looked conflicted and seemed unusually nervous.

I swore to myself.

Dammit! Now what's going on in her head?

I wished it were easier to figure out what she was thinking. I hated that I rarely knew.

Is she possibly feeling shy about undressing in front of me?

If that was the case, then she was acting ridiculous. I had already seen every beautiful inch of her bare flesh. But despite what I thought, I realized offering her a bit of privacy might put her more at ease. I was about to mention it but stopped short when she began to undress.

My breath immediately caught in my throat.

There she stood, unbuttoning her damp blouse and allowing it to slide down her shoulders slowly. I froze, completely mesmerized by the stunning woman before me.

It was easy to tell her movements were not meant to be provocative, and she was just trying to keep the chilly material away from her skin. But no matter what her intentions were, it was all I could do to keep myself from throwing her down on the bed and possessing her. She defined the meaning of perfection. Desire gripped at me, and I suppressed a groan.

Tearing my eyes away from her delicate and creamy skin, I gathered my own things to change into. Feeling frustrated, I stripped out of my current attire and tossed everything into a pile. Pulling on a new pair of jeans, I fastened the button of the Armani denim and secured my belt. I was extra careful not to glance in her direction. For I knew, only one look at her half-naked body, and it would be all over.

I pulled a T-shirt over my head. When my head slipped through the neck hole, I was completely blindsided by the sight greeting me. I staggered back a step. Krystina had moved her position slightly and was once again in my line of sight. She stood with her back to me, neatly folding her damp clothes into a stack, wearing nothing but a sweater and panties.

My eyes ran up the length of her flawless legs and settled on the curvature of her impeccable ass. A vision of those limbs wrapped around me flooded my brain.

Not yet.

But then she bent over to slip into her jeans, and any willpower I had was thrown to the wayside.

To hell with this. I'm not made of fucking iron.

I closed the distance between us in three short strides, grabbed her around the waist, and pulled her back against my chest.

"Alex—" she started to say.

"Shh. Don't, angel. Please," I implored. "I need to feel you."

I was precariously close to begging, something I had never done in my life, but it didn't matter. I wanted her more than I ever wanted her before. It was an unexplainable need of epic proportions. Perhaps it was the weeks we had spent apart. I didn't know. I only knew I was desperate to be inside her. To feel her velvet heat.

Sliding my hands under her sweater, I cupped her breasts from behind.

Christ...she doesn't have her bra on.

I twisted each nipple for a moment, relishing the weight of her bare breasts in my hands, before spinning her around. Then, lifting the sweater from her body, I tossed it aside and took a ridged peak into my mouth. She gasped in surprise, but she didn't fight me as I sucked and rolled her around my tongue. Instead, she tilted her head back and released a small sigh while I said a silent thanks to all that was divine for giving me this moment—for giving me this woman.

Moving up to claim her mouth, I pushed my tongue past her waiting lips and devoured her. She moaned, the vibration from her lips sending an electric shock straight to my groin.

"Wait—wait, Alex," she said, pulling back as if all of a sudden remembering herself. "We can't."

I was past the point of no return. *Can't* was not in my vocabulary. Waiting was not an option. Cruise control had turned into overdrive, and I was fully engaged.

"Tell me that you don't want this," I murmured into her mouth, grazing my teeth over her lips. "And tell me like you mean it."

I worked my way down her neck, savoring the feel of her pulse hammering beneath her skin as I breathed in her scent. She smelled like rain-kissed vanilla.

"I... I can't tell you that, but—"

"No but's. Don't think. Do you want this?" I whispered as I nipped up her neck to her earlobe. She lolled her head to the side and allowed me better access. I pulled her tighter against me, and she sighed her appreciation. I knew then that I had her.

"Yes," she finally conceded.

I didn't hesitate for a second after gaining her consent. I crushed my mouth against hers again. I wanted to kiss her senseless. I didn't want her to think or to question anymore.

Lifting her, I wrapped those glorious legs around my waist and pinned her against the wall. The heat of her sex through the lace panties pressed against my abdomen. She pushed forward, grinding against me, telling me her need was hot. I could have buried my cock in her right then. Against the wall. To drive into her like the wild animal she made me. But she merited better than that. Krystina deserved worshipping.

Carrying her to the bed, I laid her down on the silver and blue satin comforter. Moving down her body, my tongue raked across her skin like a needle on vinyl, arousing sensual sounds from her with every rotation and creating music for my ears. I slowly and deliberately pulled her panties down her legs, adoring every inch of her as I went. I trailed kisses up her legs, savoring the delicious taste of her skin.

"Oh, angel," I said, pressing my cheek against her inner thigh. "Do you know how much I thought about you when we were apart? The number of endless nights I spent missing you? How many nights went by, Krystina?"

When she didn't answer, I nipped hard at her thigh with my teeth. Hard enough to make it hurt.

"Thirteen," she squeaked out. "Thirteen nights."

My face hovered over her glistening sex, her lips lush, pink, and inviting. I was happy to see she had maintained a smooth shave even in my absence. I blew softly, and she began to pant.

"Thirteen too many. I won't spend another night apart from you again. Do you understand?"

"Alex—"

I swiped my tongue over her clit, and her breath hitched.

"Do you understand?"

"That can't—I can't—" she sputtered.

But I would not be denied. Burying my face in her soaking wet heat, her back arched, and she cried out, the persistent motion of my tongue silencing whatever words she was trying to say.

I reached up and took hold of her breasts, gratified to feel her nipples pebble under my palms. I twisted and pulled at the taut peaks. The pulsing in her clit signaled she was already near release, but I kept her on edge and didn't allow her to come. I circled and teased as her hands fisted at the sheets that had balled up around us. I deliberately drove her to the point of madness, not wanting her to be able to deny me when I asked again.

I pulled away suddenly, leaving her gasping for air and confused as to why I stopped.

"Not another night alone. Do you understand?" I repeated. Her breath was ragged when she looked down at me, eyes wild and full of passion. She reached to push my head back to her sweet spot, but I shifted so that I was just out of her reach. "Do you understand?"

She threw her head back on the pillow in frustration before looking at me again. Her cheeks were flushed, and her gaze was desperate. I could see the desire pooled in the depths of her eyes. But I could also see conflict. I held my breath in anticipation, although I was fairly confident she would give in.

"Not another night alone," she finally said.

"Not. One."

I shoved her legs up roughly and spread her wide. Then I devoured her. I ate her like a starving man who could not get his fill. And I couldn't. Until my dying day, I would never have enough of Krystina.

Within seconds, I could feel the throbbing of her clit intensify. Not a moment later, she cried out and exploded over my tongue. Her juices, the sweetest of all nectars, coated my lips as I suckled every last drop of her release.

I felt a tremble course down her legs, and I smiled in satisfaction.

She's going to need a minute or two to come down from that one.

Taking advantage of her lithe state, I got off the bed to undress. Removing my belt, I placed it on the bed before shedding my boxers and pants. My cock sprung free, happy to be released from the confines of the restricting jeans. Climbing back onto the bed, I straddled her waist. She looked up sleepily at me.

"You're a sneaky bastard. Do you know that?"

A low chuckle reverberated through me.

"Oh, baby. I've only just gotten started."

Taking hold of her wrists with one hand, I reached back and grabbed my belt with the other. I wrapped the leather around her hands to bind them together, then used the remaining slack to secure her to the bedpost.

This is a mistake. I should keep it vanilla for now.

Strapping her to the bed was a risk. It may have felt normal for me, but I didn't want to push the kink after what happened at Club O.

I looked back at her face to see if she showed any level of resistance. Her lips had parted slightly, and her eyes were dark with want. However, she showed no sign of unease.

"Are your hands comfortable?"

"Everything is just fine, Mr. Stone," she said deviously with a wanton smile. "Now that you have me all tied up, what are you going to do with me?"

I returned her lascivious grin.

"I'm going to bury my cock inside you. Deep. I need to feel you. I need you to feel me. All of me."

I slid my hand down her belly and over her mound to find her wet slit. One finger. Two fingers. I slowly and deliberately stretched her, preparing her for my invasion. I wasn't going to hold back. She would feel *all* of me, something I had held back in doing because I feared I might hurt her.

When I felt she was ready, I positioned myself at her waiting entrance and slowly eased my way in. Her breath caught, and her mouth went slack as she absorbed each stab of pleasure. I moved slowly, in and out, working her into a desperate frenzy.

"Alex, make me come again. Please! I need to come around you!"

"I've got you, angel. You will," I kissed the sides of her face and down her neck and shoulders. I continued to push into her body until she began to tense a bit from the pressure of me being so deep. "Relax your body. Take all of me. You can do it."

She exhaled and closed her eyes. Grabbing her right leg, I brought it up over my shoulder. I pushed forward another inch. Then another. I didn't stop until the tip of my cock was pressing against her very core.

"Oh!" she gasped in shock.

White-hot pleasure rocketed through my veins as the walls of her vagina constricted to adjust to me. She wrapped me in heat, pulsing with desire.

"I'm going to move now. Feel me, Krystina."

I pulled back slowly, then drove home again. And again.

"Alex!" she screamed out. Her body writhed with pleasure, her climax already vibrating around my cock. But I didn't stop. Instead, I pounded into her over and over, taking all I could—giving all I could.

I wanted to flip her and take her from behind, to make her ass a rosy pink with my palm, but I didn't want to give up my view. She was like a goddess with her head thrown back in passion—her lush curls splayed over the pillow and her breasts bouncing as I rode her. I pushed her leg up higher and gave her bottom a light smack.

"Yes!" she screamed out. "Again!"

Holy fuck.

To think I was worried for a moment about taking the kink too far, but now here she was, shocking me to hell by asking for more.

I smacked her again, this time a little harder. I gauged her reactions and continued with her encouragement. With every spank, she increased her movements, matching me thrust for thrust. Her enthusiasm brought our lovemaking to new heights.

Lovemaking? Since when did it stop being a fuck?

I pushed away the unexpected thought, not wanting to dwell on it while in the heat of the moment.

She pulled at the belt restraint and matched my every thrust, rocking and moaning as I possessed her. I took her higher and higher until, all at once, I felt her stiffen as a third climax rocketed through her body. Her sex tightened like a vice around me, and I knew I wouldn't last much longer.

I gripped her hips hard.

"Krystina, I'm right there!" I hissed through clenched teeth.

"Let me feel it deep. Please, Alex!"

Her spectacular cry was enough to send me over the edge. My mind went blank before a bright awareness spread through me. I plunged deep and held the position, allowing my seed to erupt into the intimate recesses of her body. My connection to the phenomenal woman beneath me was complete.

I collapsed down on top of her, panting and sated. After several minutes, our breathing returned to a somewhat normal rhythm. I reluctantly rolled to the side and unbuckled her hands. There were red marks on her wrists.

"You shouldn't pull so hard on the restraints. You could injure yourself," I scolded as I tried to massage the redness away.

When I released her, she wrapped her arms around my neck and pulled me close. She let out a sigh of contentment and began to trace small circles on my back with her fingertips.

"I shouldn't have walked away," she told me. "It was a gut reaction, and I wasn't thinking clearly. I realize that now. I know we have a lot to talk about, but I want to start by saying I'm sorry I didn't give us a chance. I won't run again, Alex. I love being with you too much."

I felt my heart tighten.

Love?

There was that word again.

It's pillow talk. She didn't say she loves me, but only that she loved being with me.

I tried to push it away once again, only for it to come roaring back with a vengeance. It didn't matter what Krystina meant with her statement. The certainty lay with me.

I do love her.

Fuck.

How in the hell did I allow that to happen?

Not sure what to do with the sudden discovery, I said nothing. This was a first for me, and I could barely even think, let alone process it. I only knew I could not say the words out loud. At least not yet, not while I was in such a vulnerable position. The clock was ticking. I had my moment with her. Now it was time to talk.

It was time for Krystina to learn the truth.

6

Krystina

I lay there in Alexander's arms feeling very conflicted over the events of the evening. Overall, my emotions were a befuddled mess. Everything had evolved so fast. In fact, fast was the best word to describe our entire relationship.

And complicated.

I should not have had sex with him again so soon, but I also felt like it was a necessity. It was a hurdle we needed to overcome before we could move forward. My heart was bursting with joy, yet I felt like crying tears of sadness at the same time. I was confused about how I should feel.

Don't think.

That's what Alexander had said to me, and he was right to do so. My tendency to overthink everything was constantly getting in the way. Perhaps he knew me better than I gave him credit for. I only wished I could shut my mind off, like the flipping of a light switch. But, unfortunately, that was not the way I was built.

Resuming our physical relationship was a game-changer, and I knew it would be impossible for me to walk away from him a second time. I had meant what I said about not running again. My plans to deal with my own troubled past had been thrown out the window the minute he kissed me on the side of the highway. It didn't matter that there were trust concerns between us, and I didn't care if he was clinging to secrets. Lying naked in his arms broke every shred of determination I was narrowly hanging on to, and it was because *he* was different.

I couldn't point out what it was exactly. Alexander had always been a generous lover, but he had given more this time. It wasn't just sex. There was an emotional connection that hadn't been there before, and I didn't know how to sort it out.

Just go with it. Everything will be okay.

I closed my eyes, took a deep breath, and willed away the angst. It was high time I stopped getting lost in my own head. Attempting to settle into the comfort of Alexander's arms, I focused on his hand that lightly massaged the top of my head. I pulled him closer, appreciating the feel of his warm and naked skin.

Yes. Everything will work out just fine.

"So," Alexander began. "Allyson mentioned you were at a job interview today. Tell me about it."

Damn her!

"I'm just exploring my options," I said, trying to sound more confident than I felt. I knew where this was headed.

"The text I sent you last week – that offer still stands. The job at Turning Stone is still yours. I want you to take the position, Krystina."

"I don't know what to do," I confessed truthfully.

"What is your gut telling you to do? Or in your case, what are your angel and devil telling you to do?" he teased. He poked me in the ribs, and I jumped.

"Hey! Cut it out!" I exclaimed, completely embarrassed that he was bringing up the angel and the devil—the childlike subconscious I'd foolishly admitted to during a drunken stupor. "Don't make fun of me, Alex."

"Well?"

He waited patiently for my answer. I thought hard, searching for the right path to take. I still didn't know what to do. I knew I wanted to give our relationship another shot. That alone was a giant leap. I just wasn't sure if I wanted to stake my financial future on something that may not work out in the end.

"Your offer was a better one," I mused, attempting to buy myself more time.

"Of course, it was."

"You can be so arrogant sometimes. Do you know that?"

"I've been told from time to time. So, what's it going to be, angel?"

I took a deep breath and frowned.

"Honestly, a lot happened today. I feel like I can't get my bearings, let alone talk about a job. So let me sleep on it. Maybe I'll have the answer tomorrow."

"Fair enough," he conceded. "Are you hungry?"

"Not really," I admitted. I skipped dinner and should have felt famished, but self-imposed worry seemed to kill any sort of appetite I may have had.

"You have to eat dinner. Let's go see what I can round up from the pantry."

Alexander kissed my forehead and rolled off the side of the bed. Completely unabashed over his naked state, he began collecting our clothes that were strewn about in various points of the room. I could only lie there and admire the view. I would never tire of looking at his elegant and masculine physique, so incredibly powerful and strong.

His solid build was perfection from head to toe. From the broad span of his shoulders to his chiseled abdomen, not a scar marred his flesh. His hands, large and strong, could make miracles happen over my body. I flushed as I thought about the way they felt running up the insides of my thighs as he looked at me with penetrating sapphire blue eyes – eyes that could see through to my very soul.

He was truly beautiful, and he set my world on fire.

He slipped into his jeans, and I inwardly sighed. I loved when Alexander wore jeans, although I couldn't say why. Perhaps it was because I rarely saw him in anything other than dress slacks. Whatever it was, there was something incredibly sexy about the way he wore denim.

I continued to watch him as he pulled a T-shirt over his head. His hair, already wild from sex, became further mussed. He ran a hand through the dark waves in an attempt to smooth them. That one simple action may have been the sexiest thing I had ever seen. He made me feel like a giddy schoolgirl, and I had to stifle a giggle. I forced myself to tear my gaze from him before I did something embarrassing.

I really am thinking like a lust-crazed teen.

I spotted my underwear hanging haphazardly off of a

small lamp on the nightstand. It was like something you might see in a college dorm room. The giggle that was imminent escaped me.

"What's so funny?" Alexander asked curiously.

"I just appreciate the decorations," I told him, pointing to the black lace panties.

The edges of his mouth curled up in the sexiest of smiles.

"I like it. I think I'll make those a permanent fixture in here."

"Maybe you'll start a new trend," I laughed as I untangled myself from the sheets. I made a move to retrieve the undergarment, but Alexander grabbed my hand.

"I was serious. Leave them there."

"Don't be silly. I need my underwear."

"No. You don't."

There was no mistaking the command in his tone. I tilted my chin up in defiance and looked him in the eye. His gaze held a wicked gleam. It was as if he was daring me to try and challenge him.

"Fine. I don't need them."

"I see you're finally learning," he said with a slight chuckle. I scowled at the roguish grin he flashed me, but inside I was melting.

I'm such a sucker.

"Don't push your luck, Stone."

After I finished dressing, minus the underwear, I followed Alexander out of the master suite and into a handsomely decorated entertainment area with a large flat-screen television and lounge seating. But what captured my attention the most was the dramatic glass staircase at the far end of the room. It climbed up to who knows where on this massive vessel.

Moving through and into the dining area, a large table with a beautiful onyx top greeted me. However, Alexander didn't give me much time to admire the details of the breathtaking piece. Instead, he just strolled past it and motioned for me to continue following him into a small and narrow kitchen.

He began to peruse the contents of one of the mahogany cabinets. My stomach gave a slight rumble, letting me know my appetite had returned. I peeked over his shoulder to see what the offerings were. The pickings were slim.

He opened the mini-fridge and pressed his lips together in annoyance. Just like the cabinet, there wasn't much to choose from—only a few condiments, a half-empty container of cranberry juice, and a block of cheese.

Before I could comment, he pulled his phone from his pocket.

"Hale," he barked into the receiver. "Go over to the marina restaurant and pick up dinner for Krystina and me. We'll both have the spinach and walnut salad. Raspberry vinaigrette on the side."

"Alexander! Don't send him out. We can make do with—"

He waved me off and continued talking.

"Yes. Grilled chicken with feta will be fine for the main dish."

Oh, hell no.

I was aghast at the way he could issue such harsh commands. Having the luxury of a manservant or not, I had come to like Hale. I'd be damned before I allowed Alexander to order him about on my behalf. So, I did the first thing that came to mind. I marched over to where Alexander was standing and ripped the phone from his hand.

"Hale, you will do no such thing!"

Alexander stood there looking shocked and furious at the same time, but I had stunned him into silence. Hale, on the other hand, was sputtering on the other end of the line.

"My apologies, Miss Cole. But Mr. Stone—"

"Yes. I am fully aware of what Mr. Stone said. And he said you could have the night off, which is exactly what you are going to do. Isn't that right, *Mr. Stone*?" I finished, looking to Alexander for confirmation.

Hale stayed silent. Alexander and I faced one another. It was a battle of wills, two participants in a staring contest of the likes I had never once partaken. The silence stretched on for what seemed like forever before Alexander held his hand out to take the phone.

"Apparently, *Miss Cole* isn't hungry this evening," he said to Hale, mimicking my tone. "Scratch the order and take the rest of the night off."

Without saying goodbye, he ended the call.

"We can make do with what's here," I began to say, but he held up his hand to silence me.

"Don't ever do that again, or else...."

I narrowed my eyes at him.

"Or else what?"

"Don't test me, Krystina."

His eyes flashed. He was fuming. The angry tick of his jaw made me realize I may have pushed him to his limit. In retrospect, I probably should not have interfered with him and a member of his staff. But either way, we really *could* make do with what was already on the boat. There was no sense in bothering Hale with it.

"I won't interfere again," I said, conceding to that one thing only. "However, I will not apologize. Just because you can summon people to do your bidding whenever you damn well please, doesn't mean you should. Now, I am starting to get a bit hungry, and I'm sure you are too. So please, step aside so that I can see about fixing us something to eat."

Not saying another word, I went to work.

Alexander

IT WAS NOT her place to interfere with my staff. I was no stranger to a power struggle. People have tried but failed miserably. I always come out on top. Yet, somehow, Krystina thwarted me.

Who the hell does she think she is?

But I knew who she was. She was an incorrigible woman, sassy and bold. A terrible submissive and a poor match for someone like me. The way she had stood there on the phone with Hale, her hand on her hip and a challenge in her eyes...

Fuck me, but I think I've fallen even more in love with her.

I stood there like a dimwitted fool while she went back and forth between the pantry and refrigerator, pulling out various items. She procured a can of tuna from somewhere. And capers.

Where did she manage to find those?

I never eat capers.

A million thoughts raced through my mind while I

watched her whip together a tuna salad. I was at a complete loss for words as I tried to assess the situation.

She takes my phone, orders an employee to disobey my wishes, and proceeds to tell me what I should and shouldn't do.

We had yet to achieve a proper Dom-sub relationship, so her bold actions should not have come as a surprise to me. She was incapable of following any sort of direction. She questioned my every move and fought me every step of the way.

And I let her do it.

A sense of unease began to grow in the pit of my stomach as I thought about the many other things I'd allowed Krystina to get away with. The list was not a short one. I should have predicted a performance such as tonight. It didn't matter that it was just a telephone conversation. It was the principle of what she had done.

The gravity of what I allowed to transpire hit me square in the chest.

I lost control.

I suddenly felt as if I were choking. During the course of our relationship, I had lost sight of crucial discipline and all of the reasons why I needed to be surrounded by it. She made me forget why I had to keep order in my life.

Perhaps it's because of the idea that I love her.

However, I knew this was highly unlikely. Love developed over a long span of time, not just a few weeks. Years of study taught me this was the truth. I was most likely mistaking lust for love. My physical needs were just messing with my psyche and causing me to forget who I was.

Or perhaps it's the stress of having to tell her about my past.

The mere thought of having to release the buried

demons was nauseating. Darkness began to settle over me, and a momentous weight felt as if it were pressing against my chest, building, and building until pure panic threatened to erupt.

What is she doing to me?

She made me feel unbalanced, slowly teetering back and forth on the edge of a precipice. I was the one who was supposed to call the shots and make all the decisions—both in and out of the bedroom. Life was simpler that way. It allowed me to maintain order. My world, always sensible and controlled, suddenly felt like it was wavering.

This will never do.

I had to take it back.

In two strides, I closed the distance between us and pulled her back against my chest. She shrieked in surprise and struggled to get away.

"Alex! I'm trying to make a salad. Let go of me!"

"No," I told her firmly. I felt like the walls were closing in around me, pressing tighter and tighter until I could barely breathe. I locked her in place by keeping a firm arm around her waist and wrapping a hand around her neck.

She has to be still. Just for a minute.

She drove me to the point of madness. I just needed a moment to find one rational thought within the hurricane of my mind. Perhaps then I could regain some measure of order. I had to teach her. To show her why she had to obey me. It was imperative that she understood. There was no other way.

"Alexander," she said, her voice eerily calm. "Let me go."

"What are you doing to me?" I whispered into her ear and gripped her tighter.

"Please let go of me," she repeated, her voice strained and raspy.

"I feel like I don't know who I am anymore!"

"Alex, you're hurting me!"

I jumped, her choked words stinging like an electric jolt. I staggered back a few steps. It was as if I was floating, looking down at the scene below. Except I wasn't looking at Krystina and myself—I was seeing my mother and father. I shook my head to clear it.

When I focused again, I looked to Krystina. She was staring at me with eyes full of hurt and accusations. She rubbed her neck and tried to catch her breath. There were faint red marks on her throat, fingerprints from where I had squeezed. Guilt overcame me, and I thought I was going to be sick. I looked away, utterly appalled.

What have I done?

Childhood memories flashed before my eyes. The universe had suddenly come full circle. History did, in fact, repeat itself. For the first time in my adult life, I truly lost all sense of self-control. Everything I swore I would never become had come to fruition in an instant. I crossed the line and became what I feared the most.

I have become my father.

I reached out to touch her shoulder, but she jerked away.

"Don't touch me!" she shouted. Her eyes flashed angrily.

"Krystina..."

"Don't you 'Krystina' me. What the fuck was that all about?"

"I'm sorry. I don't know what came over me," I began, but the words tasted like ash in my mouth. They were the exact words I'd heard my father say to my mother, and he said them more times than I could count. "I'm bringing you home."

Away from me. Where you can be safe.

"No," she said stubbornly, taking me by surprise. "You promised me the truth. I'm not leaving until I get it. But let me make one thing extremely clear. You will *never* touch me like that again. Ever."

I cringed at the harsh tone in which she spoke, even though I deserved it. I looked at her sadly.

Oh, angel. If only you knew.

"I'd like to tell you I wouldn't do it again, but...I can't."

"What do you mean you can't?" she fumed.

It means my father's blood runs through my veins! I tried to warn you that day in my conference room! You should have listened to me when I said I wasn't the right man for you!

I wanted to shout the words, but I couldn't. I had to keep my emotional state in check. I already lost it once, and I refused to do it again. I couldn't afford to do it again.

Continuing on this path would destroy me.

I rubbed my hands over my face and took a deep breath.

"There are things you don't understand," I tried to explain.

Our eyes locked, and her scrutiny was intense. It was as if she could see right through to the secret blackness of my soul. She walked toward me and placed a hand on my cheek. Her expression softened, forgiving almost, and she didn't appear so angry anymore. It just made me feel that much worse.

I'm such an asshole.

"Alex, talk to me," she said with a mystified look.

I leaned into her hand, so warm and inviting. I closed my

eyes and focused on her fingertips as they brushed my cheek. Her simple touch chased all the darkness away.

Once upon a time, a devil fell in love with an angel...

I wanted to give her a fairytale. I wanted to pull her close and pretend my past didn't exist. But I had to face reality. It was time to tell her about me, my mother, sister, and everything else in between.

Including my father.

"I've stalled long enough. It's time."

7

Krystina

Stunned by Alexander's statement and his erratic behavior, I pulled my hand from his face and slowly backed away from him.

I told him I wasn't going anywhere until I heard his story, but every bone in my body was telling me to run. I should have booked out of there the minute Alexander released his grip from my neck. But for some reason, I could not will myself to leave. Instead, I found myself softening, unable to bear the look of pain and guilt on his face.

This can't be happening. He choked me! Why wouldn't he concede to never doing it again? What did he mean when he said he couldn't?

A nervous pit began to grow in my stomach.

I should go.

I glanced around, looking for the closest escape route

from the boat. I tried to remember how we had come to be in the kitchen, but I wasn't paying attention along the way.

"Go out to the dining room and make a left," Alexander said quietly.

"What?"

"You want to run. I can tell you do. You have that fight or flight look. I certainly can't blame you."

My middle name should be Captain Obvious.

"No. I'm fine," I denied stubbornly. To prove my point, I turned back to preparing our food.

I'm not going to run again. I can do this. I can do this.

I repeated the line in my head over and over again as I vigorously mixed up a tuna salad.

He said it's time. Time for what? His story? Round two of Strangle-the-Girlfriend?

But I'm not his girlfriend, am I?

I looked down at the bowl in front of me. The salad would soon be a puree if I continued mixing it to death. I stopped the assault on our food, took a deep breath, and tried to gather my thoughts. I couldn't get lost in my head. Not now. It was better if I remained focused on the task at hand, even if it was something as trivial as preparing a simple meal.

Plates. We need plates to eat. And forks.

I poked around in the cabinets of the galley-style kitchen in search of plates and utensils. Out of the corner of my eye, I saw Alexander coming towards me. Reflex caused me to flinch without meaning to.

I'm stronger than that! Acting like a scared wallflower is just plain asinine.

"I-I was just looking for plates," I sputtered out, trying to cover up for the way I cringed upon his approach.

However, it was apparent he saw my instinctive reaction. When I looked at him, the guilt in his eyes spoke volumes.

"I'll get them," he muttered.

Slowly reaching above my head, he pulled down two plates from the overhead cabinet. His movements were cautious, almost as if he thought moving too quickly would scare me.

Together, we walked out of the kitchen and into the dining area. Without uttering a word, Alexander set the table and retrieved us a couple of bottled waters. I opened a box of crackers. The crinkling of the packaging was almost deafening, and it drew attention to how awkwardly quiet we were. The room was wrought with tension of the worst kind, making the difficult silence absolutely brutal to endure.

He simply lost his temper. That's all. We can get past this.

I tried to convince myself of that as I wracked my brain to figure out what to do. Having never seen Alexander truly lose his cool the way he did, I came up short on ideas. I just knew I had to say something—anything to somehow cut through the anxiety in the air.

"I'm not sure if you're a fan of tuna salad. I just assumed you were since you had most of the ingredients handy," I began tentatively.

"This is fine with me."

His tone was strained. I watched his brow furrow in concentration as he added a couple of spoonfuls to my plate before filling his own.

"I thought maybe we could spread it on the crackers," I added, annoyed by the waver in my voice.

My nerves are shot. I need to get a grip.

He set the bowl of tuna down and looked at me.

"You're fidgeting," he pointed out with an ominous expression. "I'm sorry, angel. I don't want you to feel nervous or afraid."

"Oh, no! I'm just... it's okay. Really," I tried to assure, even though I wasn't. I didn't know what to say or how to react to him, as I was still torn between drilling him for answers about his behavior and running out the door. My naturally quick wit was failing me.

Instead of babbling further, I went to work on the salad and crackers so my hands could keep busy. Just as I took my first bite, Alexander spoke again.

"Who told you my mother was still alive?"

I nearly spit out my food to prevent choking from the shock of him jumping right in without any preamble. Death by white albacore tuna was not the way I planned to go.

"Excuse me," I said and took a swig from a water bottle. "Sorry. I know your story is the entire purpose of this little impromptu trip to your boat, but you kind of caught me off guard. You're normally so tight-lipped about your past. I half expected to have to drag any sort of answer out of you."

"Cards on the table. All of them. That's what I promised you, didn't I? So, tell me. How did you obtain information about my mother?"

"The day I went to The Mandarin with Ally," I told him cautiously. "Your sister was there. I overheard her talking to the person she was with."

"I had a feeling that was where you heard it. Justine needs to be more careful," he said and pursed his lips to show his displeasure. "I'm not sure how much or how little you heard, but the fact of the matter is, neither Justine nor I know if my mother is alive. We haven't seen or heard from her in over twenty years. She left when I was ten. When I told you my mother was dead, it wasn't necessarily a lie. To me, she is dead."

I froze, unable to find words. To think he had spent all those years not knowing if his mother was alive or dead was inconceivable.

"She just abandoned you and—"

He held up his hand to silence me.

"You have to listen and simply take it all in first, Krystina. I know you've had many questions, and I realize it was upsetting to you when I shut you down. But knowing you, once I start telling you everything, you're going to have a thousand more questions to ask. I need you to hold onto them for the time being so I'm not interrupted every two minutes. Can you do that for me?"

"Yeah, sure. I can do that," I quickly agreed. But secretly, I doubted my ability to bite my tongue. I was too revved up from the evening's whirlwind of events.

"What I am about to tell you, you can't tell another living soul. Do you understand?"

I paused then, alarmed by the grave tone in which he spoke. His eyes bore into mine, and his face was set firm.

"I understand," I acknowledged with a slow nod of my head.

Alexander stared at me for a moment longer, almost as if he was trying to assess my trustworthiness, and I could see the internal struggle he was having with himself. Eventually, he leaned back in the dining chair and folded his arms. It was a defensive gesture, but his face looked thoughtful as he appeared to be contemplating his choice of words.

"I guess I should start with where I grew up. If I recall, I once mentioned to you that we lived in the Bronx. Specifically, it was a housing project with stereotypical cinderblock buildings, foul odors that never seemed to dissipate, and bars on the windows. The area was riddled with crime and drugs, where gun deaths and overdoses happened almost daily. Perhaps that's why I don't see New York the way you do. You see the charm, whereas I've seen the worst of the worst the city has to offer."

"I've never been to the Bronx," I admitted.

"It's not all dire, but many areas leave much to be desired. The people who lived around us had very little in terms of material possessions. That was the norm. My family did not own a car, and we couldn't afford cable. Our phone was without service more often than not because of overdue bills. It was a struggle to make ends meet, and my mother learned early on how to stretch a dollar so that we could have a decent meal.

"My father worked, but never in one place for very long. He always had an excuse for his shortcomings as an employee, and someone else was always to blame whenever he got fired from a job. I began to value the importance of money at a very young age. Our bedtime stories were never storybook fairytales, but about the life my mother wanted us to live once we broke free from the wretchedness that surrounded us. I don't remember how old I was, but at one point, I decided I was going to be rich. I didn't know how I would do that. I only knew I wanted the life my mother crafted for us in her stories. I never wanted to worry about having enough to eat or whether my shoes fit properly."

"Well, I think you've managed to do that," I joked lightly, trying to understand what it was like to live in squalor with only the dream of a better day. My mother and I had our fair share of struggles, but never to the extent he described. It was hard to imagine Alexander without the wealth that surrounded him.

"My father was angry all the time for one reason or another," he continued. "He was the worst sort of man you could imagine. He defined the meaning of the word misogynist, and that's putting it mildly. He was emotionally and physically abusive towards my mother—me too, for that matter. But for some reason, only my mother's beatings are the ones that really stick out in my mind. She got the worst of it."

His tone was entirely detached, as if he were speaking about someone else's life and not his own. However, I did notice he'd barely eaten a thing. If talking about this bothered him, his lack of appetite was the only sign he gave. It was either that, or he really didn't like tuna salad.

As if noticing I was looking at his uneaten food, Alexander picked up a cracker to nibble on before continuing.

"Her first trip to the hospital was when I was seven years old. I returned from school one day to find her beaten to a bloody pulp. She couldn't even stand. I remember being scared half to death," he said. His voice was full of contempt, and he shook his head. "She begged me not to call 911, so I called my grandparents instead."

"The grandparents you used to live with?"

As soon as the question came out, I wanted to slap my hand over my mouth for interrupting him.

Well, I guess I should be proud I lasted this long without a question.

I was so engrossed in what he was saying that I didn't think twice about it. However, despite the fact he asked me not to pose questions, he took this one in stride.

"Yes. My mother's parents. I never knew my paternal grandparents. They died long before I was born. From what I've been told, my paternal grandfather was very much like my father," he scowled, and his voice turned bitter. "The apple never really falls far from the tree, does it?"

"Alex," I began. I intended to offer words of reassurance, but his resolute expression made the words fade from my lips. Eventually, he rubbed his hands over his face as if he were trying to collect himself. When he spoke again, his tone was once again detached.

"My grandfather took her to the hospital. My grandmother brought my sister and me back to their house. We stayed there for a few days while my mother recovered. We made the most of our time there, as it was the only reprieve we ever had from the chaos that was our life."

He paused, and I decided to chance another question.

"Where was your father during all of this?"

"Most likely on a bender trying to drown out his guilt. He wasn't an alcoholic, but he would drink himself into a stupor for days after beating up on my mother," Alexander added, his voice revealing a slight hint of resentment. "My mother was released from the hospital a few days later. Stitches. A broken arm. I don't recall the extent of her injuries. But after that day, my mother changed. She became quieter, mousey almost. She never laughed anymore, too terrified of setting him off. There was a time when she'd try to stop him from coming after me, but that ended too. It was like she was dead inside."

"Alex, I'm so sorry. It had to be awful."

He frowned at my offering of sympathy.

"Don't pity me, Krystina."

"I'm not, I'm just—"

"You are, but I guess that's human nature. Well, for most people, it is," he sardonically added.

My heart broke for him. I was saddened by the resignation I heard in his voice. I hurt for the poor little boy who could not count on his mother to help him against a tyrant of a father. I saw the way he tried to act unaffected, but his eyes were beginning to betray him. I could see the pain in them. I didn't want him to have to relive it all just to appease my need for answers.

"You don't have to tell me every detail of what happened," I offered sincerely.

"I appreciate your understanding, but much of what happened during that time is irrelevant to the story anyway. I only mentioned portions so you could understand the endless cycle in which we lived. I'll fast forward to three years later, right after my tenth birthday. That was the major turning point," he paused again, long enough for me to see anger flash hot in his eyes.

"What happened?"

"My father went after Justine. He had never touched her before. I don't even remember what she did to upset him. I only remember how small she was at the time. Slight in build. Just past six years old. She was defenseless to stop him. I just stood there, too afraid to do anything but watch. And I... I didn't protect her as I should have."

Alexander's voice wavered over the last line, showing genuine emotion for the first time since he began speaking about his past. I was reminded of the way I heard him talk of his sister and about the way I had once seen them embrace from a distance. Although I had never formally met his sister, I knew they shared a special connection. But now, I realized their bond stemmed from their need to survive.

Seconds ticked by, perhaps minutes, while Alexander remained adrift in a memory.

"Alex..." I trailed off, hoping the warning tone of my voice was enough to stop him from going further.

I wanted to cry for him. Tears pricked at the corners of my eyes, and I shook my head in disbelief. The man I knew to be so confident and self-assured looked vulnerable all of a sudden. I looked into his eyes, and all I could see was a ten-year-old boy staring back at me. He was the child version of Alexander Stone, riddled with guilt over not protecting his baby sister.

"I know what you're thinking, but it was my job to protect her. I was the only person she could count on. I should have done something to help her."

"Alex, you were only a child," I tried to assure.

"Perhaps," he mused. "My lack of response on that day may or may not have changed the outcome, but the violence towards Justine did result in sparking a bit of life back into my mother. For the first time in years, she fought back. It didn't end well. She only succeeded in landing herself another hospital stay. A day or two later, she was released, and we went back home. The house was empty, and none of us expected to see my father for a few days. But even without him there, the air was tense. We all dreaded the sound of the front door opening."

"That's a horrific way to live. The constant fear—" I stopped short, unable to find the right words of comfort. He didn't need me to reiterate what it must have felt like. He lived through it.

"I never did end up hearing the front door open," Alexander continued, but this time his voice was flat and completely devoid of all emotion. "He came back when I was at school. I found him that day. Dead. Laying in a pool of his own blood."

8

Alexander

I could still smell it even after all this time—the metallic scent of blood mixed with urine. I fought back the bile welling in the back of my throat.

"Oh my god!" Krystina exclaimed. Her hand clasped over her mouth, and she wore a look of complete horror. "You found him?"

I closed my eyes, hoping and praying the truth would present itself—the truth I had been in search of for as long as I could remember. But as usual, I came up blank. I grappled with trying to find the right words to explain the events from that day.

"He was laying on the family room rug. Shot in the abdomen. The blood," I said, seeing it like it was yesterday. "It was everywhere. Justine was there. I found her hiding behind the sofa. She didn't go to school that day—sick with a head cold, as I recall. But she has no memory of how he was shot."

I squeezed my eyes shut tight and tried to will away the images of Justine sitting on the floor, her tattered pink shirt splattered with blood. She had been crying and holding our father's Glock pistol in her hand.

Fuck, I wish I could just forget about this.

But no matter how hard I tried to forget, those few moments in time would never be erased from my mind.

"Justine! What happened?"

"I don't know," she says through her sobs.

"Why do you have dad's gun?"

"Mommy's going to be so mad. I ruined my shirt!"

I shake her.

"How did this happen?" I ask her again.

Her face goes blank, and she looks strangely at me through vacant eyes.

"Alex, do you know where my blue dress is? The pretty one with the flowers. Mommy likes when I wear it."

"Justine!"

I shake her again, but it's like she can't hear me. I follow her to the bedroom we share and listen to her hum as she changes her clothes. I shout at her again, but she doesn't respond.

Fear spreads through my veins. I feel like I am suffocating.

I walk back out to the family room and pick up the gun.

A warm hand covered mine, ripping me away from a dark time and back to the present. I looked down at the slender fingers, up the arm, until my sight landed on the face of an angel. Krystina stared back with eyes full of concern.

"Alexander, it was a long time ago," she said softly.

My throat clogged with emotion, and I tore my gaze from hers.

God, I feel like shit.

I felt unsettled and vulnerable—like every protective barrier I built to protect the past had violently come crashing down.

I pulled my hand from hers and looked out the boat cabin window. The sky was dark and bleak, matching my current mood. A part of me couldn't believe I was actually speaking out loud about my past. It has always been private. Even Justine and I never spoke specifics to each other anymore. It was better off buried. But now that I'd started, I knew I had to finish. There was still so much more to tell.

"Angel, if you're through eating, what do you say we take a break and head up to the main deck? I could use a soak in the hot tub and a stiff drink."

"Well, I ah... I suppose we could do that," she stumbled, sounding slightly shocked at the change of course. "Did Hale think to pack me a bathing suit?"

"Hale is extremely thorough. I'm sure he did. But it's a fairly dark night. You won't need one."

She smirked at me.

"I suspect we won't finish talking if we're naked. Just saying."

She laughed lightly, and I could tell she was trying to lighten the mood. I returned her smile, although I wasn't really feeling it. I stood and went over to the minibar to mix us a couple of Winston Cocktails. I knew she preferred wine, but the pickings on the boat were slim. I made a mental note to keep a decent stock of whites come the spring.

"I can't believe I'm going to say this, but you can relax," I assured her as I mixed a dash of Grand Marnier with cognac. "For once, sex with you is not on my radar at the moment. Talking about all of this shit is kind of a total mood killer."

I tried to come off as nonchalant, but she wasn't buying it. She still had a worried expression and stayed quiet for a time. I hated that I was the reason for her concern.

It made me feel weak.

"If you say so, then lead the way," she eventually agreed.

Leaving the remains of our makeshift dinner on the dining room table, I handed her the mixed drink and led her to the spiral staircase that would bring us up to the main deck. Once we were outside, I took a deep breath. The night air was cold in my lungs. The crispness felt good and helped to clear my head. It made me realize how stifling the air had become when we were in the dining room.

I looked around. There didn't appear to be a soul in sight. It was dark, despite the moonbeams peeking out occasionally from a passing cloud. However, moon or no moon, the location of the hot tub afforded enough privacy. Krystina didn't need to worry about being seen by a distant passerby, and I could rest assured we wouldn't be overheard.

Moving to the hot tub control panel, I pressed the buttons to raise the cover and started the jets. The water bubbled, crystal clear and inviting. I quickly stripped and climbed in. Almost instantly, the piping-hot water helped wash away some of my anxiety and unease.

Krystina followed suit, and even though I said I was in no mood for it, I couldn't help but admire her naked flesh as she slithered into the tub across from me.

She reached up to tie her hair into a haphazard knot on top of her head. With her arms raised, her lush breasts glowed in the moonlight as her nipples peeked out to bob above the waterline. Another day, I may have been instantly turned on. But today, her simple movements had a calming effect on me.

She leaned back to slide further under the water. She caught my stare and afforded me a small smile. In an instant, I was completely lost in her. I returned her smile and silently wondered what it was I did to deserve this angel that had come into my life.

We both quietly sipped our cocktails for a time, the bubbling of the jets and the billowing steam creating an almost hypnotic atmosphere. Krystina had settled back, and her eyes were closed. However, her brow furrowed on occasion. I could practically see the mouse spinning the wheel in her head.

"What are you thinking?" I asked.

She peered open one eye to look at me.

"Honestly, I'm wondering if it's okay to ask questions now."

"Fire away," I offered, although somewhat apprehensively.

"Where was your mother on the day your father was killed?"

"My mother," I spat out bitterly. The mere mention of her grated on my nerves and instantly broke the tranquil atmosphere in the hot tub. "The last I saw her was that morning before school. She made oatmeal for my breakfast, kissed me on the cheek, and told me to have a good day. I haven't seen her since."

And I haven't been able to eat oatmeal since that day either.

Krystina sat there shaking her head in disbelief.

Yes, angel. Believe it. She abandoned us.

"Since your mother was nowhere to be found, what did you do?"

I knew she would ask, but I hesitated.

Trust her. She deserves to know it all.

"Even though I was only ten years old, I knew enough to understand the severity of the situation. My father was shot dead, and I found my sister with the gun. I could only draw one conclusion at that time. I was also still filled with guilt over not protecting Justine from my father's abuse. I thought maybe, just maybe, this was Fate's way of giving me a second chance. I reacted without thinking."

"Reacted how?"

"Justine was acting strange. Looking back, I realize now it was her mind's way of protecting her from a traumatic experience. However, I didn't know that at the time. I only knew I had to help her somehow. So, I went back into the living room and retrieved the gun. I put it in my school bag and left the house, leaving her alone with my father's dead body. I headed towards the nearest subway station. I rode the train for a while, trying to decide what I should do. Eventually, I ended up at the Harlem River."

I stopped, afraid to tell Krystina the rest. She sat there wide-eyed with her glass frozen midway to her lips, waiting for me to continue.

"The Harlem River?" she coaxed.

"The police never found the gun that shot my father. I threw it in the river, effectively destroying all evidence that would lead to the truth."

Her brow furrowed in confusion.

"Are you saying you still don't know who shot your father?"

"There are theories. Some by the police, others belong to Justine or me. My mother's disappearance, of course, made her suspect number one for the police. But they didn't know her as I did. My mother was terrified of guns, and I'm not convinced she had it in her to pull the trigger."

"Who then? Was it Justine like you originally thought? She was practically a baby!"

"I don't know. She says she still has no memory of that day or the next few days that followed. Post-traumatic stress," I added and shook my head. "It's frustrating that she can't remember. She only knows what I told her about that time."

Krystina crossed the hot tub and sat next to me. Water lapped around us as I wrapped my arm around her and pressed a kiss to the top of her head.

"What did you do after you threw away the gun?" she asked quietly.

"I went home. My mother wasn't there. For some reason, I knew she wasn't going to come back, so I made sandwiches for our dinner. It's funny how the mind works," I added as an afterthought. "Through all of it, I never once thought to call anyone about the dead body in the family room. It was by pure happenstance that Hale came by two days later."

Krystina jerked back, her expression one of incredulous disbelief.

"Wait. You and your sister lived with a dead body for two days?"

The memory of my father's disgusting corpse was singed

into my brain. The long-term damage it had inflicted on Justine caused more guilt to tear at my gut.

I should have known better. I should have called someone.

"My grandmother had asked Hale to drop off a loaf of banana bread she made for us. The rest of the day was downright chaos, and the details are hazy, but I do remember eating the banana bread," I added sardonically.

"Alex, I know you'll think this is pity, but I really am terribly sorry for all you went through. And I'm sorry I compared you to your father. I would never have said that had I known everything."

But you were right. I am like him.

"It is what it is, angel," I tried to shrug off instead.

"You are not like him."

It was as if she read my mind.

"Aren't I, though? Come on, Krystina," I said bitterly. "I get off on hitting women."

"No. Not that way," she insisted and shook her head vehemently. "It's different, and you know it. You don't like to hit women the way he did."

"It doesn't matter. I am who I am. I just channel it differently. BDSM is my chosen outlet, but it's why I say I'm not good for you. I lose control of my emotions at times with you. You'd be wise to be leery of that."

"That's a load of bullshit, Alex. I'll say it again. You are not like him."

I wanted to believe her when she said I wasn't like my father. But she didn't know everything, and she certainly didn't know me like she thought she did. Even now, her chocolate brown eyes swirled with conflicted emotions as she studied me. I was sure she was questioning her own words but willing herself to believe them at the same time.

"A load of bullshit, huh? You don't look so sure that it is."

She sat quietly for a long while. When she finally spoke, it was apparent she was choosing her words carefully.

"I do not want to downplay anything you have told me tonight. You had a terrible childhood. I get why all of this is painful to talk about. But I'm having trouble seeing why this is such a big secret to you. I don't understand why you couldn't tell me all of this before."

"What do you mean you don't see why it's a secret? First of all, I am now a man of considerable means. I'm no longer a piss broke child living in the slums who nobody gives a rat's ass about. The press would have a field day with this story. Justine would never survive it. I have to protect her from that. Secondly, I'm an accomplice to murder. I threw the evidence in the river. The only other person who knows I did that is Justine. Then..." ...*my dreams.*

I shook my head, unable to finish the sentence. My dreams were my innermost secret and something I never spoke of before to anyone. They were one of the reasons why I was so hell-bent on understanding the human mind.

There was a method to my madness when I decided on psychology as my major in college. I hoped it would help me understand post-traumatic stress disorder enough to unlock Justine's memory and learn the truth about what happened to my father.

I needed that truth to discredit the theory about who might have killed him—a theory based around my own memories that would only resurface in my dreams. I wanted to quell the nightmares that haunted my childhood, visions that made me see the possibility of another reality I didn't want to believe. However, education didn't get me anywhere, and I still didn't have any answers.

Krystina reached up and cupped my face in her hands. Her eyes were soft and comforting.

What would she think if I told her about the dreams?

However, I immediately dismissed the idea. If the dreams rattled me, they would be sure to terrify Krystina—especially after the way I had squeezed her neck just a few short hours ago.

The shameful memory of my horrendous behavior made me cringe.

"Alex, I can see how conflicted you are over this. We don't have to talk anymore about it tonight."

Grateful she was giving me a reprieve for the time being, I pulled her tight to me and buried my face in her hair. I was emotionally spent, yet I also felt like I could finally breathe.

It was then that I realized how much of a struggle my days were and how exhausting it was to maintain order in all things surrounding me. It was as if each day I was climbing a mountain, hand over hand up an endless rope to a peak I could never quite reach.

With Krystina, there were times when I felt like I was free-falling into an abyss. However, there were also moments when I thought I didn't have to worry about the rope breaking or that I'd hit rock bottom. As unbalanced as I sometimes felt with her, she somehow had the ability to keep me grounded.

Fuck the psycho-bullshit I've read. I do love her.

A feeling of melancholy settled over me. I knew loving Krystina came with consequences, as I couldn't tell her my deepest concerns about what might have happened all those years ago. I could only give her the truth as I knew it to be. In a perfect world, we could complete each other. And as I held her close, I silently wished that could be our reality.

She merited nothing short of perfection and deserved so much more than I could give her.

9

Krystina

I awoke to the early dawn sunlight streaming through the curtains of the cabin window. Alexander lay still beside me, a pleasant change from how he had been throughout the night.

I gave in to a silent yawn, exhausted from not getting nearly enough sleep. When we eventually climbed into bed, it had been well past midnight. Alexander passed out within minutes. However, I lay awake for hours contemplating everything he told me. I dozed off sometime around three in the morning, only to be startled awake an hour later by Alexander's thrashing.

He had obviously been having a terrible dream of some sort, but I had been afraid to wake him. Alexander's words about his sister's post-traumatic stress had echoed through my mind, and I worried about the possibility that Alexander might suffer from the same. It would certainly explain the unprecedented choking episode from the night before. However, I didn't know enough about the disorder to make that diagnosis. I only heard of the dangers that could occur upon waking a person who could potentially have PTSD.

I watched him sleep and listened to the sounds of his breath coming soft and even. His face was so peaceful, and it was hard to believe how restless he'd been just a few hours earlier. I wanted nothing more than to snuggle in closer and stay in his arms all day.

Unfortunately, nature called. I shifted my weight slowly towards the side of the bed, careful not to disturb his slumber. Then, tiptoeing as quietly as possible, I made my way to the bathroom.

When I looked at my reflection in the mirror, I winced. I had worn one of Alexander's T-shirts to bed, and it sagged limply over my shoulders. My face was pale from exhaustion, only emphasizing the dark rings circling my eyes. My hair was an absolute disaster, with ends sticking up every which way. I sighed.

Will mornings ever agree with me?

I splashed some water on my face with the hope it would shock a little bit of life back into my pale complexion. I tried to smooth out the unruly curls, but they refused to be tamed. I knew nothing short of a shower would suffice this morning.

Thankfully, there was a shower stall in the bathroom. It was small but larger than I would have expected a boat to have. I turned on the faucet, adjusted the temp, and stripped out of Alexander's T-shirt. As I was pulling it over my head, I paused to breathe in the scent of it. The shirt smelled like him—that familiar sandalwood scent that never failed to make me quiver inside.

After showering quickly, I wrapped myself in a towel and headed back out to the bedroom, searching for clothes. Alexander was awake but still in bed. He was propped up by pillows and looking at his phone. He appeared extremely relaxed. If he recalled having any sort of bad dream, he wasn't showing it.

"Good morning, angel. Sleep well?"

"Like a baby," I lied. I wasn't sure if I wanted to mention his tossing and turning during the night. We shared such a tense and stress-filled evening. I didn't want to start the morning off on the wrong foot.

"Come here," he said and patted the mattress next to him.

I went over to the bed and plopped down next to him. I tried to ignore the way the sheet slid down around his hips to reveal the beginning of the delectable V that would leave any woman swooning.

"What's up?"

"Are you familiar with The Stonework's Foundation?" he asked.

"That's your non-profit charity, right?"

"Yes. Our latest project is a woman's shelter in Queens. Justine is heading it up. The final fundraiser before the grand opening is on Friday. It's a charity gala. I'd like you to accompany me."

Woman's shelter?

I vaguely remembered reading something in a newspaper article about Alexander opening a shelter for battered women. At the time, I half wondered what his interest in that would be. Now it all made much more sense.

I hesitated with my response as I recalled the many press

releases that I'd read about Alexander. Some were about business dealings; others were about the women who decorated his arm. Considering how shaky our relationship was, I wasn't sure if I was ready for it to become open to public speculation. The last thing we needed was a gossipmonger's scrutiny while we were trying to work things out.

"Is this a black-tie sort of thing?" I asked, trying to gauge how big of an event it would be.

"Kind of. Think more along the lines of Moulin Rouge, the French cabaret. Justine is taking advantage of the post-Halloween season to spice things up. She's hoping to make it stand out from the typical charity gala, which can be dull and extremely boring. She decided to go with turn-of-the-century costume themes—tuxedos, top hats, and feather boas. I must say, I was skeptical at first, but her idea worked. At a thousand dollars a ticket, the event sold out."

A thousand dollars a ticket!

There was no doubt about it. This event was a huge deal.

"It sounds like it will be great, but I'm not really sure if it's something I should go to."

"That's completely absurd. Why wouldn't it be?" His brow furrowed in confusion as he ran a hand through his hair and regarded me carefully.

I shook my head and sighed. "It's the press, Alex. You've said it yourself—you are often in the public eye. We haven't made any sort of public appearance together. I'm not sure if I'm ready to see my picture in the morning newspaper. Or the tabloids, for that matter."

"There's no reason for you to have concern. Let me worry about the press."

"I'm not necessarily concerned about the press per se. It's just that we are still trying to figure out *us*, you know? I don't know if I want us to be so public yet." I shrugged like it was no big deal and moved to get off the bed, but he rolled over and pinned me beneath him. "Alex, what are you doing? I need to get dressed."

He ignored me and kissed the tip of my nose.

"Angel, the press is always going to be around in one way or another. I usually do a good job of avoiding them, but sometimes it can't be helped. You need to accept that."

"Yes, but—" I stopped short when I saw his gaze drop to my chest. The towel I had wrapped around me had fallen open to expose one of my breasts. I would have moved to fix it, but my arms were trapped in the grip of his powerful hands. I held my breath and waited to see what he would do.

His lips parted slightly, and he leaned down towards me. His eyes were a violent inferno of desire. He took the lobe of my ear between his teeth before tracing the outline with the tip of his tongue. A shiver ran through me.

"What was it you were trying to say?" he whispered. His breath was hot as he nibbled his way down my neck. A rush of heat crashed between my thighs.

"No-nothing," I gasped out, my voice barely recognizable as another shiver raced down my spine.

"Are you sure?"

Using one hand, he positioned my arms above my head and worked his way around my collarbone.

"Yes."

"I thought maybe you were going to start a fight with me," he teased. His free hand softly brushed over the side of my breast, down to my belly, then back up to flick at a rigid peak. My breath caught in my throat. "You wouldn't want to have a disagreement over something as silly as the press, now would you?"

"Never."

Wearing nothing but his boxers, he continued to straddle my hips and kept me pinned in place. He made another trail down my belly with his fingertips, never quite reaching the mark because of how he was positioned. I pushed up with my hips and strained against him, but that only served to send another rush of heat to the junction of my thighs. He was driving me absolutely mad.

"A bit eager this morning?"

Yeah, you think?

The man had the ability to turn me on in an instant. I couldn't control my need for him if I tried. I wrenched one arm free from his grip and pulled at the waistband of his boxers, suddenly desperate to have nothing between us. I tugged until he finally shifted so they could be removed. I reached to pull him close to me, only to have my grasp come up empty when he climbed off the bed.

"Don't move," he told me.

"Wait. What?"

Where the hell is he going?

"Be patient, angel. I'll be right back."

He was only gone for a minute or so when he returned, holding a bottle of champagne set in a bucket of ice and a glass of pinkish-red liquid. I assumed it to be cranberry juice, as it was one of the few things remaining in his near-empty refrigerator. I bolted up to a sitting position.

"Poinsettia cocktails?" I asked incredulously. "You left me

hanging so you could mix a damn drink at six-thirty in the morning?"

He chuckled.

"We've already established you're a terrible submissive, but the least you could do is try. Didn't I tell you not to move?"

I scowled at him as he placed the bucket and glass on the nightstand. Then, to my surprise, he turned and left the room again.

Where is he going now?

I was utterly exasperated and full of impatience. With a harrumph, I tossed myself back onto the bed and waited.

When he returned this time, he carried a black silk scarf, a towel, and a tapered candle. I wanted to point out the ambiance of candlelight usually worked better during the evening hours, but curiosity swayed me to keep my mouth shut.

"Sit up and close your eyes, angel," he told me. "Don't open them, or I might have to punish you."

I frowned but did as I was told.

This better be good.

I closed my eyes and could hear him moving about the room. I chanced a tiny peek at what he was doing. He was fashioning a knot in the black silk scarf.

What's he going to do with that?

However, I had my answer a moment later when he covered my eyes with it. After it was secured at the back of my head, I was one hundred percent blind.

Blindfolded sex. Well, well. Now this could be interesting.

Taking hold of my shoulders, he slowly lowered me back down to a laying position on the bed. Gone was the cool, silky feel of the sheets against my back. Instead, I felt a coarser texture of woven cotton. I could only assume he placed a towel behind me before I laid back. It struck me as somewhat odd, although I had yet to figure out what he was up to.

I waited for what he would do next, but everything went dead quiet. I couldn't even hear footsteps about the room—only silence. Just as I was about to speak, something ice-cold slid across my abdomen. I jumped and gasped from shock. But as soon as I felt the icy sensation, it was gone.

"That was freaking cold! What was that?"

I jerked my head to the side when I felt his breath near the side of my face. With his stealthy movements, I didn't realize he had come so close to me.

"It doesn't matter what it was," he whispered in my ear. A shiver raced down my spine. "This is about how your body reacts and feels without being able to see. That's what sensory deprivation is, angel. I am going to fuck your mind and watch as your body collapses from arousal."

Holy shit!

That one statement was the most profound aphrodisiac, lighting every square inch of my body on fire. The heated pulse between my legs turned into a fervent ache. I didn't think it was possible to want him more than I did at that moment.

Alexander went silent once again. The only sound that could be heard was my labored breathing as I waited in anticipation for what would come next.

Goosebumps pebbled my skin as cold drips of some unknown liquid hit my erect nipples.

Melted ice? Juice maybe?

The cool liquid slid down the sides of my breasts. I quivered again, but not in a bad way. On the contrary, it was a thrilling sort of sensation.

"Open your mouth, Krystina."

I did as I was told as his fingers traced the outline of my lips. He dipped his finger into my awaiting mouth, and the tart flavor of cranberry reached my tongue. Almost simultaneously, something shockingly ice-cold landed between my legs.

I sharply sucked in a breath. I may have protested, but I was prevented from speaking by his finger still lolling about in my mouth. Whatever frozen object he put between my thighs was held in place against my sex until the cold was almost burning.

Icy rivers flooded down my seam as he dipped more cranberry into my mouth. The taste was followed by something crisp and bubbly.

Champagne.

Wet fingers roamed down my belly, pressing against my abdomen and intensifying the ache in my pelvis. His teeth latched on to one of my nipples, his mouth both cold and warm as he rolled a piece of ice around with his tongue. I arched against him as his hand traveled further south between my legs.

I was rewarded by his sharp intake of air.

"Oh, angel. You're so wet," he appreciated. He pinched my icy cold clit between his fingers before plunging them inside me. Instantly, heat crashed over my body. I strained my hips up against him, only to be disappointed when he pulled out.

"Ah," I moaned in frustration.

His fingers entered my mouth once again. They tasted like cranberry, yet different. It took me a moment to realize it was cranberry mixed with my own juices. It was a philter like no other, and I vigorously sucked his fingers clean.

"Good girl," he appreciated.

He pulled his fingers from my eager lips, and the room fell silent again. I heard a slight rustle to my right before recognizing the chafing sound of a lighting match. I half wondered what the purpose of lighting the candle would be since I wouldn't be able to see it, but then the memory of a list we'd made not so long ago flashed before my eyes.

Wax.

I recalled what he wrote about wax on the list of soft and hard limitations. He said he wasn't a fan of wax play.

He wouldn't mess with that. Or would he?

"Alex," I began to protest and sat up.

"Shh. Lay back down," he scolded.

Feeling extremely nervous about what may or may not be coming, I lay back on the bed and tried to relax. I breathed a sigh of relief when I felt a feathery soft material trace the outline of my sternum before moving down my body. Whether it was silk or satin, I couldn't be sure. I was just grateful it wasn't something burning hot running over my skin.

Ice-cold liquid found its way to my breasts once again as Alexander continued to run the material down the length of my torso, ending at the juncture of my thighs. The cold didn't come as too terrible of a shock this time, as I was beginning to adjust to the sensation.

Suddenly, a splash of flaming hot hit my ribcage, and I hissed through my teeth. Even though I knew it might be coming, the contrast was like an assault. The wax puckered and hardened, adhering to my skin while Alexander continued to trace soft lines up and down the length of me. My senses were overwhelmed with touches of warm and cold, soft and hard.

He continued his torture on my body. Eventually, I was beyond the point of wanting. He was driving me insane, and I was desperate, completely lost in an ocean of sensations. I couldn't think. Nothing seemed real anymore. I was panting, unable to concentrate on anything other than the blind sensations he made me feel.

He slipped a finger inside me. Then two.

Finally! Release!

Alexander circled my walls as his thumb pressed against my clit. Within seconds, I could feel the orgasm on the horizon as he plunged his fingers deeper and deeper into my core. He kept me on edge, never quite allowing me to get there. I bucked involuntarily, craving the relief I was so close to getting.

Oh, please!

I wanted to scream out of pure frustration.

"Tell me what you want, Krystina."

"You! Now! Let me feel you inside me!"

I felt the bed shift as he grabbed hold of my knees and roughly pushed my legs apart. He moved in until the weight of his erection settled just outside the mark. My need was quenched when he plunged into me, filling me to maximum capacity with his magnificent length. I tugged at his hair and clawed at his back, the avid tightening in my belly intensifying with every thrust.

He released a satisfied moan. "I will never stop pleasing

you, angel. I will stretch you and bend you in ways that are beyond your wildest imagination. Now give it to me, Krystina. Come for me."

Instantly, my insides constricted, and my mind went hazy. His words sent me over the edge, and I was lost to him. I burst apart beneath him in a splintering orgasm as his hips continued to power forward. I tossed my head from side to side and let out a harsh cry of fantastical release.

I had barely caught my breath when the blindfold was unexpectedly removed from my head. I squinted against the harsh light assaulting my eyes and moved a hand to cover them. When my vision returned to normal, my gaze rested on the face of Alexander. He was hovering above me. His skin was shiny from the sweat of exertion, and his expression was hooded with dark carnal need.

Without saying a word, he took hold of my hips and flipped me around onto my stomach. He leaned down, so his long, hard body pressed against my backside.

"I'm going to spank you now, Krystina. It's going to hurt. Do you remember your safeword?"

Burning with unexplainable need, I choked out the word.

"Sapphire."

"I want to see the pink imprint of my palm on your ass. Get on your hands and knees."

My already rapid heartbeat increased in rhythm, fueling my veins with even more desire for him. I quickly did as I was told and braced for the imminent assault.

Placing his hands on my backside, he slowly eased into me.

"Oh, god," I sighed from the feeling of being full once more.

SMACK!

Even though I'd braced for it, I jumped from the shock of the sting. He continued his assault with another swift slap to the other cheek before pulling back and slamming hard into me. I jolted forward onto my stomach.

"Stay on your knees!" he roared. He gripped my hips, yanked me back up, and landed another hard spank. I locked my elbows in place by gripping the headboard. Confident that I wouldn't fall forward again, I matched him thrust for thrust. It was rough and hard, yet so undeniably erotic.

He brought his hand down again, and a glorious sensation spread. I groaned, reveling in his possession. Over and over again, he pounded into me until my arms began to ache. I was right on the edge, ready to come again, but I knew I couldn't without collapsing under him.

Another smack to my behind and the tightening in my core intensified. I was almost out of energy. I wouldn't be able to hold out much longer.

"Alex," I began to plead.

"Hold on, angel. I'm almost there."

I clenched around him, provoking his release, needing him to give in. I was only seconds away.

"Ah!" he thundered out a cry.

With one last plunge, Alexander's body jerked behind me, and I was spiraling into the abyss of mindless release. Completely and utterly spent, he collapsed down on top of me. A rush of breath escaped my lungs as my hammering heart slowed to a normal rhythm.

"Goddamn, Krystina," he breathed into my ear. "You don't know what you do to me."

He rolled to the side and pulled me into his arms. With a content sigh, I snuggled in closer.

"What is it I do, Alex?" I purred.

He didn't respond right away but pressed his face against the top of my head and breathed deeply. When he finally spoke, his voice was barely a whisper.

"You completely unravel me."

10

Alexander

We lay together, relaxed and sated. Krystina's arm was tossed lazily over my chest, and I found the weight of it to be comforting.

My phone vibrated on the nightstand. I frowned at the intrusion. It was most likely a business-related incoming text, and I was reminded of how little I accomplished over the past few weeks.

It can wait.

Choosing to put off work for just a while longer, I pulled Krystina in closer to me. She had me completely bewitched. Nothing was more important than being with her at that moment.

"Why did you name the boat *The Lucy*?" she asked out of the blue.

I turned my head to look at her. Her cheeks were a delectable shade of rosy pink as she looked at me with inquisitive eyes. I brushed away a lock of hair that had fallen over her brow.

"That's an odd post-sex question," I said with a small chuckle.

"Well, maybe. I was just thinking about your boat."

"What about her, angel?"

"I was thinking it's a shame the boating season is over, and we can't come back here for a while. I kind of like it here...away from the rest of the world. No distractions are nice every now and again."

"She is a great escape," I began, agreeing wholeheartedly with Krystina's sentiments. "But to answer your question, Lucy was my grandmother's name. Why do you ask?"

"Oh. I thought maybe...well, never mind."

I sat up, curious over her hesitation.

"You thought what?"

"It's silly, but I thought it might have been an old girlfriend's name or something," she muttered. Her cheeks flushed a deeper shade of scarlet.

For some odd reason, I found her embarrassed jealousy to be endearing. I was suddenly filled with a heady combination of mischief and delight. I flashed her a devilish smile and dragged her towards the side of the bed.

"I already told you. I never dated before meeting you. Now come on," I said, giving her bottom a light smack. "Get dressed while I take a quick shower. I have to go to work for a bit this afternoon and I want to show you something before I take you home."

"Um, I think I need another shower too," she said and looked pointedly at the wax covering her abdomen and breasts. I laughed.

"It's paraffin wax. It should peel right off. But, if you insist on needing another shower, you're welcome to join me."

My suggestion earned me a tossed pillow to the head.

"You're a sex fiend!" she joked.

"You make me that way, angel. Just wait until later," I promised. I ducked when she threw another pillow at me.

I laughed to myself as I headed towards the bathroom. Before going in, I took one last look at her. Her hair was wild and curling over her shoulders. Her eyes were luminous with a I've-just-been-properly-fucked sort of look. I had half a mind to keep her here all day.

Oh, Miss Cole...the things I would have done to you if I had the proper tools on the boat.

I smiled as I closed the door for the bathroom, thinking of all the possibilities we could explore once I had her back at the penthouse.

After we dressed and gathered our belongings, I led her out to the entertainment suite, and we climbed to the top of the spiral staircase. The walls disappeared and the open deck surrounded us. I squinted at the wash of sunlight and pulled my sunglasses from my pocket.

I inhaled deeply, taking in the crisp morning air, and looked around. Even docked, the serenity *The Lucy* offered was exquisite. When I took her out of the confines of Lake Montauk, away from everything and everyone, there wasn't anything quite like an Atlantic wind when I opened up the throttle.

Krystina is right. It really is a shame The Lucy *is going to dry dock in a few days.*

A vision of Krystina's long brown curls, blowing in a salty Caribbean breeze, came to mind. I pictured her on the bow with the morning sun behind her, casting a glow around her angelic face.

I could make that happen.

I pulled out my phone to send Laura an email about having *The Lucy* commissioned to go south, rather than storing her in dry dock. I knew I might be hard pressed to find a crew this late in the year. But if there was any decent company available to handle the job, I knew my assistant would be able to find them.

"It looks so different in the daylight with the sun sparkling off of the water," Krystina observed, looking out towards the shoreline. "Is this what you wanted to show me?"

I held up my finger to signal I would be with her in a minute. I quickly reread what I had typed. Satisfied, I hit send and turned back to Krystina.

"I wanted to give you a quick tour of the upper deck, seeing as it was too dark last night." I placed my hand at the small of her back and led her around the deck. She remained unusually observant while I pointed out various attributes of the boat. When we reached the pilothouse, I explained how I had it modified to create a more open floor plan. "The switchboard design, captain's chairs, and extra wide console have all been redesigned according to my specifications. The emergency mechanisms –"

I stopped when I saw the blank look on her face.

"I'm sorry, Alex. I really don't mean to be rude," she apologized with a shrug. "I can see you're really proud of this. Talk to me about cars and I can hold my own. But I know jack about boats."

I raised an eyebrow, amused by her confused expression.

Wrapping my arms around her waist, I pulled her tight to my chest.

"Am I boring you, Miss Cole?" I asked into her ear.

"Oh, no! I just –,"

I bit down on her lobe and she gasped. Backing her up slowly, I pinned her against the main console.

"Don't you want to hear about *Lucy's* state of the art navigation system?" I teased.

I worked my way down her neck, nipping and swiping my tongue over her delicious skin as I went. She leaned back, bracing her weight on her hands. Her hips pushed against mine as she tilted her head back.

I felt as if all the blood in my body went straight to my groin. I groaned, wanting to take her again. Right here and right now.

She shifted slightly and there was a click. I froze.

What did she hit?

When the deck merely flooded with loud music, I breathed a sigh of relief.

Just the stereo.

Fucking her up against a half a million dollars' worth of equipment probably wasn't the brightest idea anyways.

"Oh, no! Sorry! How do you turn it off?" she asked, sounding completely mortified. I laughed as she scrambled around to find the switch she accidentally pressed.

"Don't worry, angel," I assured as I reached to lower the volume to a less deafening level. "I may have bored you to tears with *Lucy's* specs, but you may appreciate her sound system."

Her eyes lit up.

"Actually, the sound is great!" she admired and began to hum. "I love this song, too."

I smiled at the way she swayed in place, her hips moving subtly but not quite so much that it could be considered dancing.

"Dance with me," I said and took hold of her hand.

She snorted.

"That's the craziest suggestion you've ever made!"

"Oh, is it now?" I said with a wink. I positioned an arm around her waist and spun her in a circle.

"Alexander Stone! Let go of me right now!" she squealed. Her hands shot up in resistance as she grabbed my biceps, but I was steadfast with my hold.

"Never, angel. I plan to have many dances with you. This is only our first," I murmured into her ear.

She stopped squirming and tilted her head back to look at me. Her eyebrows were raised, as if she were shocked by what I had said. I half surprised myself with the truthfulness of my statement. I truly did want Krystina dancing in my arms for a long time to come. I pulled her tighter against me and we fell into a rhythm.

The feel of her body pressed against mine was soothing. I breathed in the scent of her hair, enticing and familiar, and so uniquely Krystina.

"Early morning waltz with the Captain of the ship. Is this how you impress all the ladies?"

"You're the first," I admitted.

"Yeah, right," she laughed in disbelief.

I pressed my lips together in tight line. The fact she didn't take me seriously was annoying.

"It's the truth," I reinforced. "I've never brought a woman aboard *The Lucy* before."

"Then I guess this is more than just a first dance, isn't it?"

So, it is, baby. So, it is.

"I seem to have a lot of firsts with you," I whispered, more to myself than to her.

"What am I to you, Alex?"

Her question caught me off guard and I pulled back so I could see her face.

How can she not know what she is to me?

After everything we had been through, she had to have some idea. I chased her. Begged her to come back. Bared my soul. She unnerved me with her ability to tear me apart yet keep me whole at the same time. No woman had ever affected me the way she did. She was the sunshine in the darkness. The lightning to my thunder.

Holy hell. Since when did I become such a damn poet?

Perhaps it was Dan Reynolds' heart wrenching ballad about smoke and mirrors. Or maybe it was because I found myself unexpectedly in love. I pursed my lips and frowned.

Careful, Stone. Find the balance.

I needed to get back on track. I made my position perfectly clear in the beginning. I told her no strings attached and she was in complete agreement. However, what I wanted had unexpectedly changed. I wasn't sure if Krystina was on the same page as I was. There was a very real possibility she didn't want more.

"You belong to me. There's no question about that," I began cautiously. "But I don't like the terms boyfriend and girlfriend. It sounds childish."

"Um, okay..." she trailed off and her brow furrowed. She appeared disappointed by my response.

"You don't sound okay."

"I guess I'm just concerned over how I'm going to be introduced to others at this charity gala thing. If the press is going to be there, I'd kind of like to be prepared with an answer."

Ah, now I see.

I smiled to myself, pleased she had come to her senses and decided not to argue further over going to the gala.

I may just tame her yet.

"We could say you're my date, but I'd like you to be distinguished as more than just that."

"Okay, significant other maybe?" she suggested. "No, never mind. That sounds lame."

"Perhaps I could introduce you as my plus one? Or arm candy might work," I joked with a wink and spun her in a circle.

She scoffed and swatted my arm.

"Be serious!"

I grinned, having only just gotten started.

"Okay, how about my old lady?"

"Old lady?" she laughed. "Now you're just talking nonsense!"

"My paramour? My steady?"

"Ha! Did we just transport back in time to a different century?"

She was laughing hard when the song came to an end, the sort of deep belly laugh that left your sides aching.

I took her face in my hands. She stopped laughing when she saw the serious set of my jaw. I kissed her softly on the lips, sealing the end of our first dance together. I lingered for a moment before pulling back to look into her rich chocolate eyes.

"Angel, as long as you know you are mine and I am yours, we can be whatever you want us to be."

11

Krystina

I walked up the pathway to my apartment building in Greenwich Village. It had been an interesting twenty-four hours, but the magical escape to Alexander's boat was over – and it had been truly magical for the most part. Last night was stress laden, but the morning sun seemed to chase it all away. It was as if there were no issues between us, no barriers, no problems or concerns. For a minute, we were able to be just two people alone in our own little world.

Unfortunately, it was now back to reality. I couldn't ignore the many things that needed to be sorted out.

I learned our individual pasts defined us in many ways. I finally understood Alexander's need for control. He had once told me he only wanted to control me in the bedroom. However, his actions showed otherwise at times and his history of assumed arrogance had flared my temper more times than I could count. But after hearing his story, I now realized his need to control all things in his life wasn't a preference. It wasn't alpha or macho. It was about survival.

On the flip side, maintaining control over my individuality was something I embraced. It was something I needed to hang on to, so I didn't repeat the mistakes of my past. Even though I could understand both ends of the spectrum, I still didn't know if I could let go enough for him to be satisfied. I only knew I had to try.

I stepped over the threshold to enter the lobby of my building.

"Good morning, Phil," I greeted to the doorman.

"Morning, Miss Cole," Phillip returned. "A package arrived for you about ten minutes ago. It's a heavy one. Would you like some help bringing it up the stairs?"

He pointed to a large box sitting beneath the long rows of tenant mailboxes.

I wonder what that could be?

I lifted the box. It was bulky, but it wasn't anything I couldn't carry. I saw it was postmarked in Manhattan. More than likely, my mother must have arranged for a store delivery when she was in the city shopping a few weeks back.

"No. I think I can manage. I'll just take the elevator up, rather than the stairs."

"Okay, then. Enjoy the rest of your day," he said with a nod.

"Thanks, Phil."

Carrying the box into the elevator, I set it at my feet and punched the number for my floor.

My thoughts drifted back to Alexander and all the issues we still needed to work out. I knew it was going to be an uphill battle. But, for the first time since meeting him, I was ready for it.

There's also the job offer to consider. I'll need to make my mind up about that soon.

When the elevator came to a halt, I headed down the hall to my flat. When I walked through the door, I found Allyson sitting at the kitchenette drinking a cup of coffee and reading a magazine. She was tapping her foot to an Elle King song that was blasting from the speaker dock on the counter.

A small stab of betrayal hit me.

In all the craziness with Alexander, I had forgotten about the way she set me up. It didn't matter what her intentions were. Even if everything worked out fine with Alexander, it didn't change the fact I had been ambushed.

"Hey, Krys," she said when she noticed I had come in.

"Hey, yourself," I repeated back just a little too harshly. I set the box on the floor unnecessarily hard.

She looked up from whatever she was reading, a curious expression on her face.

"What's in the box?"

"I don't know," I clipped.

Don't be a bitch to her. She meant well.

"Well, you just caught me," she stated and stood up, completely oblivious to the fact I was annoyed. "I was just about to leave for work."

"Actually, we need to talk if you can spare a minute."

Then she seemed to really look at me for the first time.

"What's wrong?"

I snapped.

"Don't 'what's wrong' me. You know exactly what's wrong!"

She plopped back down in her chair and smirked.

"Don't you dare yell at me, Krys. I know why you're peeved. I did what I thought was best. And since you didn't come home last night, without texting me I might add, I'm assuming things went well?"

I went over the iPod dock and shut off the music. Once it was silenced, I turned and looked pointedly at her.

"Whether they went well or not is beside the point. You totally set me up."

"So, what?" She stuck out her chin in defiance.

I looked at the stubborn set of her jaw. She was somewhat right, even if I wasn't happy with her way of handling things. And if I were to be completely honest with myself, I really didn't feel like lecturing her at that moment. What I really wanted was a friend to talk to about everything. I had been deliberately holding things back from her and we were long overdue for a good heart to heart.

I took a deep breath and sighed.

"Look, I'm not thrilled about what you did."

"He's a good guy, Krys. I could see it in his eyes."

"He is a good guy, but there's..." I trailed off, not sure where to begin. Before we left the boat, Alexander had reminded me of his need for privacy, reiterating I could not even tell Allyson. I had to be careful with what I said so I didn't betray his confidence.

"There's what, Krys?" she prodded.

"He's got a really shitty past, Ally."

"So do you, or at least I assume you do," she added dryly.

"Yes, but –" I stopped short as her words about assuming

hit me. That's when I saw her hurt expression. "What's that supposed to mean?"

"It means you told him about Trevor."

"I had to!" I tried to defend.

"But you never told me," she stated flatly. "Just like you haven't told me what's been going on these past couple of weeks."

She had me there, but I chose to ignore the last part of her statement. The past few weeks were something I had to work out for myself.

"Allyson, you knew what Trevor did to me. You had to of known!"

"No, not for sure," she said and shook her head vehemently. "I only assumed what happened."

I closed my eyes and pinched the bridge of my nose.

"You don't understand. It wasn't that I was trying to hide it from you. It was just, for some reason, I was ashamed by what happened," I tried to explain. "I went through periods where I blamed myself. There were times when I thought that nobody would believe me if I revealed the truth. Trevor came from a wealthy family and their potential influence made me afraid."

Her eyes softened.

"There is nothing for you to feel ashamed or embarrassed about, doll. You are the victim."

"I know, Ally. But it took me a long time to realize that. Please don't be mad that I didn't talk to you about it. It was just too painful. I wanted to forget the whole thing ever happened."

"So why did you tell Alex?"

"I had to tell him. There are things about him you don't

know."

"Actually, I know enough. He enlightened me about his kinks, which was something you only briefly alluded to," she pointed out and frowned. "That's some scary shit, Krys. Are you really okay with all of it?"

My thoughts drifted back to the morning I shared with Alexander. It had been quite the illuminating experience.

And then some...

I smirked to myself when I recalled the blindfold. And the wax.

However, Allyson was right to call attention to the issue. I may have been receptive to everything he had to offer to date, but I really needed to figure out what my own personal limits were. Scenes from Club O were never very far from my mind. Alexander's kinks, and how extreme he planned to take things, would eventually need to be addressed.

"I don't know," I answered truthfully. I glanced at the clock. "There's so much I have to tell you, but I don't want you to be late for work."

"Work can wait. Besides, it's Saturday. I'll make up some bullshit about unexpected traffic or something. Don't sweat it."

Allyson took her job very seriously, and her decision to be late was not one made lightly. I took a seat across the table from her.

"Okay, then. I'll try to be quick. It's just a question of where to start," I began.

"Alex brought me up to speed on most. It ended with the night he brought you to that freak show."

"Ally, it wasn't a freak show."

"Whatever you say."

"Forget about that. It's not important when you consider the grand scheme of things. For Alex, it's just part of who he is. The question is whether or not his past is dictating his lifestyle. That's what I am unsure about."

"Well, tell me about his past. Maybe I can help."

I told her as much as could, careful not to divulge key details Alexander made me swear not to tell. And even though I promised to be quick, it took me a solid thirty minutes to get to the end of the story. Allyson carefully studied me the entire time, having not uttered a word since I began speaking.

"Bottom line is he thinks he's like his father," I finished. "So, what are your thoughts?"

"I think any sort of comparison to his father is ridiculous. His father was a wife beater. That's not what Alex is. Look, Krys. I think I'm right to have some reservations about the two of you together. But if you're into it, who am I to judge? I may not be into that sort of thing, but it certainly doesn't mean Alex is abusive. Has he hurt you at all? I mean, you know," she alluded with a little shrug. "Like, not in a kinky way."

The memory of Alexander's hands squeezing my neck instantly came to mind.

Don't tell her. She wouldn't understand because she wasn't there.

"No," I lied, but immediately felt guilty. My little angel friend, who had been conspicuously absent over the past few weeks, suddenly reappeared. She was frowning and shaking her finger at me.

Ugh, not you again!

I struggled to drive away the guilt about lying to Allyson.

"Well, if you're truly okay with his kinks, then what's your concern?" she pushed.

"I'm just afraid of history repeating itself. Look at my history and what happened with Trevor. Combine that with Alexander's jacked up past..." I trailed off and shook my head. "I really want to make a go at this with him, but I can think of a million and one reasons to end it before it really takes off. Sometimes I worry I'm too wrapped up in him. He's very possessive and domineering. So was Trevor, but in a different way. I don't want to become a statistic, you know?"

"Krys, I know what you're doing. Don't over think this. I listened to him talk about you yesterday. The man was completely torn up. I'd even dare to say he might be in love with you."

"Now *that* is what's ridiculous. Alex isn't the happily ever after type, Ally. I knew that about him going in."

"Don't count him out, doll. He may surprise you."

I thought about what Alexander had said to me when we were dancing on the boat. There had been a firm, no nonsense set to his jaw while his intense sapphire eyes held mine.

"*...We can be whatever you want us to be.*"

I shook my head, not wanting to look too much into something that wasn't really there.

"Maybe I'm the one who isn't ready to get serious," I suggested.

"You keep on telling yourself that. I'll be here later to tell you I told you so," she added with a wink. "In the meantime, I'm going to head to work. The traffic excuse will only buy me so much time."

"Yeah, I've kept you long enough," I agreed.

"Sorry. I don't mean to cut you short."

"No worries. Besides, I have to call my mother." I stood up, retrieved the box from the floor, and set it on the table. "I'm guessing this box is related to her shopping excursions."

"Good luck with that," she laughed. "But hey, what does your schedule look like this week? Let's plan a girl's night out and we can talk more."

"That sounds like a good idea," I mused as I tore open the box. I had expected to find clothes or something of the like, but it was full of files. There was a hand-written note placed on the top.

Krystina,
Enclosed are the client files for Turning Stone Advertising. I thought you might want to review them before you start work on Monday morning.
Yours, Alexander

I BLINKED and read the note card again, completely taken aback by his presumption. I never gave him an answer about the job.

I tabbed through the files quickly. Wally's Grocery was among them, as well as quite a few other prominent names. My curiosity piqued.

Damn him!

Once again, he was assuming. I could envision him standing in front of the floor to ceiling windows of his self-made empire, wielding his authority and issuing orders from his command center. He would always be the master of all that surrounded him. I pursed my lips in annoyance, knowing this was just his latest power play.

Some things will never change. There's no use fighting it.

I looked up at Allyson. She was collecting her keys and purse from the island in the kitchen.

"Let me know what day works for you," she said as she headed for the door.

"Um...actually, I'm not sure what my schedule is going to look like this week. Apparently, I'm going to be starting a new job," I stated dryly.

"Oh, that's good news! Your interview must have gone well. I didn't realize LD Marketing made you an offer."

"They did, but that's not where I'm going to be working."

She paused at the door and a knowing look slowly spread over her features.

"Really?" she said, almost too innocently. "So where will you be working?"

"Turning Stone," I mumbled.

She flashed me a beaming smile and flipped her blond hair over her shoulder.

"Why, Krystina Cole, I think things are going to turn out better than you think."

12

Alexander

I walked into my office at Stone Enterprise with a satisfied smile on the face. Having just come from the floor that held the Turning Stone offices, I was remarkably pleased with the result. Kimberly and Josh did a fantastic job with the design and construction. I was looking forward to seeing Krystina's reaction come Monday morning.

I glanced at the wall clock.

She should have received the files by now.

I sat down behind my desk and pulled my phone from my pocket to send her a text message.

11:42 AM, Me: *I trust Hale dropped you off safe and sound.*

Her response came almost immediately.

11:44 AM, Krystina: *Yes.*

I frowned, having expected her to say something about the files. Evidently, she wasn't going to make this easy for me. However, there was always the possibility she hadn't received the delivery as of yet. I would have to feel her out just in case.

11:46 AM, Me: *What are your plans for later this afternoon?*
11:49AM, Krystina: *Apparently, I'll be busy going through client files for Turning Stone.*

I smiled at the angry faced emoticon she added after her text.

There's my girl.

11:53 AM, Me: *Apparently?*
11:54 AM, Krystina: *Sending this to me was very assuming. You know that, right?*
11:57 AM, Me: *You were never going to turn me down. YOU know THAT, right?*

I could almost see the smoke billowing from her ears after reading the way I had used her own words on her.

12:01 PM, Krystina: *I'm not going to answer that.*
12:03 PM, Me: *Dinner at my place later?*
12:04 PM, Krystina: *We'll see.*

We'll see indeed, Miss Cole.

If she was that angry, she would have flat out refused. Satisfied she wasn't too upset with me, I placed the cell on the desk and chuckled to myself as I powered on my computer.

I read through various emails and responded to those that needed quick follow ups. I came across the email with the video feed attachment from Club O. I forwarded it on to Hale and requested he gather all the information he could find on Trevor Hamilton. I wanted a full-blown background check, along with any skeletons he may be hiding in his closet.

Know your enemy.

I planned to make sure the asshole never bothered Krystina again.

Once that was done, I moved on to the emails requiring more attention. I had several deals in the works, two of which were near the final stages. My inbox was flooded with floor plan schematics and property contracts from my lawyer. They needed to be reviewed and signed in order to close on Tuesday. I looked at the date and time stamps on the emails. Stephen sent most of them after I left on Friday afternoon.

I pressed my lips together in a tight line, annoyed at how little time he left me to review everything. Going through all the fine print would take most of today, as well as tomorrow. I needed to get ahold of Laura. We had a lot of work to do before Tuesday.

I picked up the phone to punch in her extension but paused when I remembered it was Saturday.

She's not in the office.

As I began to dial her cell phone, the recollection of Krystina's words stopped me from completing the call.

"Just because you can summon people to do your bidding whenever you damn well please doesn't mean you should."

Laura was a salaried employee. So were Stephen and

Bryan for that matter. There had been plenty of times when we worked through the weekend in order to meet deadlines. However, Krystina now had me second-guessing those decisions, and I began to reevaluate the amount of time I took away from my employee's personal time off.

I slammed the phone down.

Damn her!

Annoyed over the predicament I was now in, I turned back to the computer. I clicked on one of Stephen's emails and opened the attachment.

One hundred and seven pages.

Resigned to pulling an all-nighter, I hit the print icon on the computer screen. While it was printing, I typed an email to Krystina.

TO: Krystina Cole
FROM: Alexander Stone
SUBJECT: Change of plan

My Dearest Angel,
I find myself in a quandary. I had planned to dine with you this evening, then perhaps follow up with a continuation of this morning's exploration of your limits. However, I am going to have to postpone my plan for the evening until tomorrow night.
Work has unexpectedly taken precedence in a way it never has before. You see, I would have simply called in reinforcements to help me with the long and dreadful tasks ahead of me, but you've taught me I should not disturb employees on their day off.
You played your hand well, angel. Lesson learned.

I expect I'll regret my decision by tomorrow night, so be sure to get plenty of sleep tonight. There may be a punishment for this coming your way.

Yours truly,
Alexander

I hit the send button and got up to go over to the printer. The first contract was still printing. I rubbed my temples. It was going to be a long night.

I need an energy drink.

I walked over to the mini bar in my office and opened the small refrigerator. I frowned when I saw there was only flavored and regular bottled water to be found, but then recalled Laura only kept it stocked for guests who visited my office. I would have to remember to tell her to add 5-Hour Energy to the supply.

When the contract finished printing, I collected the pile of papers from the tray and returned to my desk. There was an email notification in my inbox from Krystina. Pleased she responded so quickly, I opened it and began to read.

TO: Alexander Stone
FROM: Krystina Cole
SUBJECT: Glad you're not Vader

Alexander,
I'm happy to know you've crossed over from the dark side. All things considered, any punishment you decide to dole out will be worth it if it means you will be nicer to your Padawan's going forward.

That being said, I feel it is best for both of us to concentrate on our work. You obviously have much to do, and I have barely gotten started (no thanks to your welcome aboard package). I will plan to see you bright and early Monday morning.

Your Newest Padawan,
Krystina

I may have been annoyed over the fact she was putting me off, but her terminology made me laugh. I glanced at the one hundred plus pages in front of me. Realistically, Monday was a better plan, even if I didn't want to wait that long to see her.

TO: Krystina Cole
FROM: Alexander Stone
SUBJECT: Padawan?

To my Hollywood fiend,
I must apologize, but I am not familiar with this term. Since you referenced Vader in your last email, is it safe to assume Padawan is *Star Wars* terminology?

Sincerely,
Your Paramour who needs to watch more movies

P.S. Hale will pick you up at 8 a.m. on Monday.

I was laughing out loud when I hit send. I should have gotten to work on the pending contract, but I couldn't concentrate as I waited for her response. Finally, my inbox pinged.

TO: Alexander Stone
FROM: Krystina Cole
SUBJECT: Next Date

Alexander,
This email should have been titled Jabba, as your knowledge of movies is representative to that of an oversized slug.
However, I forgot I was writing an email to a man who has never seen *Star Trek*. I should not have assumed so much as to think you would be familiar with *Star Wars*.
Scratch the hanky-panky. Our next date needs to be a sci-fi movie marathon.

Your Princess from Alderaan,
Krystina

P.S. You must really have a lot of work to do. You never let me off this easy.

I sat back in my chair, having no idea what Alderaan was, and smiled to myself.
She really is something else.
I contemplated a date with Krystina, where we did nothing but watch movies. It was an odd concept, but one I wasn't opposed to. In fact, I actually looked forward to the cliché idea of popcorn and a movie. I was amazed at my willingness to do normal couple things with her.
Love is turning you to mush, Stone.

Perhaps it was, but the fact of the matter was I *wanted* to be normal with her in every sense of the word. Nevertheless, normal never worked out well for me. Even if she was changing me, it wasn't safe for me to let down my guard enough to *be* normal. After the way I lost my temper with her on the boat, it was simply a risk I couldn't afford to take.

13

Krystina

Just as Alexander promised, Hale was waiting for me at eight sharp on Monday morning. I thought about how quickly the weekend flew by as I climbed through the rear passenger door Hale held open for me.

"Thanks, Hale."

"Yes, Miss," he replied in his ever so sullen way. He closed the door behind me and walked around to the driver's side of the black Porsche SUV.

As we pulled into traffic, I ran through all the information I read in the client files for Turning Stone. There were opportunities to say the least, and Alexander was right to say the employees at Turning Stone were mediocre at best.

Or perhaps they just need a bit more direction.

The task awaiting me was a daunting one, but I was looking forward to the challenge. When I thought about the long workdays ahead of me, I reconsidered my start time. An eight o'clock start may not suffice if I had any hopes of having free time in the evenings. I looked to Hale, wondering if he would be my ride to work each day.

Surely, I can't expect him to chauffeur me daily.

"Has Alex instructed you to pick me up every morning?" I asked him.

"No, Miss," was all he said. I pursed my lips and frowned at his reply.

Yes, Miss. No, Miss. Aren't you a regular ole chatterbox.

I should not have been surprised by his short responses, as they were in typical Hale fashion. I just wanted someone to talk to, in a shoot-the-shit kind of way. I was full of restless energy, excited for my first day at Turning Stone. I thought I might be apprehensive about working for Alexander, but after spending all day Saturday and Sunday going through the client files, I couldn't stop the enthusiasm from bubbling over. This opportunity was what I had been waiting so long for.

However, excited or not, I knew how challenging Alexander could be on a personal level. I wondered how difficult he would be to work for.

"Is it hard to work for Alex?" I mused the question aloud to Hale. He just smiled at me through the review mirror. "Come on, Hale. You packed my underwear into a duffle bag just a few days ago. I think we can drop a few of the formalities."

He snorted at my statement, his face showing more emotion than I had ever seen before. When he spoke, there was a hint of humor in his voice.

"No, Miss. Mr. Stone is not hard to work for."

"That's all you can say? You can't give me just the teeniest bit of insight?" I teased.

To my disappointment, he remained silent as we continued the short drive.

I should be happy he said that much.

I stared out the window at the passing streets, contemplating how my first day might go. When we eventually pulled up to Cornerstone Tower, my excitement had turned into a ball of nerves.

Hale got out of the SUV first and came around to open the door for me. When I stepped out onto the pavement, he took hold of my elbow.

"Miss Cole," he said, startling me. I couldn't believe he was actually speaking to me without being asked.

"Yes, Hale," I replied, waiting patiently for whatever it was he was about to say.

"Mr. Stone instructed me to tell you he will meet you in the lobby. Reception will call up to tell him when you have arrived."

"Oh, um…. Thank you."

I thought that would be it, but he didn't release his hold on my arm.

"One more thing. I can see you're nervous," he said and looked pointedly to my hands I hadn't realized were fidgeting. "Don't worry. Mr. Stone may come across as hard, but he's not as bad as you might think he is. He has a good soul."

And with that, he turned and climbed back into the vehicle. I stood on the curb, stunned speechless, watching as he pulled away.

Well…okay, then.

I looked up at the looming building before me, an impressive structure topped with a sleek ornamental spire. A feeling of déjà vu settled over me. The nerves rattling me were very similar to the ones I had when I came here for the first time.

The interview.

I smiled to myself when I thought about that day.

If I only knew how drastically my life would change...

The thought put me strangely at ease. Feeling more confident, I pushed through the turnstile doors. I was ready to start a new day. And a new life.

Alexander

I STEPPED out of the elevator and made my way through the lobby to where Krystina was waiting for me. My eyes traveled up the length of her. She looked polished in her mint green suit jacket and skirt, yet still sexy as hell. The color complimented her creamy skin and chestnut curls. I had forgotten how good she looked in shades of green. Even so, I still wanted to rip the clothes from her body.

She's damn hot. It's going to be hard keeping things strictly to business during the day.

"Miss Cole," I said when I approached her.

"Good morning, sir."

Sir.

My cock gave a slight twinge at that one little word, having rarely heard it come from her lips.

Hard is an understatement. It's going to be near impossible to keep my hands off of her if she continues to address me like that.

"Let's keep it to Mr. Stone when we're at work," I told her. Then I winked and whispered, "You can call me 'sir' later."

Her eyes widened and her cheeks flushed a delectable pink.

"Alex, not here," she hissed. "We have to try to keep it professional."

I flashed her a cocky grin and took hold of her elbow.

"No promises, angel." Leading her to the bank of elevators, I punched the button that would take us up to Turning Stone Advertising. "Your offices are located on the thirty-seventh floor. I recently had the floor completely remodeled. I trust you'll find it to your liking."

"I'm sure it will be fine," she said as the elevator started to ascend. I glanced at her and saw she was twisting her hands. I turned and boxed her in against the wall between my arms.

"Why are you nervous?"

"Starting a new job is always a bit nerve wracking, Alex."

I leaned in, wanting to take a bite out of her, but the elevator pinged to signal we had stopped. A computerized voice announced we were at the nineteenth floor.

Not our floor.

I quickly stepped away, just in time for the doors to open. A man joined us in the five by five space. Dark hair. Early twenties if I had to guess.

Patrick something or another. Mailroom employee.

I tensed when I saw the way he looked at Krystina.

Keep your eyes to yourself, buddy.

He glanced up and saw I was watching him. He quickly

averted his attention to a random spot in the corner of the elevator.

That's right. She's mine.

The doors opened again, and the employee got out.

"Jealousy is not very becoming on you, Alex," Krystina remarked after the doors closed once more.

"What?"

"I saw the way you stared down that poor boy. I'm sure it was innocent on his part. Seriously, I'm the new girl. People are going to stare for a minute. It's normal until they figure out who I am."

I stared at her, completely awed by how oblivious she was to her beauty.

The elevator chimed again, this time announcing we had reached the thirty-seventh floor. The doors slid open to reveal a long corridor of offices. The smell of new carpet and fresh paint assaulted us. I pinched up my nose and wondered how long the smells would linger for.

"Here we are, angel. Turning Stone Advertising," I announced.

"You probably shouldn't call me that when we are here," she whispered.

"It's fine for now. Nobody's here at the moment. I've instructed the staff to tie up loose ends at the old office this morning. Your team will join you after lunch. I figured you might want the morning to yourself to get acclimated."

We walked down the main hallway and I pointed to the various offices the employees would use. I led her into one of the large design rooms that could be used for both client meetings and strategy planning.

"Wow, Alex! I couldn't ask for this space to be laid out

any better," she walked around the long oval conference table and over to the large windows on the far wall. "The lighting in here is simply fantastic."

"It is, but my designer thought differently. She said you might find the late afternoon sun to be somewhat of a hindrance. She had an automatic shade installed so the light doesn't interfere with the flat screens and white board. You'll probably want to explore this room more extensively later. There's quite a bit of equipment at your disposal."

Her eyes were wide as she took in the rest of the room.

"I can see that," she murmured as her eyes settled on the state-of-the-art stereo, audio, and recording systems she could utilize for radio advertisements.

"Follow me this way. There's more for you to see," I told her, anxious for her to see the space designed specifically for her.

We walked to the far end of the hallway, where the doublewide glass doors for Krystina's main office faced us. Turning Stone Advertising had been etched into frosted glass in a large swirling black font, with her name imprinted right below it.

Turning Stone Advertising
Krystina Cole
Chief Executive Officer

"Fancy," she commented. "Wait. That says Chief Executive Officer."

"Yes. So, it does." I chuckled as I pushed through the glass doors. "Welcome to your new office, Miss Cole."

14

Krystina

I was trying to process why in the world he would have me titled the CEO, when my breath caught in my throat. The office – my office – was more than I could have ever imagined. To say it was stunning would be a gross understatement. I was speechless, unable to utter a single word, as I took in the magnificent space.

The room was wide, traveling the entire length of the building, with my own private restroom. Floor to ceiling windows flanked the north and south walls. Plush armchairs were arranged around a glass-topped table to form a seating area off to my right. A mini bar, which included an elaborate coffee machine, was to my left. The fact he remembered my penchant for caffeine made me smile.

A polished wood desk sat centered on the west wall, made of an eclectic blend of reclaimed antique hardwoods that was simply stunning. However, despite the beauty of the craftsmanship, I couldn't tear my eyes away from the artwork behind it.

It was a mural of a single white lily against a black and gray backdrop. It spanned the entire length of the room. The colors swirled together in a downward pattern, creating a waterfall effect with the lily as the focal piece. Above the lily, a quote was inscribed.

"There's something which impels us to show our inner souls. The more courageous we are, the more we succeed in explaining what we know."
-Maya Angelou

The quote was one of my favorites.

"Do you like it?" Alexander asked. If I wasn't mistaken, he sounded nervous.

"Like it? Alex, I..." I trailed off, unable to find the right word to describe what I was thinking. "Everything is perfect."

"Because of all the framed quotes you have in your bedroom, I thought it was safe to assume you had a fondness for Maya Angelou. I picked a quote that I felt best suited you."

I looked at him then, having realized I hadn't given him enough credit. His attention to detail and the way the office was crafted specifically to reflect my personality, showed how well he knew me. Suddenly overwhelmed with emotion, I blinked at the sting of tears beginning to form.

"I couldn't have picked a better quote myself. Really, Alex. Everything is beyond compare," I said sincerely.

"I just wanted you to be happy and comfortable here, angel. I know you were apprehensive about taking the job."

"Well, you're doing a fantastic job of convincing me this was the right decision," I laughed.

"Good, because there is one more thing. I made a few modifications to the contract I originally presented to you. I think you'll find the adjustments in your favor. I left it for you in the top drawer of your desk. Take your time and look it over," he said. He kissed the top of my head and moved towards the door.

"Wait, you're leaving? Don't you want to go over it with me?"

"I have to get back for an appointment. If you need anything or have any questions about it, you can find me in my office."

"Oh, okay. I'll probably be up a little later," I said distractedly, still trying to take in my surroundings.

After he was gone, I looked more closely at my office space, wanting to absorb every single detail of it. I smiled to myself and wanted to squeal with delight. Walking behind my new desk, I took a seat. As I pulled out the revised contract, Allyson's words echoed in my mind.

You were right, Ally.

Things are definitely turning out better than I thought they would.

Alexander

I SAT at my desk and looked over the invoices for the upcoming fundraiser. I pinched the bridge of my nose and looked at the clock. I still had a lot to prepare for before tomorrow.

I don't have time to be dealing with this.

Normally, I would have passed this sort of task on to Bryan to handle. However, Justine was adamant we go through everything together.

I should be with Krystina right now.

I was anxious to see how she would react to my new offer. The contract I left for her was not an employment contract, but a transfer of ownership. I didn't want her financial stability to be looming over our relationship. Turning Stone would all be hers once she signed on the dotted line.

The phone on my desk buzzed.

"Mr. Stone, Ms. Andrews is here to see you," Laura said through the speaker.

"Send her in please."

Justine, as usual, entered my office like a whirlwind.

"Alex, I feel like my head is spinning. The fundraiser is less than a week away and I'm running out of time. I need to steal Laura from you for a couple of days."

"That's not happening, Justine. I have a major deal closing tomorrow with Canterwell, and I need her too much at the moment. You're going to have to handle this yourself," I told her firmly. I knew Justine was perfectly capable, but she lacked the confidence at times.

"Fine. Be that way. But if something isn't done right, don't blame me," she said petulantly.

"I hate it when you pout," I said with a frown.

"I'm also worried about Charlie showing up. I don't know why, but it's always in the back of my mind."

I took a deep breath and tried not to lose my patience over her obsession with her ex-husband showing up unannounced. In my eyes, she was acting paranoid.

"You need to relax. Don't worry about Charlie. I handled him. Things will be fine. I just read over the invoices. You've done a fantastic job. This will be the most profitable fundraiser The Stoneworks Foundation has put on yet."

"The numbers work, but I wish I could have cut down on a few of the costs. I'm hoping the silent auction makes up for it. That's what I wanted to go over with you. I figured you might see an opportunity I missed."

"Well, there is –"

The door to my office came crashing open. Krystina was red faced and holding the contract I'd left in her desk.

"Are you out of your mind?" she exclaimed. Laura was trailing in her wake.

"Mr. Stone. I'm so sorry. She just – she wouldn't listen," Laura sputtered. I had never seen my assistant so flustered. I smiled to myself.

Welcome to my world.

"It's fine, Laura. I'll handle it," I assured her before looking to Krystina. "Krystina, have a seat."

"I will not have a seat, Alex! You need to explain this!" she yelled, waving the fistful of papers around angrily.

"Krystina, sit down," I said more firmly. I motioned to Justine. "I'd like you to meet my sister, Justine Andrews."

"Your sister? Oh!" Krystina's flushed face turned ten shades redder when she noticed Justine sitting there. She shook her head as she tried to collect herself. "Oh my gosh.

I'm so sorry. You must think I'm crazy. I'm Krystina Cole. It's nice to meet you."

Krystina walked over to Justine and held out her hand. Justine was wide eyed as she accepted the handshake. She looked as if she had been stunned into silence. More than likely, she was shocked I'd allowed a scene such as this to happen. Nobody ever came to my office unannounced, let alone screaming and yelling. Justine knew that better than anyone.

I looked at the two women. They were among the most exasperating individuals I had ever encountered. I contemplated how I should handle them being in the same room together.

I leaned forward and propped my elbows on the desk.

"Krystina is taking over the Turning Stone division of Stone Enterprise. Today is her first day," I informed Justine. "She has yet to learn the protocol."

"Yes, about that," Krystina began, but I didn't let her finish.

"Justine and I were in a meeting. We were going over some of the numbers for the charity gala this Friday. Since you are going to be my date, perhaps you'd like to partake in our discussion."

"Your date?" Justine choked out, having finally found her voice.

"Yes. I told Krystina about your Moulin Rouge vision. She thinks it's a great idea."

"I do?" questioned Krystina, obviously taken aback. I smiled innocently at her.

"You do. In fact, we'll be going shopping on Wednesday for the appropriate attire. What do you suggest we wear,

Justine?" I asked, turning back to the other incorrigible woman in my life.

"Oh, um..." she trailed off as her eyes shifted back and forth between Krystina and me. "The women will be in cabaret style dresses, the men in coat tails and top hats. There's a great shop on West 25th Street. They have an excellent selection of vintage style clothing for the occasion."

"It's settled then. That's where we will go," I announced.

Daggers were shooting from Krystina's eyes, and they were aimed straight at me. She was seething, but I could tell she was trying to keep her temper in check in front of Justine. For some odd reason, I found the situation to be incredibly amusing.

"Sounds perfect," Krystina said, her voice laden with sarcasm. "I'm going to go and let you two finish up. It's nearing lunchtime, so I expect the Turning Stone employees will be arriving shortly. I want to be there to greet them."

She looked as though she wanted to stomp her foot. I had to put my tongue in my cheek to contain my grin as I watched her stalk from the room. Once she was gone, Justine rounded on me.

"What was that all about?" she demanded.

"It was nothing."

"Alex, I know you too well. That wasn't *nothing*. She wasn't *nothing*."

I sighed and leaned back in my chair. I rubbed my hands over my face, already exhausted from the conversation. My relationship with Krystina was my own personal business. Justine did not need to know the details of it.

"It's complicated. I'd prefer to not get into it."

Justine eyed me suspiciously for a moment, before her eyes went as wide as saucers.

"Oh my god! Are you dating her? Like, *really* dating her?"

"What if I am?"

"For starters, you never date. Secondly, she's an employee. Since when do you mix business with pleasure?"

"That's not your concern," I told her firmly, not bothering to mention Krystina's employment status would change the minute the new contract was signed. Technically, she will no longer be working for me, but for herself.

Justine crossed her legs and looked pointedly at me, but my determination to maintain my privacy was unyielding as I stared her down. She looked away and began picking at a chip in her finger nail polish.

"She doesn't look like your type," she mused.

"I didn't realize my type had a look," I replied dryly, but she just ignored my comment.

"I don't think bringing her to the gala is a good idea, Alex. Suzanne will be there."

"Christ, not this again!" I threw my hands in the air, having finally gotten to the root of what Justine's thought process was. I was incensed that she would even bring Suzanne into question.

"Come on, Alex! Don't be insensitive. You know she'll be crushed to see you with someone else."

I shook my head and took a deep breath.

"I can't help that, and you know it as well as I do. I've always just considered Suzanne a friend and nothing more. The minute I realized she had other ideas, I stopped asking her to accompany me to various functions. I know you're loyal to her, but I could never give her what she was looking for."

"Yeah, so you've said," she commented with a smirk. "I believe you told her something about not being the dating kind."

"That's correct," I said cautiously.

"Suzanne knows a lot about our past, Alex."

I was about to tell her I told Krystina nearly everything already, and that it was no thanks to Justine's big mouth that Krystina was alerted to the past in the first place. However, I stopped short when I saw the worried expression on her face. Justine told Suzanne everything. I knew that.

How much does Suzanne know exactly?

"What are you saying?"

"I'm saying that you're playing with fire, Alex. Don't say I didn't warn you."

15

Alexander

T he sun is hot. My house will be even hotter. I don't want to go inside. He gets angry when he's hot.

I look at my bike lying in the ugly dead grass.

I should pick it up, so I don't get yelled at. Mom says Grandma bought me that bike and I should take better care of it.

I'm too sweaty. I'll put it away later.

I go into the apartment building and pinch my nose. The hallway always smells like a toilet. I need to get to my door where it doesn't smell so much inside.

I hear yelling. Is that him?

No. It's the crazy lady down the hall.

My backpack is so heavy.

I can't wait to put it down.

Not on the floor, though. He'll get mad if he trips.

I look at the numbers on the doors I pass. Ten. Eleven. Twelve. Three. The one is missing. I think it is supposed to say thirteen.

Almost there.

I reach the door that has the number fifteen and place my hand on the knob.

I BOLTED UPRIGHT, the sound of the alarm clock ringing shrill in my ears. I reached over to the nightstand to silence it. I shook my head and tried to will away the images of the night. And the smells.

What the fuck?

At the very least, I was thankful the alarm woke me before the dream went any further.

The last thing I need to do is to start the day off analyzing that shit.

My brain felt foggy. I needed Krystina. I sat up in bed and tried to remember what day it was.

Wednesday.

I scowled when I remembered I hadn't spoken to Krystina since Monday. I was partly to blame for that, as the Canterwell deal took more finesse than I anticipated. What should have been a simple sign and go, wound up being dinner and drinks with George Canterwell about another potential property sale.

And the greedy bastard still wouldn't budge on the price.

I rubbed my hands over the stubble on my face as I thought about the past two days. Despite my busy schedule, I still called and texted Krystina multiple times, only to receive a short response or be ignored all together. I tried to stop by her floor but found her conveniently busy in closed-door meetings with the employees from Turning Stone.

I knew when I was being put off, and I suspected it was

because she was still upset over my proposal. It was safe to assume that she'd be stubborn about accepting, but I hadn't expected her to be outright angry.

Transferring ownership of Turning Stone to her was meant to put her more at ease. I didn't want her employment status to be looming over us and potentially get in the way of our relationship. I understood the meaning of financial instability. I never wanted her to worry about having that stress. Giving her Turning Stone was merely a drop in the bucket, despite Stephen and Bryan's arguments. It was a portion of my business I had little time for anyways. My focus had always been, and always would be, real estate.

Enough is enough. She can't continue on like this.

Feeling frustrated, I threw the blankets off and climbed out of bed.

I need a work out and a shower.

After completing a solid thirty minutes of cardio, I took a quick shower and dressed for the day. As I knotted my tie, I eyed up the line of clothes I'd purchased for Krystina. They took up an entire row of the walk-in closet, bright and colorful, and such a contrast to the utilitarian colored suits I wore. The closet was hers as much as it was mine.

She belongs here. Regularly.

I toyed with the idea of convincing her to move in with me as I retrieved my cell from the dresser, and I made my way to the kitchen.

One thing at a time, Stone.

I opened the refrigerator and was pleased to see Vivian had recently gone grocery shopping. Fresh fruit had been cut and placed in airtight containers. My housekeeper was a godsend.

I sat down on one of the kitchen bar stools and began sifting through emails on my phone while I ate an assortment of melons and berries. I spotted one from Krystina and immediately opened it first.

TO: Alexander Stone
FROM: Krystina Cole
SUBJECT: Your Offer

Alexander,
After careful consideration, I have decided to accept your proposal. However, a few changes needed to be made to the plan you laid out. I have attached a modified version of the buyout.
If you are in agreement, I would like to formally discuss it this afternoon. Please let me know what time works for you.

Krystina

Buyout?
The contract was not a buyout. I was giving her the company straight out. Curious, I clicked on the attachment and read through it.

Her plan was no longer a transfer of ownership, but a buyout similar to a rent-to-own. She had researched fair market value for a firm the size of Turning Stone and renegotiated her salary to be a considerable amount less. The difference in her salary, as well as a portion of Turning Stone profits, would be paid to Stone Enterprise in the form of monthly payments with a term date.

I sat back in my chair, stunned over how well she played

her hand. Her idea made sense, and I couldn't believe I didn't think of it myself. I should have known Krystina would not accept an entire company for free, but rather work to obtain it on her own.

Miss Cole, you will never cease to amaze me.

Her revised plan would certainly stop Stephen and Bryan from balking so much. I forwarded her email on to them and requested they meet in my office to discuss the new proposal at three o'clock. I then typed a quick response to Krystina to let her know what time to meet us, and also reminded her of our shopping appointment later after work.

I hit send and smiled to myself, looking forward to having a very interesting day.

Krystina

I SAT down behind my computer with a steaming cup of coffee. I sipped it slowly, waiting to feel the surge of caffeine through my veins while I reviewed my calendar of appointments and list of things to do for the day. My first two days on the job had been long and tiring. I was beginning to understand why Alexander wanted someone to take charge of Turning Stone Advertising.

While the company was profitable, it was apparent it was not Alexander's main business focus. Between getting to know the somewhat reluctant-to-accept-change employees and sorting through existing and future ad campaign opportunities, I quickly learned I had my work cut out for me. The employees, while creatively competent, could use some formal guidance. That fact alone was intimidating. I knew I could handle the job aspects, but there was a big difference between being a boss and a leader. Having never had my leadership skills put to the test, I could only hope I was up for the challenge.

I exited out of the calendar application and opened my inbox. The first thing to populate was an email from Alexander. It was in response to the one I sent that morning.

That was quick.

Nervous butterflies danced in my stomach. I wasn't sure how he would take to my offer, but his reply came remarkably quick. I hesitantly clicked on the email.

FROM: Alexander Stone
TO: Krystina Cole
SUBJECT: Re: Your Offer

I'm glad you've finally decided to break the silence. And here I thought I would have to take you over my knee. I may still do exactly that, as just the mere thought is more than a little bit appealing. You've been away from me for too long, Miss Cole.

I've scheduled a meeting for us with my accountant and lawyer. Come to my office at 3 P.M. today so we can discuss your proposal with them further. I don't imagine it will take very long. We should be done in plenty of time to follow through with our plans to costume shop tonight.

Alexander Stone
CEO, Stone Enterprise

I frowned after reading his email, not knowing what to think about it. He didn't give me any inclination as to whether or not he was going to accept my offer. To me, it wasn't up for debate. I had thought long and hard about Alexander's proposal, which was the reason why I avoided him for two days. I needed to think on my own without the interference of his intensely determined sapphire eyes.

Ultimately, I concluded taking Turning Stone free and clear was simply something I could not do. I would have been perfectly okay with managing the company or exploring partnership possibilities down the road, but I could never accept it freely if I hadn't earned it. There was no pride in that. I valued the rewards that came from hard work too much.

I reread his email, looking for some sort of clue in regard to which way he was leaning. He said he wanted us to meet with his accountant and lawyer, which could potentially mean he was considering the revised deal. That was a good sign. However, I knew Alexander. He was anything but predictable. I needed to be braced for anything he might throw at me.

I glanced up when I heard a knock on my office door.

"Come in," I called.

Clive, the lead marketing coordinator for Turning Stone, came in.

"Good Morning, Miss Cole."

I shook my head at the way he so formally addressed me. He, along with the other employees at Turning Stone, were used to Alexander's ways. I wanted them to be more relaxed with me, as I believed totalitarian rule over them would only result in stifling their creativity.

"Clive, I've already told you. There's no need to be so formal. Krys is fine with me," I said with a light laugh.

He smiled sheepishly.

"Sorry, old habits die hard. I'll try to remember in the future."

I returned his smile, hoping to put him more at ease.

"Don't sweat it. So, what do you have for me?" I asked, noting the large portfolio case he was carrying.

"Billboard designs for Wally's. Carol and I just finished the layout. If you have a minute, I'd like to go over them with you."

"Sure thing. Let's see what you came up with," I said and stood up to walk over to the small conference table sitting in the corner of my office.

Clive pulled six different billboard designs from the portfolio case and spread them out over the table. The designs were sleek and polished, clearly displaying the diversity of the city while using catchy phrases to emphasize the high-quality product standards of the grocer. However, I couldn't help but feel like they were missing the essence of what Wally's truly was.

"What do you think?" he asked.

"Overall, I think you and Carol did a fantastic job with them."

"I sense a 'but' in there," he remarked somewhat dejectedly.

"Well, I do have a suggestion to make. Wally's is a family owned business and a staple in so many communities. I think we could use that to our advantage with a few very subtle changes."

I went on to tell Clive my thoughts on what to do, as well

as share my firsthand knowledge about the company. At first, he seemed skeptical, but he listened attentively. I watched him carefully while I spoke, not wanting him to think I was putting down his creativities, but merely wanted to explore the possibility of capturing an additional audience. When his expression changed from being doubtful to enthusiastic, I knew I had broken through.

"This is all great info!" he exclaimed. "I'm going to get with Carol again. We need to think out of the box on this one."

I smiled at his newfound excitement over the Wally's campaign. It was contagious.

"We do. Just keep in mind, Wally's is trying to make a recovery after falling on hard times. I suggest we keep our long-term activities to ads proven to work, but still incorporate fresh ideas into shorter term ads in order to see what sticks."

"I think we are going to have to appeal to each individual community separately," he mused.

"I agree. Communities are the best place to start. Do you think you can have the new designs done by Friday? I have a meeting scheduled with Walter Roberts and I'd like to show him what Turning Stone has come up with."

"It will be tough because we're kind of backlogged, but I can shuffle a few things to make sure it is."

I frowned at hearing that, as I had been thinking about the staff's workload just that morning during my cab ride into work. I had concerns over the many clients still waiting on design proofs.

"Clive, what do you think about hiring a few temps to get us caught up?"

I could see the relief sag in his shoulders immediately at my question.

"That would be extremely helpful, Miss Cole."

I raised my eyebrows at him.

"Miss Cole?"

"Sorry. That would be extremely helpful, *Krys*," he said and grinned.

"Thanks," I laughed. "Let me see what I can do about our staffing issue. There may be a temp agency Mr. Stone already uses that could be of help. Either way, when we start looking at candidates, I'll want your input on who we bring onboard."

Clive, who had begun putting away the billboard designs, stopped what he was doing at looked up at me in surprise.

"You want my input? Really?"

"Yes, really. You're the lead marketing coordinator. Why wouldn't I value your input?"

"Well, I just..." he trailed off, and appeared to be searching for the right words. "When we heard Mr. Stone was bringing someone in to take over Turning Stone, we all assumed you would be some hotshot New York City know-it-all. Those sentiments grew stronger once we saw how he pulled out all the stops for this new office. But I must say, I'm happy to see you've been proving otherwise. I think I'm going to enjoy working for you."

"I'm happy to be here," I said earnestly.

Smiling to myself, I headed out of the planning room feeling relatively pleased with how day three at Turning Stone was shaping up to be. I could only hope my meeting with Alexander would go just as well.

16

Alexander

I glanced at the clock. It was nearing three o'clock and I was expecting Krystina at any minute. Stephen and Bryan were sitting in my office, both arguing their opinions on what I should and shouldn't do about Krystina's offer.

"I like her tenacity, Alex. She could have just taken the company free and clear but decided to earn it instead. I think her proposal is smart and well thought out," Stephen argued.

"That's why you're the lawyer and I'm the accountant," Bryan quipped. "You're not looking at these numbers. Yes, she is offering fair market value, but I am looking at the long-term loss of potential revenue."

I shook my head at Bryan.

"Bryan, I'm not concerned about the long-term loss," I reiterated. "Turning Stone was a venture designed to help the businesses that have lease agreements with me, nothing more. It was never a get-rich plan. I think you're over stating the loss."

"What if she defaults on the payments? Then what?" Bryan pressed.

"She won't. And if she does, Stephen has included a lien clause just to appease you," I rebuked. "If the payments are not made, the company defaults back to Stone Enterprise. However, I highly doubt it will come to that. I trust her capabilities. In fact, I think she'll succeed in making Turning Stone a very lucrative business."

"That's just more reason to not sell it off," Bryan muttered.

The phone on my desk buzzed. It was Laura.

"Mr. Stone. Miss Cole is here," she said somewhat tersely.

I smiled to myself, imagining the possible scene outside of my office. After the way Krystina had burst in here on Monday, I was fairly certain Laura considered moving furniture to block Krystina from entering without permission ever again. I had to refrain from laughing at the idea as I leaned forward to press the intercom button.

"Send her in please," I said into the speaker.

When Krystina came in, her brilliant brown eyes locked on mine. She looked determined, but wary at the same time as she moved to take a seat in between Bryan and Stephen.

"Hello. I'm Krystina Cole," she said politely and extended her hand to each of them.

While they exchanged introductions, I couldn't help but to take in her appearance. She was wearing a navy-blue suit, the jacket outlining the curve of her waistline and breasts in the most delectable way. It was the same suit she wore when she came to my office for the very first time. And when I saw the triskelion necklace I bought for her clasped around her neck, my cock instantly sprung to life.

Yes indeed, Miss Cole. I have been away from you for far too long.

I looked at Bryan and Stephen. They were both carefully assessing her. I expected as much but planned to just observe them for the time being. They needed a minute to get to know the woman I nearly handed a division of my company over to.

"We were just discussing your plan to buyout Turning Stone," Stephen said to her. "It appears you did your research."

"Alexander put a lot on the table. I felt it was important to know what I was getting into," she replied evenly as she eyed me ever so subtly. I couldn't help but to think there was a double meaning behind her words.

"Yes, and I couldn't agree more with her idea," I told the three of them. "It's the best solution for all parties involved."

"So, you're open to it?" Krystina asked and her eyes lit up.

"Of course, I am. I'll admit it wasn't something I considered until you presented it, but it makes perfect sense. I understand why you wouldn't accept the company outright."

"I'm curious, Krystina" Bryan chimed in. "I was highly against the original offer, but it was extremely beneficial to you. What made you decide to not accept it?"

Bryan's tone was sarcastic, and a stark contrast to the cordial attitude Stephen took. But Bryan was different from Stephen, especially when it came down to money. He was testing her, and it pissed me off. However, just as I was about to rip into him for it, Krystina spoke. Her tone was light, but her eyes held a fierce determination.

"Look, gentlemen. Neither one of you know me," she began and looked back and forth between them. "I understand your hesitations and suspicions when it comes to me."

"It's our job to protect Stone Enterprise's legal and financial matters," Bryan stated bluntly. "That's what we are paid to do."

"Hey, Bryan. Chill. Just hear her out you old scrooge," Stephen joked.

Bryan sat back in his chair, folded his arms, and looked pointedly at Krystina.

"I'm sorry, but I can't help but to think Alex's personal interest in you is clouding his judgment."

"I've thought the same thing," Stephen commented offhandedly.

"Enough!" I snapped. "Neither one of you should be concerning yourselves with my personal life."

My temper simmered below the surface, just waiting to erupt. Friends of mine or not, they were both precariously close to being fired.

"It's okay, Alex," Krystina interjected. "If I were them, I would be thinking the same."

"This is not an attack on your personal life," Stephen explained calmly, the voice of reason as usual. "Stone Enterprise has been very successful because of sound business decisions made by you, Alex. Bryan is just doing the job you've asked him to do, and the same goes for me. If we weren't questioning this, then we'd be shirking our responsibilities. Krystina, Alex just spent the last hour expressing his belief in your capabilities. And while he isn't a stupid man by any stretch of the imagination, I think I speak for both Bryan and I when I say we would like to hear your testimony on the matter."

"Stephen, don't treat this like one of your court rooms," I warned. "Regardless of what Krystina says, the decision to sell off Turning Stone lies with me and me alone."

"Alexander the Dictator," Krystina remarked.

Stephen immediately started to laugh.

"You've got that right!" he goaded.

I looked to Bryan and saw the corners of his mouth twitch. Krystina, on the other hand, merely sat there with a smirk on her face. I shook my head, somewhat amazed by the effect her quick wit had on people. In just three words, even if she was poking fun at me, she managed to instantly defuse the tension in the room.

When she began to speak again, she looked pointedly at me.

"I will succeed with this, Alexander. I'm too stubborn to let Turning Stone fail. But it's more than just that to me, which is why I refused to accept your original offer. There is something to be said about pride and self-worth. I believe hard work and diligence enhances an individual's character. It gives a broader appreciation of one's own achievements. Taking a handout isn't my style, even if given with the best intentions. Perhaps that's a foolish way to view it, especially considering the fact I was offered a golden opportunity. But to me, accepting would give me no sense of accomplishment. I need to know I succeeded all by myself."

I smiled at her, knowing she said exactly what Stephen and Bryan needed to hear. The way they looked at her, it was almost as if they were seeing her for the first time. And in a way, they were.

Yes, gentlemen. This is the woman who has turned my world upside down.

"Well then," Bryan said and smiled. He seemed more at ease, and not nearly as suspicious as he did a few moments before. "It looks like we have a contract to review now, doesn't it?"

17

Krystina

I climbed inside Alexander's Tesla at five o'clock. After I buckled in, I leaned my head back against the seat and looked to him as he sat down in the driver's seat.

"I can't believe how relatively easy you changed that deal for me," I told him.

"I can be reasonable, Krystina. You should have given me a chance before deciding to ignore me for a day and half. Don't do that again," he warned.

I threw my hands up in mock surrender.

"Sorry, but I thought I was going to have to fight in order to get you to agree to it. The research took some time and I wanted to make sure I had all of my ducks in a row first."

"Honestly, I would have preferred if you just took the company free and clear. But in hindsight, I should have known you would have never accepted it. I can understand your reasoning, as well as appreciate it. Besides, your way of thinking sat much better with Stephen and Bryan."

I thought about the meeting with Alexander's accountant and lawyer that began two hours earlier. Initially, they seemed more than just a little bit hesitant. It was as if they were sizing up the woman who Alexander wanted to hand a portion of his company over to. If I were in their shoes, I wouldn't trust me either. We ended our meeting on a more positive note, but I still had some reservations.

"Do you think they approved?"

"It doesn't matter if they approve or not. That's not what I pay them for. This is a business arrangement between the two of us. They were just there to work out the figures and the legalities."

Alexander assumed I was talking about the deal, but I was more concerned over whether they approved of *me* or not. After watching the three men together, it was apparent they were more than just business associates. Their casual banter was too friendly at times. If they were truly his friends, their approval meant significantly more to me for some odd reason.

Why do I care if they approve of me or not?

I stayed quiet, choosing to not clarify what I meant or voice my concerns.

Alexander flipped on the car stereo and backed out of the parking space. Green Day's latest release pumped through the speakers as we made our way to the costume shop in Chelsea. I began to wonder what sort of outfit I should buy. Having never been to an upscale costume ball of sorts, I didn't know how elaborately dressed people would be.

"A penny for your thoughts," Alexander said after a time. "I was just thinking about how decked out people may or may not be. I don't want to look stupid."

Alexander laughed.

"Angel, you could never look stupid."

"That's debatable," I said dryly.

Apprehension crept into my veins. I still didn't know if I was ready for this extravaganza.

When we pulled up to the front of the shop, I looked out the window. A red awning hung over the entrance with the name 25th Street Vintage written across it. There were mannequins in the storefront windows – each one dressed in 1920's styled long and flowing gowns in a kaleidoscope of colors. The jewel tones of them were simply breathtaking.

Alexander came around to my side of the car and opened the passenger door for me. He took my hand as I climbed out.

"Ready to have some fun?" he asked, his eyes full of mischief. I was still eyeing up the dresses in the windows. Each one looked as if it might weigh fifty pounds.

"Ready as I'll ever be, I guess. Let's go."

We entered the boutique and bells chimed on the door. Almost instantly, we were face to face with a young, cheery faced girl. She didn't look to be a day over seventeen years old.

"Hello and welcome! My name is Brielle. What can I help you with today?"

"Thank you. We are in looking for –," Alexander began. He was cut off by a woman who exited from a curtained off room.

"You must be Alexander Stone," she announced. I looked to Alexander. He appeared to be taken aback by the woman.

"Why, yes I am. And you might be?"

"I am Dejah," she said in an accent I couldn't quite place. As she came nearer to us, she began to chuckle. "Don't look so surprised, dear. I'm not a psychic. Your sister telephoned me to tell me you would be in this evening."

"Ah, Justine. I can only imagine what she said to you. She can be a bit overzealous at times," Alexander said lightly.

"Oh, not at all *monsieur*! She said I should be on the lookout for a tall, dark haired man, most likely wearing a suit. However, she failed to tell me how handsome you were," Dejah added with a wink.

Alexander afforded her compliment a small smile. I may have been jealous, but the thick streaks of gray flowing through her long black hair told me she was easily twenty or thirty years his senior. Between that and her oversized jewelry, she reminded me of a carnival gypsy.

"Dejah, this is Krystina Cole. Both her and I are in need of specific attire for a function we will be attending together. Did Justine explain to you what we are here for?" Alexander asked.

"Yes, of course. She told me all about the event. It sounds like it's going to be a marvelous occasion."

"Yes, it will be," he replied.

"If I might add, I'm rather envious over missing it. I can just see it now – the costumes, the setting, the air of a French cabaret come to life," Dejah rambled on wistfully.

Alexander cleared his throat, albeit somewhat impatiently.

"About the costumes," he began.

"Yes, yes. I talk too much. Your sister did say your time is precious. Come with me and we will start going over everything you will need. You've come to the right place!"

She spun on her heel and began walking away from us. I looked to Alexander, but he just shook his head and motioned for me to follow the eccentric woman.

She took us past long rows of clothing from eras gone past. Everything seemed to be organized according to decade, starting with Gucci trends of the 90's all the way back to treasures from the turn of the century. I expected our shopping to take place in this area of the store, but the woman motioned for us to follow her up a set of wooden stairs.

"This way, please. The second floor is what you need."

When we reached the top of the stairs, I gasped at the archival collection before me. It was literally a living museum of burlesque fashion. From the frills and ruffles of the can-can dress, to the beaded corselets of some long-ago courtesan; Dejah's collection was astoundingly authentic.

"This piece here," she said as she ran her hand along the lacy lines of an ivory colored gown. "It is rumored that it was worn by Mistinguett at the Moulin Rouge. However, I have been unable to verify the truth of that rumor, as many photographs and records were lost after the Second World War."

My eyes widened in surprise.

"Are you saying this clothing is the real thing? Not just costume replicas?" I asked incredulously.

"Of course, my dear. My shop is not called 25th Street Vintage for nothing," she proudly stated. "Now, I'll leave you two to look around for a bit. When you are ready to try something on, give me a holler and I will assist you."

I looked at the displays surrounding me. I walked slowly over to a rose-colored silk dress. It was a beautiful gown, but not as ornate as the others in the room. I peeked at the price tag. Not surprisingly, it had a four-figure dollar amount attached to it.

I moved over to a different dress, one that was a breathtaking emerald green with black lace. Rhinestone buttons secured the front of the bodice, while crisscross ties laced up the back. I fingered the satin material as my eyes traveled down the long train and over the beaded detail. The dress was exquisite, and I could picture myself wearing it. However, it came with a five-figure price tag.

Yeah, there's no way can I buy anything from here.

I turned to Alexander.

"That green dress would look stunning on you," he remarked.

"Alex, this is a little out of my price range."

"Who said you were paying?"

"These dresses are outrageously priced. You'd be a fool to pay that much for something I'll most likely only wear once. I'm sure we could find someplace cheaper."

"It's only money, Krystina. And I have plenty of it."

"Well, now that's arrogance for you," I said sarcastically. He frowned.

"This is not about money. It's about you being my date. And as my date, you will need to dress appropriately for the occasion."

"This is asinine. I mean, these costumes are beautiful,

but I highly doubt the other women in attendance will be dressed so extravagantly."

He ignored my comment and walked over to the stairway.

"Dejah," he called down. "Miss Cole would like to try on the green dress you have on display up here."

"Alex! I do not!" I hissed.

"Yes, you do. I could tell by the way you were looking at it. Now be quiet. Dejah is on her way back up. I'll not have an argument with you in front of her."

I half wanted to stomp my foot like a child but refrained when Dejah reached the top of the stairs.

"Lovely choice, dear," she said as she began to remove the dress from the mannequin. "We do alterations on premise, but you may not need them. This looks to be about your size."

She held the dress up against me.

"The color will suit her," Alexander commented. I scowled at him.

"Yes, yes it will," Dejah mused. "Fitting area is just this way. Once you have it on, I will help you tie up the back."

I begrudgingly went behind the curtain she pushed aside for me and took the dress from her hands. I expected it to be heavy, but it wasn't too bad considering my assumption about the dresses in the storefront.

As I stripped out of my clothing, I could hear Dejah and Alexander talking. She was explaining the various items he could wear, pointing out which would go best with my dress.

My dress.

I scoffed to myself as I stepped into said dress. I slipped my arms into position and arranged the sleeves until they felt comfortable. There was not a mirror in the cordoned off fitting area, so I could only assume I put it on correctly.

"Dejah," I called out to her. "I think I'm ready to be laced up."

She came behind the curtain, spun me around, and began to roughly tie up the laces. From the base of my spine to the middle of my back, the higher she went the tighter she pulled. All I could envision was the scene from *Gone with the Wind*, where Scarlett O'Hara was yelling at Mammy to tie it tighter.

Women from back then had to be out of their minds. If she pulls any tighter, I won't be able to breathe!

When Dejah finished, she spun me around.

"Come out here so I can look at you properly, dear." I followed her out of the fitting area to where Alexander was looking at a display of suit coats with tails. Dejah stepped in front of me and gave me a slow look over. "Oh, *monsieur*. She is stunning. Absolutely stunning."

Alexander turned at her words and took in my appearance for the first time. His eyes lit up with appreciation.

"Is it okay?" I asked him. "There wasn't a mirror in the fitting room so I couldn't see."

"Oh, how mindless of me!" Dejah exclaimed and motioned to her left. "The mirror is right over there."

I stepped over to the full-length mirror and slowly turned in a circle. The front of the dress was shorter than the back, leaving the tail of the train to barely brush the floor as I turned. Black beads were woven into the lace detail, sparkling as they caught the light. Sprigs of glittery feathers were used to accent the bust and waistline, giving the dress a luminous appeal.

I truly loved everything about it. Not only did it look astonishingly elegant on me, but it also made me feel mysterious – like I could be anyone I wanted to be when wearing it. However, I was still silently fretting over the extravagant price Alexander would have to pay for it.

"It fits well. Perfect actually," I said hesitantly and ran my hands over the bodice.

Alexander stepped up behind me and placed a simple headdress of rhinestones with green and black feathers upon my head. He ran his hands down my arms as he took in our reflections.

"Krystina, it's more than perfect. Dejah, we'll take the dress."

18

Krystina

"I still think it was a ridiculous amount of money to spend," I insisted as we entered the kitchen of Alexander's penthouse. I dropped my purse onto the breakfast bar and bent over to take off my shoes. I sat on one of the bar stools and began to rub the balls of my feet. After a ten-hour workday and four hours of shopping, my feet were killing me. I resigned myself to the fact that shoes and I would always have a love-hate relationship going on.

"Forget about it. You're going to look fabulous, and that's all that matters," he insisted for what may have been the ninety-ninth time.

"Are you sure I won't be too overdone?"

"Krystina," he said in a warning tone. "I thought we settled this in the car."

"Okay, okay. I'll let it go," I conceded, even if I still thought the expenditure was beyond insensible. He came over to where I was sitting and placed his hands on my shoulders.

"I want to buy you things. I enjoy spending money on you. Why can't you accept that?"

"I don't know. I just..." I trailed off, unable to find a suitable argument. He could spend money on whatever and whomever he wanted. I should be grateful he was choosing to spend it on me. However, the independent side of me always wanted to resist.

"We've talked about this before. I've explained what it means to me to be a Dominant, even if you fight over every aspect of it. Please, allow me this much," he said and placed a soft kiss on my lips.

"About that," I murmured against him.

"What about it?" he asked and pulled back to look at me.

I contemplated how I should broach the subject of his kinkiness without seeming like I was dwelling on past issues. I looked up into his sapphire eyes, so intense that it felt like he could see right through me. I couldn't think when he looked at me that way, so I stood up and began pacing the kitchen.

"Well, I was thinking about that night at Club O, at least the part before everything went bad."

"Yes," he said cautiously.

"I've been thinking about how far you'd like to take things. Don't get me wrong; things have been great between us. Perfect actually. But I feel like we have a lot of unfinished business there."

His blue eyes flashed as he narrowed his gaze on me. I stopped pacing and tried to get a read on what he was thinking. However, before I could explain further, I found myself pinned up against the wall with Alexander's hard torso pressed against mine.

"You're impossible. Do you know that?" he growled.

"I don't mean to –"

"Stop. Now," he demanded.

"This is important to me, Alex. I can't just let it drop. You've done stuff with other women, a lot of stuff I can't even begin to imagine. I'm not very well versed on these sorts of things and I don't know what to think about it. I don't know what my limitations are."

"Kristina, listen to me. Yes, I have done things many consider taboo in the past. I have been with countless women and have pushed their boundaries. I've shown them pain and I've given them pleasure, but never once did I give them a second thought afterwards. Now it's all about you. I only want what you can give me. Nothing more. We have spent the majority of our time together talking about what was or what could be, but that isn't going to happen anymore. Going forward, we will be living in the present."

"I won't argue with that, but there are –"

"Have you enjoyed everything we've done so far?"

"Yes, of course," I told him, taken aback that he might think otherwise.

"Do you feel secure enough to use your safeword if needed?"

"Yes, Alex. But, again, there is –"

"End of discussion," he said, completely cutting me off for a third time.

"You're not being reasonable," I pointed out.

"Actually, I'm making perfect sense," he said, his voice noticeably lowering an octave. He gripped my hair into a ponytail and gave it a slight tug. "You need to trust me. I've already sacrificed and given up so much of who I am for you, Krystina. I won't let you take this from me, too. Your body will always be mine to do with as I please. I will own it and you won't question it."

The command in his voice sent a delicate shiver of delight down my spine. I looked into his eyes. They swirled with a dark primal need, but there was also a challenge in them. It was almost as if he were daring me to push back, like this was a test.

He will own me. I am not allowed to question it. Can I do that?

He tightened his grip on my hair and yanked a bit harder. Pulling my head back, he placed his mouth on the shell of my ear and grazed his teeth over the delicate skin. I shivered again when I felt the hardness of his erection straining through his pants and pressed up against me. A familiar tingle began to form in my belly, rapidly intensifying until I was astoundingly aroused.

"Tell me, Krystina. Say you'll fully submit to me. Give me the words I need to hear," he said gruffly as he tightened his hold.

There was an edge to his voice that was an aphrodisiac to my senses. I found that I didn't want to challenge him on this. I wanted Alexander to take complete and total control over my body. I wanted to feel like that woman on the stage at Club O and let go of my inhibitions. She trusted her Dominant to take complete and total control of her body. Her Dom was her entire universe and nothing else mattered.

I wanted to surrender myself to Alexander, and not just in the physical sense. I had finally reached the point where I trusted him enough to give my full emotional surrender as well. He was just waiting for my consent.

I looked deep into his eyes. I saw a yearning I could no longer deny him of. This is what he needed.

"I'm yours," I said.

A slow and satisfied smile spread over his features, before turning into something darker and full of promise.

"I'm going to be hard on you, angel. You will be completely at my mercy. You don't need to be concerned about my limits anymore. Tonight will be about learning your own. I won't stop unless you use your safeword."

I closed my eyes and let his words wash over me.

Will I enjoy what he does to me? Or will he push me too far?

"What happens if I use my safeword?" I asked hesitantly.

"Don't sound as if that's something you should be ashamed of. You have a safeword for a reason, and I *will* stop if it's used. Repeat it to me so I know you'll call on it if needed."

"Sapphire."

"Good girl," he appreciated. "Without that word, neither one of us will know how high we can go. You need to let go and trust yourself. But more importantly, you need to trust me. Now, go to the bedroom and take off your clothes. I want you kneeling on the floor in the submissive position."

He released his grip on my hair and took a step back. Without hesitation, I hurried to the bedroom, my heated pulse hammering through my veins.

I was wildly aroused, almost to the point of being dizzy. Now that I'd openly agreed, the idea of exploring was unexpectedly exhilarating. My little devil friend was back, and he was rocking out to Madonna's "Erotica" on my shoulder. I *wanted* to do this more than anything.

As I quickly undressed, I began to wonder about the limits in which he would push me to. I was slightly apprehensive because I didn't want to chicken out and disappoint him. However, I shook off the worry almost immediately. He had already shown me so many things I never thought I'd be open to. I felt confident that Alexander was the master of giving both pain and pleasure. I might not know what my limits were, but I knew he would find the balance.

I had already assumed the proper position when he came into the room. He was shirtless and carrying two glasses of wine. He raked his eyes over me, and I saw the desire in them flash hot.

He stepped up to me and placed a glass at my lips.

"Drink," he told me.

I parted my lips so he could tip some of the crisp white wine into my mouth. When he pulled the glass away, a small amount dribbled out of the corner of my mouth. I ran my tongue over my lips to catch it.

He set the glasses on the dresser, then turned back to grasp my chin in his hand. He tilted my face up towards his.

"Do that again," he told me.

"Do what?"

"Your tongue. Run your tongue over your lips and look into my eyes when you do it." I felt somewhat foolish but did as instructed. My eyes locked on his. The carnal need I saw in them sent a rush of heat between my legs, as I slowly slid my tongue over my bottom lip.

He groaned and pulled me to my feet.

"God, what you fucking do to me," he growled and crushed his mouth to mine.

I moaned against his mouth, my body moving against his as the kiss deepened. Alexander cupped the back of my neck with his hand and gripped firmly as he pressed his hard body along my entire length. My hand ran over the span of his broad chest, digging into the muscles as I searched for his sensitive nipples with my fingertips.

He gave a sharp slap to my bare behind.

"Slow, angel. You're too greedy."

He abandoned my lips, leaving a trail of fire down my neck. I tilted my head down and nipped at his ear. Satisfaction filled me when I sensed the shiver running through his body after my teeth dug into his lobe.

Alexander ran his hands up and down my sides, past my breasts without making any real contact. He was torturing me on purpose. I released a moan of frustration. I pressed my body to his, brushing my taut nipples against his chest. I needed to feel his hot skin against mine. I clung tight, trying to will him with my mind to quicken his pace, but he would have none of it.

"Take off my pants, Krystina. Slowly."

Moving back to my knees, I positioned myself in front of him. I could see his erection prominent beneath his pants. On impulse, I leaned forward and pressed my face against the bulge of material. He hissed in surprise and I smiled with satisfaction.

He said slowly. Two can play at this game.

Using my teeth, I deliberately bit down, exerting enough pressure to make him tremble. He hissed again and pulled away.

"I said to take off my pants! I never gave another direction. You need to follow my instructions."

"My apologies," I lied. I wasn't sorry at all. I suppressed a grin, knowing I'd likely be chastised again for being disobedient.

I looked up at him only to find his eyes narrow with suspicion.

"You're a terrible liar. Get up."

"I thought you wanted me to take off –"

"Get up!"

I scrambled to my feet at his command. He took hold of my arm and ushered me over to the corner of the bedroom. He grabbed the edge of the settee and spun it around.

Oh, crap. The spanking horse.

Before I could even process what was about to happen, I found myself bent over the horse, watching as Alexander secured leather cuffs to my wrists. Locking me in place, he stood up and ran his hand lightly over the line of my jaw. He disappeared from my line of sight and I felt leather straps circle my ankles. Spreading my legs apart, he secured them to the posts on the bench.

Stretched over the bench, with my ass high in the air, I was completely vulnerable. I tugged lightly at the restraints but found there was no give. I was rendered immobile and helpless to his whim.

I could hear Alexander moving about the room, but I couldn't see what he was doing. I heard the jingling of keys, then a door opening and closing.

The toy closet.

Music suddenly filled my ears. It started off quiet, but Alexander increased the volume until it was bordering on loud. The electric pulses from the music mixed with the singer's soul-searching lyrics wreaked havoc on my senses and sent my desire into overdrive. It made me desperate for whatever it was he planned to do to me.

The soft feel of leather trailed down the middle of my back. I immediately recognized it as the flogger. A chill raced down my spine in anticipation, wanting to feel the fiery sensation of the leather against my skin.

Alexander leaned down and whispered into my ear.

"I'm going to mark your skin. And I mean it when I say that. It won't be like the last time. I will raise welts that you will feel tomorrow and be reminded of how they got there," he said in a husky voice. "Do you understand?"

"I understand," I told him and nodded my consent. For some strange reason, I had little concern over what he said he was going to do. A part of me knew he only needed me to acknowledge the intensity of what was to come.

His hand slid over my backside, massaging my cheeks before slipping down between my legs. I gasped when he came in contact with my opening. He slid his fingers around the rim, spreading the moisture over the folds to my tingling clit.

"Oh, angel. I love that you're always ready for me."

He pinched and held the pulsing nub between his fingers. I quivered with need, as the painful ache grew until I was desperate for release. I tried to push against him but was prevented by the restraints. I was right there, already so close to the threshold of amazing bliss.

Just as the familiar build up began, he pulled his hand away.

"Ah!" I cried out in frustration.

"Not yet. I want you on edge while I flog you. I'm going to make you mindless. Your ass will burn. You'll be begging for relief, desperate for the release only I can give you. But even then, I won't let you come," he said. His hand slid over my backside and pushed against my puckered rear hole. "I won't let you come until I've taken you in a place no other man has been before."

I couldn't even form a coherent response. His words were like silk in my ears, clouding the reality around me. His statement brought my arousal to a new height, the darkness of his promise an aphrodisiac like no other.

I sucked in a sharp breath as a loud snap of leather jolted me back to awareness. It didn't fall on my flesh but was just made to let me know the first blow was coming. I braced myself for the first lash of fire.

CRACK!

Pain blew over my skin like a rushing inferno and I jumped, unable to stop my reaction to the first blow. I waited for the next, knowing the pain would eventually move to an incredible and pleasurable height. The second one came, but in a different place from the last. I breathed through the burn until it passed. On the third blow, a different kind of burn began to overtake me, one that pulsed and throbbed in my core.

He continued to pepper my backside, one lash after another. After every other whip of the leather, he would reach down and massage my burning clit until I was wild with desperation. I craved the orgasm that was so near, and I didn't think I could take much more of his torment.

"Alex, please!" I shamelessly begged.

He didn't give in but stayed relentless with his assault.

"You will not come until I let you," he reminded me.

He picked up his speed, each blow coming closer and harder than the last. Everything started to get hazy and a feeling of euphoria settled over me. It was as if time ceased to exist, and the only thing that mattered was holding onto the pleasure within the pain.

All at once, he stopped. His palms glided softly over the curvature of my ass, a sharp contrast to the previous sensations.

"Your ass is beautifully red from my marks. It looks fucking magnificent," he murmured. His voice was thick and heavy with desire. I closed my eyes and tried to envision what he was seeing.

He pressed a kiss to one cheek, then the other, the tender action almost worshipful as he spread them apart. I vaguely heard a click sound before being shocked by a cool liquid sliding down my crack. When he began to smear it over the entrance to my seam, probing against the tight hole, I was instantly ripped out of my clouded state and jolted back to reality.

Lube.

When he mentioned taking me where no man had ever been before, I thought he was speaking metaphorically. I didn't think he would actually *do* it.

"Alex, wait –"

"Shh. Trust yourself, Krystina. You can do this."

Oh, yeah sure. I can do this. No sweat.

I rolled my eyes, thinking I just may be out of my damn mind. Tonight was supposed to be about finding my limits, and I was hard pressed to think of a truer test. I lay there, all but dangling helpless, very conflicted over whether or not I should use my safeword.

The music changed to a more edgy tune, the female singer's voice chillingly raw, as Alexander continued to lubricate my backside. Every so often, he would reach through my tender folds to massage my swollen clit. I moaned every time he did it, as I was still dying for the release that I had been deprived of for what seemed like eons. His deft fingers moved up, over, and in, stretching and preparing me for his invasion.

When I felt his erection press against me, I tensed.

"Relax. If you don't, this will hurt. I don't want to hurt you, angel."

Moment of truth, Cole. Safeword or no safeword?

He reached around under my belly and moved his fingers over my pulsing nub, exerting just enough pressure to get me closer to the edge I so desperately wanted to fall over. Taking advantage of my distraction, he pushed himself forward, nudging against my tight ring. My body protested the slight penetration, but he persisted. I gasped when he finally broke through, the painful intrusion overriding any magic he was working on my clit.

"Breathe through it," he instructed. "Don't hold your breath. The pain will pass if you relax your body. Allow yourself to embrace the sensation."

I did what he told me to do and took a few deep breaths. Alexander didn't move but ran his hands up and down my back to help relax me further. Eventually, the tension began to dissipate, and he pushed forward once more. Inch by inch, he made his way in, stretching me impossibly wide.

With one final thrust, he was all the way in. I cried out

and tried to move away instinctively, but the bonds held me firmly in place. Alexander stilled his body and waited for me to adjust to his massive girth, yet never once ceased the stroking motion of his fingers on my clit.

"I'm going to move now, angel. Are you ready?"

I was panting and gasping for breath, trying to absorb the foreign sensation that was both painful and pleasurable. It was an odd sort of feeling and I didn't know which one outweighed the other.

"I'm ready," I whispered, trying to keep my body relaxed.

He pulled back ever so slightly, and I was shocked to discover that I wanted him to stay put. It was as if his backwards motion left a vacancy I *needed* to have filled. Just as I was about to moan a complaint, Alexander thrust forward once again.

"Fuck, Krystina," he said in a rasping tone. "You're sucking me in like a greedy fist."

A dark and edgy sensation began to creep through my veins, propelling me back into the state of euphoria I was in before as he continued to drive forward. Deep and hard, he savagely thrust into me. He said he was going to go hard, and he would show me no mercy. He promised to push me to my limits, and that's exactly what he was doing. Alexander was showing me what it meant to be truly dominated.

This was a demonstration of his power – forceful and utterly alpha. I was helpless to his every desire, yet I relished the vulnerable state he put me in. He was giving me a taste of his complete domination, and I was like an addict. I would never get enough of his power and control. It would forever be like a drug, calling to the deepest and darkest parts of my soul.

I was close to the breaking point, my orgasm just within my reach. The room began to blur around me. I wouldn't be able to hold out much longer.

"Alex, I'm too close!" I cried out.

He slowed his pace and leaned down so his torso was pressed against my back. He smoothed away the hair that had fallen over my face.

"I want you to come, angel. You've earned it."

Returning to a standing position, he reared back before slamming into me. He brought his hand back to my clit, rolling the sensitive nub between his fingers. Over and over again, he pumped his hips forward, the power of his possession overwhelming. But just as I thought it would be too much, pleasure rocketed through me, up and over until it exploded like a firework. I shook uncontrollably, buzzing from a high I had never before experienced.

19

Alexander

I gave her a moment to come down before pulling out. She gasped in shock as I stepped away.

I hear you, baby. I could have stayed in there all night.

I crouched down to remove the restraints at her ankles, then moved around to the front to unfasten the cuffs at her wrists. She didn't budge but continued to lay there relaxed and sated. I coaxed her into a standing position, but she was as flaccid as a wilting flower.

"Come on, angel. I haven't finished with you yet," I said and scooped her up into my arms. I brought her to the bed and lay her down on top on the black satin comforter. "I'm just going to get cleaned up. I'll be right back."

She mumbled something incomprehensible and I chuckled to myself as I made my way to the master bathroom. For the first time, Krystina had truly given me her full submission. And it was a beautiful thing. Given fully and irrevocably, it was something to be cherished. She deserved nothing more than to be worshipped for the rest of the night.

When I returned to the bedroom, she was curled up on her side with her head resting on her hands. I climbed onto the bed next to her and her eyes fluttered open.

"Round two?" she lazily asked.

"Oh, angel. We're still only on round one," I said with a wink. "Roll onto your stomach."

She eyed me suspiciously for a minute but did what I asked without question. I smiled to myself.

I love it when she obeys.

I popped open the cap for the aloe I had brought in from the bathroom and squirted some into my palm. Taking my time, I massaged the cooling gel over the welts covering her ass.

"That feels nice," she murmured. I rubbed my hands around the globes, over her hips, and down her legs, marveling over the sheer perfection of her body.

She's exquisite.

Once I was satisfied that she was feeling more soothed from the aloe, I turned her onto her right side, knowing she wouldn't be comfortable laying on her backside for a while yet.

"Spread your legs for me, angel. I've been dying to taste you. I want your come all over my tongue."

Almost immediately, I heard her breathing increase. Her response was like an electric shock straight to my groin. Before the night was over, I planned to taste every inch of her delectable skin. No part of her would be left unexplored.

I positioned my head between her legs, taking a moment to appreciate the sheen of moisture glistening on her delicate folds. Unable to resist, I brought a finger up to graze her clit before tracing the line of her small opening.

She was dripping with desire, so wet and so moist. She was ready and I could have taken her right then, but I wanted to take my time with her. She had been so generous and so willing to push her boundaries – she deserved more than a minute or two of spoiling.

I continued to stroke and prod until she began to tremble.

"Alex..."

Her plea sounded desperate as her body began to tighten. I smiled and grazed the inside of her thighs with my teeth, before inhaling deeply to take in her scent. I parted her lips and blew softly over her clit. I flicked my tongue over it, satisfied by her immediate intake of breath.

Gripping her hips, I pushed my tongue down harder. Encouraged by her response, I thrust my tongue into her well of honey, not wanting to waste a single drop of her desire. She pushed against my mouth and pulled at my hair. I ate her like a starving man. And for her, I was. I would never get enough of her taste. Her scent. A groan escaped me, as I wanted nothing more than to bury myself in her heat.

"Alex, wait. Stop!" she cried out. Her frantic and broken scream made me pause.

"What's wrong?" I asked, alarmed by the desperation in her tone.

"What we did," she said in between pants. "I loved it, but

I need to feel you where you belong. I want you inside me when I come."

I breathed a sigh of relief.

"Now that, my sweet angel, is an easy request to fulfill."

I loved that she wasn't holding in her desires. She wasn't keeping anything back. She was just being Krystina. It was then I realized how much strength it took for her to relinquish all the control over to me and to trust me so implicitly. I had dominated her in the most intimate of ways and she barely uttered a protest. She simply gave.

It was time I gave back in return, and not just in the physical sense. I could bring her to new heights all night long, but that wouldn't be enough of a repayment for what she gave me tonight.

I moved up alongside of her and pulled her tight to me. In one swift motion, I turned onto my back and dragged her across my chest. Her hair fell to the sides, curtaining our faces that were mere inches apart.

"Ride me, Krystina. Take control."

Her eyes widened in surprise. The shocked look on her face made me smile.

"You want me..." she trailed off.

"Yes, angel. But don't get used to it," I joked.

Her stunned expression turned dark, and her eyes burned with a need I couldn't describe. Her pupils dilated with a provocative and sultry glow, as she slid her hands down my stomach and wrapped her slender fingers around the base of my cock. Positioning her body above mine, she slowly lowered down.

The groan that passed my lips came from the gut, deep and guttural as she took me fully. I felt her constrict around me, encircling me in pure ecstasy. She was like the smoothest of silks, wrapping me in her warmth. I could have spent the rest of my life inside her and died a happy man.

When she began to move, I couldn't stop my eyes from traveling the length of her. Her eyes were closed, and her head was thrown back in unabashed bliss, her tits bouncing with every drive. She was like a goddess as she rode me, her pace destined to drive me over the edge.

I was so close, but I couldn't come yet. Not without her. I wanted her orgasm first. This was supposed to be all about her. It was no longer about pushing her limits, but about her pleasures. Her needs. I had taken, but now I had to give as much as I took.

"I'm right there, Alex," she breathed. Her eyes looked glassy, sluggish almost, as if she were caught up in another world.

"I'll wait for you, angel," I promised. My cock throbbed and pulsed, just aching to explode. The pleasure was like liquid gold running through my veins.

"Meet me there," she pleaded.

Her desperation almost broke my sanity and I nearly lost control. The beautiful goddess above me would be my undoing.

I'm lost in her. In this. In this moment.

I thrust up hard against her, matching her movements while she drove me to an unbelievable height. Our gazes locked and I felt her tighten around me. I pushed up one more time and she cried out my name.

"Alex!"

"Give it to me. Give it to me now, Krystina," I croaked out, my voice sounding raspy even to my own ears. "Let go."

At my words, she went off like a bomb and her scream of pleasure sent me over the edge. Instantly, my body went taut, straining so tight I thought I would burst apart at the seams. There was a flash of white, before everything went blank. She continued to grind against me, never stopping despite her own climax, jetting my release into the deep recesses of her core.

Krystina collapsed down on top of me. I could feel the way her heart raced in her chest, matching my own hammering pulse. I traced small circles along the line of her spine, as a feeling of warm contentment settled over me.

I really do love this woman.

The words were on the tip of my tongue. I wanted to tell her so badly, but I knew it wasn't the right time. A part of me wondered when that right time would be, as Krystina had never given any inclination that she shared my sentiments.

It's too soon. I can't tell her yet.

Eventually, her breathing returned to a normal rhythm and I turned to shift her weight to the side. She barely moved on her own accord, having already fallen into a dreamlike slumber.

I should wake her. She needs water.

I knew she'd reached subspace while on the spanking horse. Her lithe state afterward told me as much. Aftercare was something I never wanted to neglect with Krystina, as neither one of us knew how hard she could potentially crash. But as she lay there, her breasts rising and falling with every breath she took, I didn't have the heart to wake her.

Instead, I pulled the comforter and sheet out from underneath her and spread them out over the both of us. I spooned up alongside of her and brushed a curl from her forehead. I watched her for a long while, wondering what it was that I did to deserve someone like her. She was feisty and spunky, and everything I thought I would never want. Yet, she was exactly what I needed.

I closed my eyes and settled into her warmth. Within minutes, I fell into my own peaceful sleep.

20

Alexander

Ten. Eleven. Twelve. Three. The one is missing. I think it is supposed to say thirteen. Almost there.

I reach the door that has the number fifteen and place my hand on the knob. It feels sticky. Justine must have forgotten to wash her hands after eating the sucker from Grandma.

I twist the door handle and go inside. Everything is quiet.

Good. Quiet is always better than yelling.

I hear a noise. It sounds like Justine crying. I hate when she cries. I need to find out why she's upset.

I go to the kitchen. She's not here. Maybe she's in the family room.

I see her little feet peeking out from behind the couch. She's hiding.

He hates that.

"Justine," I whisper. "We are not supposed to play hide and seek in the house."

*I go behind the couch to get her. Her face is all scratched up
and blotchy. There is red stuff all over her clothes.*

"Justine! What happened?"

*"I don't know," she says. She picks up Dolly and squeezes her. I
see something shiny.*

"Why do you have dad's gun?"

"Mommy's going to be so mad. I ruined my shirt!"

I shake her and Dolly falls out of her hands.

"How did this happen?" I ask her again.

*"Alex, do you know where my blue dress is? The pretty one
with the flowers. Mommy likes when I wear it."*

She looks weird. What is wrong with her?

"Justine!"

*I shake her again, but she isn't paying attention. He did
something to her to make her act funny. I know it.*

This is his fault. I need to find him.

*I hear Justine humming mommy's favorite song. I need to help
Justine.*

I need the gun first. He can't hurt me if I have the gun.

There it is.

I pick up the gun.

I see him lying on the floor. Lazy bastard is probably sleeping.

That's what grandpa says. Says he's a lazy bastard.

"Hey!" I yell to him.

He doesn't answer.

*I walk around to the other side of him. I need to wake him up.
I need to tell him not to hurt Justine anymore.*

He's awake. His eyes are open.

"Hey!" I yell again. He doesn't answer me again.

I'm angry. So angry. I hate him.

People who do bad things need to be punished. He did

something bad to Justine. He does bad things to mommy. Like the time he banged her head against the floor and made blood everywhere.

He needs to learn a lesson.

I point the gun at him.

"ALEX!" I heard someone call. "Alex, wake up! It's just a dream!"

Krystina.

I bolted upright and the room tilted. My heart was racing at a fevered pace, fueled by absolute rage. I glanced down at my hands.

Large hands. My hands. Not the hands of a child.

But more importantly, the hands I looked at were empty. I breathed a sigh of relief.

No gun.

I shook my head to chase away the images belonging to a ten-year-old boy. When my vision cleared, I saw Krystina sitting in the bed next to me. From the light of the moon coming in through the windows, I could see her expression. She looked severely alarmed.

"I apologize. I didn't mean to wake you," I mumbled and shook my head again.

"Alex, what was that all about? You were yelling your sister's name and you were saying you hated him. Who do you hate?"

I ran a hand over my face and through my hair, trying to rid myself of the disturbing dreams that haunted me.

"It was nothing," I tried to dismiss. But as usual, Krystina pushed.

"Your father?"

Fuck this.

I threw the covers off and got out of bed.

"I said it was nothing. Just forget it," I said harshly. "Go back to sleep."

"Where are you going?"

"To the den. I need to work on my speech for Friday night."

"Your speech? Alex, it's barely four in the morning," she pointed out skeptically.

I felt edgy. Unbalanced. My temper was ready to flare up at any given moment. I had to get away from her, away from this burning need to lash out at someone. Anyone.

Get it under control, Stone.

I took a deep breath and went around to her side of the bed. I kissed her lightly on the forehead and tried to adapt a more patient tone.

"I know what time it is. Please, just try to go back to sleep."

Not waiting for her response, I left her, and I made my way to the den where my home office was situated. I sat behind the desk and leaned back in the chair.

Dammit! I usually wake up before the dream goes that far. If Krystina hadn't been there...

A chill raced down my spine.

But she was there.

The fact she'd heard me talking in my sleep was disturbing in itself. But I was more bothered by the amount of anger I felt when I awoke from the dream. I was filled with hatred of the worst kind, and I had this unexplainable need to physically harm something or someone. It was another reminder of why I wasn't good for Krystina. I felt like a ticking time bomb waiting to go off at any moment. I was a threat to her safety.

I need to get a goddamn grip.

I was no stranger to the nightmare, but I was concerned by the frequency as of late. The dream that had come almost daily as a child had eventually dissipated throughout my adult years. I grappled with trying to find a reason why they were becoming more regular after all this time.

I glanced at the bookshelf against the wall to my right. It was full of old college textbooks, as well as modern psychology studies on the many complex ways the human mind works. I had spent hours on end, scouring those books for answers. My fingers itched to pick one up again.

However, I was too keyed up to delve into research at that moment. I knew the dream was too fresh for me to take an unbiased stance on the material. Until I had the right frame of mind to research what the trigger may be, a distraction was in order. I needed to take my mind off the past, my nightmares, and all the ways it could affect my relationship with Krystina.

I reached behind me and turned on the stereo. Linkin Park streamed through the speakers and I quickly switched it to a classical music station.

Mozart's 'Jupiter'. Good. I could use something a little more relaxing.

Turning back to my desk, I fired up my laptop and opened a blank plain text document. My speech for the charity gala still needed to be written, and I couldn't think of a better time to do it.

"Alexander."

I looked up and saw Krystina in the doorway. She was wearing one of my T-shirts, her hair falling in loose curls over her shoulders. She looked beautiful standing there, perfect in every way. She took my breath away.

I don't deserve her. She's not safe with me.

I pushed aside the nagging worry that I may someday unintentionally hurt her and focused on the words I had spoken to Krystina earlier.

Live in the present.

I flashed her an easy smile and was careful to keep my tone light.

"I've always considered myself a silk and satin kind of guy, but you look damn sexy when you wear my T-shirts. Have I ever told you that?"

"Don't try to avoid the issue," she said gently and shook her head. Walking over to me, she sat down on my lap and fingered a hand through my hair. "Talk to me."

I embraced her in my arms and squeezed tight. She felt so good. Soft and warm. And such a sharp dissimilarity to what I had been feeling just a few minutes before.

After a moment, I pulled back and looked into her rich chocolate eyes. They were full of patience as she waited for me to speak.

"Angel, it was just a nightmare. People have them."

"Not like that, Alex. Whatever that was, it wasn't normal."

"You're right. Normal people don't have nightmares like that. But we've been through this. You already know I'm not normal," I said bitterly.

"Alex..." she trailed off. "Your childhood was horrific. All things considered, I think the fact it still bothers you is a very normal thing."

None of it is fucking normal.

I closed my eyes and took a deep breath. I knew I should tell her about the dreams. She deserved the whole truth and she had the right to know what she was getting into.

"Krystina, when I told you about my past, I didn't tell you everything."

She pulled back, and her brow formed the shape of a V. I fought the urge to smooth the wrinkles away. I preferred it when she smiled. If it were up to me, she'd never frown again.

"What didn't you tell me?"

"I've told you everything as best as I can remember," I began. "This might sound strange, but I think my memories are muddled by my dreams. The dream I had tonight is a reoccurring one. I've had it since I was a child."

The sound of the gun shot rang through my mind; the smell of gunpowder prevalent in the air. I shuttered and tried to will it all away.

"What's the dream about?"

I pinched the bridge of my nose and I wrestled with trying to find the right words to explain the sequence of how it all happens. I had come this far, and I knew I had to tell her the rest. Even still, I couldn't help but feel like I would gag on the words I had never before spoken out loud.

"The dream is very similar to my memory. There's only one difference. In the dream, I didn't come home to find my father already dead. I'm the one who shot him," I choked out.

There. I said it. It's finally out in the open.

"But, Alex. It's only a dream," she said softly. "You said

yourself that the police never found out who shot him, and Justine has no memory of it."

I stared at her in shock, astounded by her innocence.

"Krystina, don't you understand what I'm saying? I think there is a very real possibility I was the one to pull the trigger. Not my mother. Not Justine. Not a random criminal. Me."

She stood up and began to pace back and forth in front of my desk.

"Tell me the details of the dream."

"Angel, I'd rather not get into it. At least not tonight. Another day maybe."

"Fair enough. So, we'll look at a different angle. There was an investigation, right?"

"Yes," I told her, not sure where she was going with her line of questioning.

"Did anything ever come out about your mother's whereabouts?"

"No. It was like she just vanished. Her picture was all over the newspapers; the police questioned everyone we knew. They came up empty."

I recalled that time period, and how hard it was for Justine and me. The school had been informed and teachers were questioned. It was only a matter of time before our classmates caught wind of it. Justine came home crying more often than not.

Kids are so damn cruel.

I, on the other hand, had started skipping school all together. Overnight, I became a problem child for my grandparents who were just trying to do their best with the hand they were dealt. Bitter and resentful, I was a recluse during my teenage years. After discovering my desire to hit women at the tender age of sixteen, I deemed myself unsafe to others. I trusted no one, including myself. If I hadn't met Sasha, the girl who introduced me to the world of BDSM, I may have never gotten my life under control. At eighteen, she became my only outlet for years of pent up anger and put me back in control of my emotions. By the time I was twenty, I had mastered the art of balancing patience and self-restraint with power and control. It became my identity and my way of life.

Until now.

Since meeting Krystina, everything felt out of balance and my carefully honed instincts were awry.

"There had to have been something. Some little clue as to where your mother went," Krystina said, tearing my thoughts away from that dark period of my life.

She stopped pacing and came to stand before me. I could see the way her mind was turning, like she was trying to put together a puzzle that came with missing pieces.

"There's no use trying to figure it out. I've tried. I wish I had the answers, but I don't. She may be dead, or she may still be out there somewhere for all I know."

Krystina tilted her head to one side and looked curiously at me.

"Is that why you decided to open a woman's shelter?" she asked softly.

I narrowed my eyes at her, finding it somewhat uncanny that she came to that conclusion.

"What makes you ask that?"

"Well, I don't know," she said with a shrug. "My original thought was you were opening it because you could sympathize with women who came from abusive situations. But now I'm thinking there might be more to it. Like perhaps you're wondering if one day your mother will show up there."

"In a perfect world, angel. In a perfect world," I mused with a shake of my head.

"Do you want her to be found?"

I didn't know the answer to that, as I had asked myself the same question over and over again. A part of me hated my mother and never wanted to lay eyes on her again. But another part of me found it hard to believe she would just leave us so easily. I was sure Hale was tired of looking into every Jane Doe who showed up on police blotters, even if he would never say anything about my obsession to discover the truth. Justine never understood my need to find the answers either. She thought I was looking for a ghost.

"Come here," I answered instead and pulled her back down to my lap. "There is no sense in both of us being exhausted tomorrow. Go back to bed. I'm going to stay up and work on this speech."

"Honestly, I'm not really all that tired at the moment. Maybe I could help," she suggested.

"You don't want to do that," I said with a laugh, attempting to lighten the somber mood. "These things are boring and pretty standard. I have a rough idea of what I need to write, but I'll need to spice it up a bit or Justine will have my head. She says I'm too dry and I need to show more heart."

Coaxing her off my lap, I guided her back to the bedroom. Krystina climbed into bed and I pulled the covers over her. When I leaned down to kiss her, she rested her palms against the sides of my face.

"I have an idea, Alex. How about you tell the truth in your speech? I can't think of anything more heartfelt than a true story."

I looked pointedly at her, kissed her on the nose, and stood up.

"That will never happen, angel."

"You should try. You may end up feeling better about what happened if you do."

I didn't give her a response, but simply dimmed the light and walked from the room. Maybe I would feel better if I told my story, or maybe I wouldn't. But it's something I would never find out. Making my story public was not an option. I refused to be the subject of speculation. Justine and I had already lived through that, and hell would freeze over before I allowed it to happen again.

Krystina

AFTER ALEXANDER LEFT THE ROOM, I reached over to the nightstand and grabbed my phone. If he thought I would be able to sleep after our conversation, he was sadly mistaken. The man was obviously grasping for answers. I was sure he had researched his father's murder extensively, but perhaps there was something he missed.

I slinked down in the bed and tucked the phone under the covers. I didn't want the light from the screen to be seen by Alexander. It was better if he thought I was going back to sleep, rather than find out I was doing research on his behalf. I knew how much he valued his privacy. I didn't want him to become upset upon learning what I was up to, even if I did have his best interests in mind.

I pulled up the browser app and thought about how I should begin my search.

I need a timeline. A date.

I subtracted his age from the current year to figure out a time frame. After doing the quick math, I typed in Alexander's name and the year he would have been ten years old. I frowned when I saw the search populated nothing of relevance. Everything I found was either a tabloid or business article related to the past ten years or so.

I tried to narrow it down by including the Bronx, the area he grew up in. I came across an article about a real estate transaction, but nothing mentioned his mother or an unsolved murder case.

Having little success with a search on Alexander, I tried using Justine's name instead. I still came up with nothing pertaining to what I was looking for. I rubbed my burning eyes, attempting to fight off the sleep that wanted to overtake me.

Perhaps his grandparents or his mother's name?

It was then I realized I didn't even know his mother's name. I knew his grandmother's name was Lucy, but I couldn't recall if he ever mentioned the name of his grandfather.

This is useless. I need more to go on.

Feeling frustrated, I placed the phone back onto the nightstand. I wished I had found just a tiny scrap of information to work off of. There had to be something that would lead me to more answers for Alexander. I thought he was putting way too much stock in a dream, but I knew he needed the truth in order to move on. If I could help him find it, maybe he would stop beating himself up so much.

I'll look into it more after work tomorrow.

Committing myself to do exactly that, I rolled onto my side and stared out the window. The sun was close to cresting the horizon, giving the sky a luminous red glow.

Red in the morning, sailors take warning.

I closed my eyes. The possibility of what the day's weather forecast could be was my last fleeting thought before surrendering over to sleep.

21

Krystina

I was amazed at how fast my workdays were going at Turning Stone. Thursday went by like a blur, despite the fact I had put in a twelve-hour day. Now here I was on Friday morning, already having almost a week under my belt. My days were jam packed, but I loved every minute of it.

"Regina," I called out to my secretary, having barely gotten used to the idea of even having a secretary.

"Yes, ma'am," she said, peeking her head into my office. It was strange to be called ma'am, especially considering the fact she was easily twenty years my senior.

"I have an appointment with Walter Roberts this morning to go over the advertising strategy for Wally's. It's tough for him to get out of the store, so I'm going to meet him at his office. I should be back no later than two o'clock. Please forward any calls to my cell."

"Will do. Anything else?"

"Actually, yes. Did you get a chance to read the email the I sent you about Sheppard's Cuisine?"

"I did, and I was already working on it."

"Great. Any luck finding info on their competitor's markets?"

"Oh, a ton! I already sent a lot of information over to Clive," she told me, referring to Turning Stone's lead marketing coordinator. "I'll tell you, I remember a day when that task would have taken days' worth of legwork. I might be showing my age when I say this but thank heavens for the invention of the Internet. It made the research a breeze."

I laughed and was about to thank her, but stopped short as her words reminded me of all the trouble I was having with my attempt to research the murder of Alexander's father online.

That's it! The Internet is my problem!

The Internet was barely in existence twenty-five years ago, so there wouldn't be any information available for me to find. I thought about the time I had wasted last night trying to find information. Alexander wanted me to spend the night at his place, but I had made the excuse of being too tired from a long day.

I'm so stupid...I can't believe I didn't think about that!

I would need to go to the library and look at newspaper archives.

"Uh, thanks, Regina. One more thing," I said absently. "I may not be back as soon as I expected. I just thought of another stop I have to make."

"Take your time. We'll hold the fort," she joked before returning to her office.

I grabbed my purse and made my way towards the

elevator. I was looking forward to seeing and working with Mr. Roberts, but I hoped he wasn't feeling particularly chatty this afternoon. I suddenly had a more pressing matter to attend to. If I balanced my time with him efficiently, I just might be able to squeeze in an hour at the library before having to get ready for the charity gala.

The elevator doors opened and, in my mad rush to leave, I smacked right into Hale.

"Oh! Hale," I said, feeling embarrassed for not paying attention. "Sorry about that. I wasn't looking where I was going."

"It's okay, Miss. I was actually just on my way to see you. Mr. Stone requested I give these to you."

He held out a set of keys.

"What are these for?" I asked in confusion as I took the keys from him.

"There is a car in the parking garage for you. It's located in spot D36. Since I'm not always available for you, Mr. Stone prefers you utilize this going forward. He is concerned about your safety on the subway or in a taxi."

"That sounds like something he would say," I said with a frown. Something wasn't sitting right with me. "Hale, is this just on loan until I can get my car fixed?"

"I can't say for sure, Miss. We didn't discuss it. I was only told to retrieve the Porsche Boxster from his storage facility and bring the keys to you."

A Porsche. That sneaky bastard.

Most likely, the car was not a loaner, but a gift. Alexander knew about the secret love affair I had for the German car manufacturer. I recalled how he had once told me that collecting cars was a hobby of his. I was curious about the extent of this collection, as well as whether or not the Porsche was a part of it. However, no matter how much I was tempted, a car was one gift I simply could not accept.

"Hale, please tell Mr. Stone I said thank you for the offer, but I prefer the cab. Besides, it's easier than trying to find a parking spot."

"Miss Cole –"

"Hale," I said and reached for his hand. I placed the keys back into his palm. "I'm taking a taxi."

"He will not be very pleased about this."

"Oh, I'm sure he'll be furious. But I can handle it," I added with a wink and pressed the button to call up the elevator once again. The corners of Hale's mouth turned up in the subtlest way. It wasn't quite a smile, but there was a hint of humor in his eyes that gave him away.

"Have a good day, Miss."

"Thanks. You too," I said as I stepped into the elevator.

Before the elevator even reached the ground floor, my cell pinged with a text notification. As I walked through the lobby, I pulled my cell from my purse. Not surprisingly, the text was from Alexander.

9:51 AM, ALEXANDER: *MUST YOU ALWAYS BE SO DIFFICULT?*

I smiled to myself. Rather than have a battle of wills, I responded with only a kissy-face emoticon and tossed the phone back in to my purse. He could either laugh at what I sent or get mad. Either way, I had a busy day lined up and fighting over a car was not on my agenda.

I walked out the main doors and was happy to see there was already a cab parked at the curb. I quickly climbed in.

"Wally's on 57th please," I told the driver.

I sat back in my seat and thought about Walter Roberts. I hadn't seen my old boss in weeks. I was looking forward to working with him again, even if the context was different than before.

My cell phone began to ring. I groaned to myself, thinking it was Alexander calling me about the Porsche. However, when I looked at the screen, I saw it was my mother calling. A part of me wished it were Alexander, as that conversation would have been easier. I hadn't spoken with my mother since she left after her last visit, and things were strained to say the least.

"Hi, mom," I greeted tentatively.

"Hello, love. How are you? I haven't heard from you in a while."

"Sorry, things have been a little hectic. I started a new job," I told her, hoping she'd be happy to hear the news. "The pay is really good. You can tell Frank I'll take care of my rent from now on."

"Good for you. I'll let him know. Anything else new and exciting?"

That's it?

She had been hounding me about a job for months. I was shocked that she wasn't pressing me for details. The cab driver took a sharp right, forcing me hard against the passenger door.

Maybe Alexander is right to have concern over my safety in a cab.

"Um...not really. Same old," I told her.

I wasn't sure what else to say. My mother usually talked my ear off, and I could rarely ever get a word in edgewise.

"Are you still seeing Alexander?"

Ah...now we might be getting somewhere.

"Actually, I am. Why do you ask?" I said, feeling somewhat guarded.

"Well, I was thinking about Thanksgiving. You usually come home for the holiday. I thought you could invite him to join us."

What is this?

It was like she was encouraging me to have a relationship. She was always so full of doom and gloom whenever the opposite sex came up, and I wondered what brought on this one-eighty.

"I could ask him. I'm not sure if he has plans or not," I said somewhat distractedly as I looked at the road ahead. I gripped the door handle for dear life as the cab came to a sudden stop.

"Excellent. Let me know when you find out. Now, I know how busy you are, so I won't keep you."

Okay, now this is just beyond the point of bizarre.

I found it hard to believe I was speaking to Elizabeth Long, the bitter woman who all but claimed all men were evil and I should steer clear of the lot of them. I pulled the phone away from my ear just to make sure it was her name on the display.

"Mom, is everything okay?" I asked her before she could hang up.

"Yes, love. Why wouldn't it be?"

"I don't know. You're just acting kind of weird," I said, feeling totally bewildered. The line went quiet. "Mom, are you still there?"

I heard her sigh.

"I'm here. I'm sorry if you think I'm acting strange. Maybe I am, but it's only because I'm trying to just let you be. I was left with a lot to think about after my last visit."

"Mom –"

"Just hear me out for a minute. I was really upset and had a long talk with Frank on the drive home from the city. Then, over the course of the past few weeks, he eventually made me see things a bit differently. I didn't realize how hard I was being on you. You know I love you, right?"

"Of course, I do, Mom. I love you too."

"I really only want what's best for you, but I know I need to take a step back. You're an adult and I can't keep telling you what to do. It's well past time I let *you* decide what is best for you."

"Uh, thanks I guess," I said with a small laugh, lacking any other thing to say. This was so out of character for her, and I wasn't sure what to think.

"You'll call me when you have an answer about Thanksgiving?"

"Yeah, sure. No problem."

"Alright, love. Then I'll talk to you soon. Bye now."

"Bye, mom."

I hit the end button on my cell and just sat there staring at the screen. Traffic passed by and horns blared, but I was seeing and hearing none of it. I was happy my mother was finally loosening the reins a bit. After all, I stopped being a child long ago. But even so, it may have been the weirdest conversation I'd ever had with her.

Alexander

It was nearing three o'clock and I was finishing up my weekly recap with Laura in order to set up priorities for the following week.

"Were you able to get a crew for *The Lucy*?"

"I did find one, sir," Laura told me. "The company comes with good references and are fully insured. They suggested you dock her in the Florida Keys rather than the Caribbean because of crime concerns. If you'd like to discuss it in more detail, I have already scheduled a meeting for you with them next week on Tuesday."

"Good. Where do we stand on the building permits?" I asked, moving on to the next order of business. "I need to know who's palm I have to grease to get things moving along."

She flipped tabs in the binder she held in her lap and ran a finger down a page.

"All of the permits for the old Rushmore building have come through from the city ordinance, Mr. Stone. I'm just waiting on your go ahead to give the contractors clearance to begin work," Laura told me.

"It's about damn time, too," I bit out in annoyance. "I bought that building nearly two years ago."

She sighed.

"I understand your frustrations, but there was no way you could have known about the structural concerns of the building, sir," she tried to assure. "It wasn't disclosed, and it was missed by the inspectors."

"Either way, the holdup is irritating, not to mention extremely costly. Where is Stephen on the legal end of that?"

"I only know he's been hitting wall after wall with trying to get compensation from Rushmore Industries. Their bankruptcy is putting a monkey wrench in anything Stephen tries to present to the judge."

"Alright. I'll get with him on that later. What else do you have for me?"

"The roof construction permits for Wally's Grocery have been applied for, and I do not expect any hold up there. The Mayor's interest in that deal has really helped to move things along."

"Good. I'll take it one step further. Call his office and try to set up a lunch meeting for us next week. I want to ensure his interest remains steadfast."

"Will do, sir. Anything else?"

"Yes. I emailed you a list of properties in lower Manhattan. I'll need all the background information pertaining to them. Scratch anything that will be a headache, then send me an updated list of what looks promising. I'll do site visits with Hale next week."

"I'll have the information by Monday morn –"

A knock on my office door interrupted her.

"Come in," I barked, annoyed by the interruption. Krystina was due to arrive here soon, and I wanted to finish business for the week. I was going on a seven-day stretch and was looking forward to taking a day or two off. The image of Krystina bound and naked had been like a carrot dangling in front of my face all day.

"Mr. Stone," said Hale as he stepped into the office.

"Oh, Hale. Good. I'm glad you're here. I wanted to speak with you before tonight. Laura," I said, turning back to my assistant. "Unless there is anything more pressing you can think of, I think we can wrap things up."

"No, sir. I'm set," she affirmed.

After Laura left, I motioned for Hale to have a seat across from me.

"Are we all set for tonight?" I asked him.

"Yes, sir. Justine would like you to be dropped off at the main doors. I didn't give her an affirmative answer to that. I thought it was safe to assume you would want to survey the press presence first. There is a back door if needed."

"Good call on that. Krystina has reservations about the media. An alternate entrance just may be needed," I contemplated. "What about the Bugatti?"

"I've already been to the storage garage and have had the car prepared as you requested."

I laughed.

"You've had a busy day over at the garage site, haven't you?"

"Just a bit," Hale said and afforded me a rare smile.

"Tell me about your conversation with Krystina earlier. Was she mad about the Porsche?"

"She didn't seem upset, but she was hard to read. We didn't talk for that long," he admitted and furrowed his brow. I sat back in my chair and listened while Hale gave a brief recap about Krystina's refusal to take the Porsche.

"I figured she would be resistant, but I thought she'd be more apt to take it from you over me. I'll handle it from here," I told him. "How are we on security for later?"

"Security is in place. I spoke to Justine and she shared a few additional concerns I've made accommodations for. I'll be there to keep an eye on things all night. If Charlie makes an appearance, we'll be all over it."

"I don't think he'll come around," I dismissed.

"Well, if he does, we'll be ready to toss him back out to the street," Hale assured. "Did you get my email on Trevor Hamilton?"

"I did, but I haven't had the chance to look it over yet. Did you find anything on him?"

"Quite a bit, sir. In fact, it's quite disturbing. That's why I asked if you received it. I have a hard time picturing someone like Miss Cole being with a man like him."

I pressed my lips together and frowned. No matter what Hale found in Hamilton's background, I didn't like picturing her with *any* man other than myself.

My phone buzzed and I glanced down at the screen. It was from Krystina and instantly my mood lightened.

3:07 PM, KRYSTINA: *MR. ROBERTS KEPT ME LONGER THAN I PLANNED. ON MY WAY UP NOW.*

Hamilton could take a flying leap. She was mine now.

3:08 PM, ME: *SEE YOU IN A FEW.*

On impulse, I added the same kissy-faced emoticon she'd sent to me earlier. I smiled, thinking about how she had the ability to bring out an uncharacteristically playful side in me.

I looked back to Hale. He wore a peculiar expression on his face and I quickly wiped the soppy grin off my face.

"That was Krystina," I told him seriously. "She's on her

way up. We plan to get ready for the gala at the penthouse. You can pick us up there at six o'clock."

"Yes, sir," he replied, but he was eyeing me with a knowing look.

"What?"

"Nothing, sir. Nothing at all."

I narrowed my gaze, fully aware of what he was thinking.

Yes, Hale. I'm completely smitten by an angel.

I honestly didn't care what he thought. In fact, I didn't really care what anyone thought. I was in love with a woman, even if she didn't know it yet. If people wanted to judge me for that, so be it.

22

Krystina

As we neared the hotel hosting the charity gala, I was already feeling like a princess. It was hard to believe I was arriving in a 1931 Bugatti. Between that and our vintage attire, I would bet even members of the British Royal Family would experience a twinge of envy. I was starting to learn very quickly that Alexander never did anything small.

When we pulled up, I glanced out the window. A sea of news reporters was there at the ready. All of my excitement instantly vanished.

"Alex," I said warily as I took in the crowd lining a Hollywood style red carpet. "Are those all reporters?"

"Most likely. There was a lot of hype surrounding this event," he said with a frown. "But I will admit, I didn't expect to see so many."

"Shall I pull around back, Mr. Stone?" Hale asked from the front seat.

"The publicity will be good. I shouldn't avoid them," Alexander mused before turning to me. "Krystina, I'll need their coverage to capture the interest of future donors if tonight's silent auction doesn't pull in as much as we hope it will."

"It's okay. I understand. I can handle it."

I hope.

"Hale, we'll just get out here."

"Yes, sir," Hale replied.

Hale got out of the car and walked around to open the door for us. Alexander climbed out first then turned around to take my hand. The minute I stepped out of the vehicle, the press pounced.

"Mr. Stone, can you comment on Stone Arena?"

"What are your community outreach plans for the women's shelter?"

"Mr. Stone, when are you going to begin work on the Rushmore building?"

Question after question was fired at him, but he didn't bat an eye. Instead, he just smiled as we walked up the red-carpet hand in hand. Hale trailed very closely behind, keeping a watchful eye on the scene.

Holy crap. This is absolutely nuts!

Cameras flashed. The entire thing felt surreal. I literally felt like a celebrity.

"Mr. Stone, some have been calling you a venture capitalist," a reporter called out. "What's your position on that?"

Alexander paused at the question and turned to face the reporter. He was a tall and thin man, looking to be in his mid-forties. He pushed his glasses up the bridge of his nose as he held out a microphone in anticipation of what Alexander might say.

"My business has always been real estate. It always will be." More questions came flying, and Alexander held up his hand to silence them. "I cannot discuss the details about Stone Arena at this time. But rest assured. As soon as I can, a press conference will be scheduled."

"Mr. Stone, can you tell us the name of your date for this evening?" said a woman from behind the man with the glasses. Alexander paused and seemed to be contemplating his words before he spoke.

"This is Krystina Cole. My girlfriend," he added.

I almost started choking as the press buzzed to life once more.

"Who designed her dress?" shouted someone from the crowd.

"Her dress was purchased at 25th Street Vintage, from a lovely woman named Dejah. Now, if you'll excuse us. Stone's Hope Gala awaits us," he said before turning back to me and lowering his voice so only I could hear. "Let's go, angel."

"I thought you said boyfriend and girlfriend sounded childish," I whispered once we were out of earshot from the press.

"I did."

"What made you change your mind?"

"I don't know to be honest. Would you have preferred something different?"

I smiled to myself.

Not at all.

"Oh, I could get used to it I suppose," I said nonchalantly.

"Maybe I should have stuck with arm candy," he mused. However, he couldn't keep the smile from showing through in his voice. I looked up at him as we walked through the entry doors Hale held open for us. Alexander's eyes twinkled bright with amusement.

"The day you refer to me as your arm candy is the day I start calling you cupcake," I joked.

He laughed, the sound echoing through the lobby of the hotel.

"You really are something, Miss Cole. It's occurred to me that I might actually enjoy myself tonight." He stopped walking as we came upon a set of great double doors. He bent at the waist and made an exaggerated swooping motion with his arm. "My lady, I am honored to have you here as my date."

Looping his arm in mine, we walked through the doors of the ballroom. When we entered, I was completely awestruck.

"Oh, wow!"

Deep red and black satin swooped down from the ceiling, with an ornate crystal chandelier as the centerpiece. The same deep red covered the tables, accented with black and white dinnerware. Roses set in gemstone colored vases adorned each table.

Framed replicas of Toulouse-Lautrec posters covered the walls, adding to the authenticity of the setting. There was a massive stage at the far end of the room, with a backdrop of red velvet curtains lined with gold sequins. A band of musicians wearing top hats and three-piece suits with striped vests was already playing. Their lead singer was a woman decked out in swanky black dress and long strands of pearls. They swayed around her neck as she sang a cover of "Alone" by Patricia Kaas.

"It looks like my sister has out done herself," Alexander commented.

"You can say that again! This place looks amazing! Actually, glamorous would be a better word for it. I feel like I've just walked into a turn of the century movie."

People mingled about wearing elaborate attire. The women wore everything from the sleek and sexy dresses of a courtesan, to the more revealing burlesque fashions of the time. The men were in costume as well, their style similar to Alexander's striped tuxedo and top hat. Any reservations I may have had about my costume vanished. I was dressed perfectly for the occasion.

"Alex!" called a female voice. I turned and saw Justine coming towards us. She looked striking in a long gown of deep purple, the coloring complimenting her jet-black hair that was twisted into a stylish knot with pin curls on top of her head.

"Justine, you look lovely," Alexander complimented and kissed her lightly on the cheek. "You remember Krystina, right?"

"Yes, of course," she said and turned to me. "I just love your dress! How was Dejah? She didn't talk your ear off, did she?"

"She was fine," I said and laughed. "Alex was sure to keep her in line."

"I bet he did!"

"Alright, alright. No tag teaming allowed tonight," Alexander joked. "Krystina, let's head over to our table and leave Justine to do whatever it is she needs to do."

"Actually, I need you to come with me," Justine interjected. She made a quick glance over her shoulder and lowered her voice. "Mrs. Van Rensselaer is already here. I could use your help with persuading her to open her checkbook. You know how she is. I need you to work your magic on her."

Alexander looked to me.

"It's okay," I assured him. "Go on ahead. I can find our table without you."

"Are you sure?" He looked doubtful, ignoring Justine as she tugged on his arm.

"I'll be fine, Alex. Go work your magic on Mrs. Van Rensselaer," I teased with a wink.

"I won't be long."

After Alexander and Justine walked away, I headed over to the table holding our seating place cards. I located our table assignment easily enough, as we were seated at the head table near the stage. When I sat down, I fought the urge to kick off my shoes. They had been on my feet for barely an hour, but I was already feeling the pinch in my toes. I was regretting my choice to give in to Dejah's insistence over the Edwardian era shoe.

"Justine said you didn't look his type," said a female voice from behind me.

I turned to see who was speaking. A slender red headed woman in a royal blue dress leaned against the table behind me. She was drinking from a champagne flute. I recognized her immediately as the woman Justine was with at The Mandarin Day Spa. She was also the woman whose face appeared in news articles, photographed next to Alexander, on numerous occasions.

Suzanne Jacobs.

Since we had never been formally introduced, I played the innocent card.

"Hello. I'm Krystina Cole," I said and stood to offer my hand to her.

She glanced down at my hand but didn't accept the handshake. Instead, she polished off what little amount was left in her champagne glass and signaled a waiter for another.

"You're a little young for Alex," she drawled. She peered at me through glassy eyes. It was then I realized she was well on her way to being drunk.

Already? The night has barely gotten started.

"I'm sure I don't know what you're talking about," I told her.

The situation had disaster written all over it. I turned my back to her and reclaimed my seat. I was not about to have a confrontation with a drunken woman I had never met before. But, much to my dismay, she pulled out the chair next to me.

"Allow me to introduce myself. I'm Suzanne. Suzanne Jacobs."

I know that already, you nitwit.

I smiled sweetly at her.

"It's nice to meet you," I stated, trying to be polite as possible.

"Look at you, sitting there all sweet and innocent," she said. Her voice dripped with contempt. "Have you ever been to an event like this?"

"Um, no. I haven't."

"Honey, you have no idea what you're in for. Trust me. I

know. In fact, I know a lot of things about these sorts of affairs. Just like I know a lot about Alex," she snorted in the most unbecoming way. "And I know he will break your pretty little heart."

She leaned forward and poked me relatively hard in the chest. I sat back, startled by this woman's aggressive behavior. It was not the time, nor the place. I looked around for Alexander and spotted him on the other side of the room engaged in conversation with someone.

I tried to remember the names of the people assigned to sit at the same table as Alexander and me. Justine had a place card, as well as Alexander's accountant and lawyer, Bryan and Stephen. There were also other names I didn't recognize, but I would have remembered reading the name Suzanne Jacobs. She was definitely in the wrong place.

"You might want to go find out what table you were assigned to. I don't recall seeing your name listed for this one," I told her, hoping she would take the hint.

"Trying to get rid of me already? Oh, no honey. I'm just getting warmed up."

"No, you're not. This conversation is over," I told her and stood up. If she wasn't going to leave the table, then I would.

She grabbed hold of my wrist, her grip remarkably strong considering how boney and frail her hand looked.

"Don't be fooled by him," she warned me. I ripped my hand out of her grasp.

"It's you who are the fool," I said, careful to keep my voice quiet and even. The last thing Alexander needed was a scene on such an important night. "Don't pretend to think you know everything about him. I know him. Alexander Stone is a good man."

"Stone? You really are naïve," she laughed loudly at some private joke. "You obviously don't know as much as you think."

I looked up when I saw someone approaching out of the corner of my eye. Justine was making a beeline towards us.

Oh, thank god.

"Suzy!" she hissed. "What are you doing?"

"Oh, relax!" Suzanne waved off.

Justine looked more closely at her friend.

"Shit. You're drunk," she whispered. "I can't believe you! You, of all people, know how much work I put into tonight. I told you that Alex was bringing someone, and you promised you wouldn't do anything stupid! And here I was worried about Charlie ruining everything!"

Who is Charlie?

I looked back and forth between the two women, not sure what to make of the situation, when Alexander came strolling up.

"Suzanne," he said with a nod. His greeting was pleasant enough, but I knew otherwise from the strained tick in his jaw. It was a telltale sign he was angry.

"Alex, call Hale immediately," Justine ordered. "Suzanne needs to be taken home. Now."

Alexander looked over to the left. I followed his gaze and saw Hale standing against a wall nearby. The two men nodded to one another, before Hale came over to the table.

Hale didn't say a word, but simply took Suzanne by the arm and steered her towards the main doors. She, of course, did not want to go willingly and protested the entire way. A few guests glanced in their direction, but for the most part, their exit was made quickly and quietly.

"I'm very sorry about that, Krystina," Justine apologized. "Suzanne is...bitter. Let's just say there's something to be said about a scorned woman."

"Don't make excuses for her, Justine," Alexander quipped. "She's a grown woman. She should know how to behave."

"Alex, I tried to warn –"

The loud static from a microphone being adjusted interrupted whatever it was Justine was going to say. The female lead singer from the band had left the stage and was now behind the podium. In all the commotion with Suzanne, I hadn't even realized the music stopped.

"Ladies and gentlemen, please take your seats," she announced. "Dinner will be served momentarily. In the meantime, I'd like to welcome up to the stage the man who has made all of this possible. He is the Chief Executive Officer of Stone Enterprise and the founder of The Stoneworks Foundation. Without him, none of us would be here tonight. So, without further ado, please put your hands together for Mr. Alexander Stone."

23

Alexander

We had the attention of the entire ballroom. I smiled and gave a brief wave before turning to Krystina.

"I have to give a speech. Are you okay?"

"I'm fine. Go do your thing," she assured.

"Justine, you'll be sitting here?"

"Yes, of course. Now get up there. People are beginning to stare!" Justine said through her teeth, never once breaking the false smile plastered on her face.

I glanced at Krystina. She smiled politely and nodded her head to me. To an outsider, she looked perfectly happy. But I knew differently. Suzanne had rattled her.

I could kill that woman.

I leaned in and kissed her lightly on the cheek, hating the fact I was going to leave her alone once again.

"We'll talk in a bit," I whispered to her.

"I'm fine," she insisted once more.

Not satisfied she was, I turned and made my way to the podium. After taking my place behind the microphone, I pulled out the speech I had written and surveyed my audience.

Christ, I fucking hate giving speeches.

"Thank you all for being here tonight," I began. "Without your generous donations, Stone's Hope Shelter for Women would have never taken flight. However, there are many other individuals who have helped to make this night possible. I'd like to take a minute to thank the staff, the volunteers, and most importantly, my sister, Justine. She is the heart and soul of tonight's event, as well as the driving force behind Stone's Hope."

I paused for a moment, allowing the crowd to give the customary applause.

"For those of you who do not know, tonight marks the fifth annual fundraising dinner for The Stoneworks Foundation. While events in the past have always gone to a worthy cause, tonight holds more significance. Stone's Hope _"

I stopped short, as Krystina's words echoed in my mind.

Tell the truth.

I scanned the crowd. Waiters and waitresses had begun serving the first course, while guests waited in anticipation for what I was about to say. I looked down at the speech in front of me. What I had written was full of insincerities with the hope of monetary gain. And if I were being truthful to myself, it was shallow.

I folded up the speech and placed it in the breast pocket of my suit coat.

"I had a speech prepared for tonight, but I'm sure you've

all heard something similar before. So instead, I'm going to tell you a story. It's about two children who grew up with a mother who could not escape from the clutches of domestic violence."

I glanced at Justine and saw she looked horrorstruck. Krystina leaned in and whispered something to her, before looking back to me and nodding her head in encouragement.

This is for you, angel.

I focused my attention back to the crowd and took a deep breath. I then began to tell them a tale about a family of four, who lived in poverty, amidst the brutality of a husband and father. I spoke in generalities, never once mentioning my name or Justine's, but I told the truth all the same. I told them about the abuse, both mental and physical, and about the endless cycle that could not be broken. I spoke of a kind woman who loved her children but didn't have enough strength to break free from a world that had beaten her down.

"They lived under a patriarchal mentality, where the man in the house had the right to judge, decide, and dole out punishments as he saw fit. The mother, fearful of her children's safety as well as her own, taught them how to behave so as not to anger their father. But there were times when her lessons were not enough to stop his fury. More often than not, she wore a blackened ring of shame around one or both eyes, while she dressed her son in long sleeved shirts during the summer to hide his bruises from school officials. She would blame herself for doing something wrong, feeling ashamed for failing in her wifely duties.

"Her children lived in constant fear. They didn't play like

most children should, as they were fearful the littlest sound would spark their father to hurt their mother. Or worse, hurt them. They were terrified of the days when their father would come home in a drunken rage, something that was a regular occurrence after he bloodied their mother. Their only option was to hide from him, sometimes for days, as their mother was rarely there to help them because she was too weak or broken to get up from the floor."

"Alex, how much longer do we have to stay in here?" Justine would ask me.

"Shh. Be quiet. He'll hear you," I'd scold.

I looked out into the crowd.

"As you all sit here tonight, I'd like you to imagine the world I'm describing to you. Imagine their home – a housing project made of cinderblock, where crime and violence were the norm; where survival was the only motivation to get out of bed every day. Imagine a man, one so dissatisfied with his life that he takes to pummeling his wife as a way of venting his frustrations. Now close your eyes and picture a six-year-old girl and a ten-year-old boy, their mother beaten so badly they have no other choice but to hide in a filthy broom closet. They had no place to go, no one to turn to. These children, so young and so afraid, only had each other."

Even after all this time, I could still picture Justine and I huddled together in that wretched closet. I could still smell the musty scent wafting from the floor. It was like old shoes that sat out in the rain for too long.

I don't want to be talking about this. I don't want to remember it.

I took a deep breath, knowing I had little choice but to continue on with the story I was now committed to telling.

"The physical and mental abuse wore m –" I stopped short, correcting the mistake just in time. I had almost said 'my' mother. "It wore this poor mother down over time. After enduring the pain of countless broken bones and witnessing the brutality raining upon her children, she realized there was nothing any of them could do to make her husband happy. But she also felt she had nowhere to go. So, she began teaching her son and daughter new lessons whenever her husband wasn't around."

As I spoke, I heard my mother's words as if they were spoken only yesterday.

"Alexander and Justine, I hope one day you will become better than this world. I want you to demand respect, but you also need to understand how to give it. I want you to live in contentment, yet still shoot for the impossible dream. Break this cycle and make a difference in the world."

"The lessons she gave them were no longer about how to avoid their father's wrath, but about perseverance and about the life she eventually wanted her children to have. She painted a picture of the individuals she wanted them to become. She knew she lacked the self-esteem and the financial resources to make this her own reality but hoped her teachings would make her children learn from her mistakes."

I continued on and told them about the mother who had dreams of a better life, and about the woman who spoke of fairytale ideals where she and her children were surrounded by happiness.

"I want you to escape and be something, and never want for anything ever again. This is my wish for you. Don't settle for

anything less. I know in my heart you can do this. Don't be like me. Strive for better."

"This mother wanted a better life for her children with all of her heart, but years of abuse had eventually broken her will. She stopped telling stories. She stopped having hope. She gave up, no longer having the energy to make a difference."

I paused, knowing I had said enough, and looked around at the faces below me. It was then I realized how much time I had spent hating my mother yet ended up doing exactly as she told me to do. I demanded respect from others, and I went after the impossible dream. And here I was, making a difference.

Because of her.

"Her story, while it echoes so many others today, took place many years ago. It was a point in time when the domestic abuse movement was still in its infancy. Shelters were not readily available in every town or city. There were no outlets for new beginnings. Our society has evolved for the better since then. Laws have been passed to recognize and protect women who have fallen victim to abuse. But it's not enough. We still have so much work to do.

"Knowing what I know about that poor little boy and his sister, I wonder how different their life would have been if their mother had another choice. A way out. An escape. Stone's Hope will give women, and their children, a chance at a better life. It will provide a roof, protection and security, and pave the way to a fresh start. But most importantly, it will give hope. Because sometimes, hope is all you need."

The crowd was silent. Not even the clinking of silverware

could be heard in the room, before everyone erupted into applause.

Instantly, I was filled with relief. They may not know of the individuals I spoke of, but I did. Because of that, a huge weight I hadn't realized I was carrying was lifted from my shoulders. For the first time in my life, I felt my past might finally be used for some good.

Justine took the stage and made her way over to me. She leaned in to give me a quick hug.

"I don't know what possessed you to do that," she whispered. "I just hope they don't put two and two together."

I returned her hug, careful to keep my smile in place.

"I was cautious. Besides, my original speech was boring."

She laughed.

"Yes, it was. I read it. This was much more..." she began and pulled back to look at me. "I don't have the memories you do. The way you spoke about her...it was heartfelt."

"That's what you wanted, right? More heart?"

"I did."

Her eyes glistened with tears.

Oh, no.

"Justine, get it together."

She sucked in a sharp breath and quickly collected herself. She smiled one more time at me before stepping up to the podium.

"Ladies and gentlemen," she said into the microphone. Her voice silenced the audience that was still applauding. "I will echo the sentiments of my brother when he said sometimes hope is all you need. Stone's Hope *means* hope."

I exited the stage and listened while Justine went on to talk about the importance of our donors. This was her area of expertise over mine. She was better at wooing people to open their wallets for a charitable cause. I was the more cut and dry sibling. I told it like it was and it usually suited me well in the business world. Tonight was a rare performance.

Heading over to the table where Krystina was waiting for me, I felt relieved over having finished my part for the evening. I was never a big fan of speeches to begin with, but this one had been a particularly difficult one to give for a magnitude of reasons.

Krystina stood when I approached her, and I pulled her into my arms.

"I'm proud of you," she told me.

"Thank you, angel. I never would have done that if it weren't for your suggestion and encouragement," I whispered into her ear. "Now, for the rest of the night, I'm all yours."

Krystina

AFTER DINNER, the first dance was announced. The largest donors, as well as Alexander and Justine, were invited to lead off the night. The band performed a version of "Dream a Little Dream of Me", a soulful yet sweet duet from the lead singer and her partner that carried across the room.

"Aside from the episode with Suzanne, are you having a good time?" Alexander asked as we swayed to the music.

"Actually, I'm having a fantastic time," I told him honestly.

"I know you're probably wondering about her."

I was curious, but at that moment, I didn't want to give the woman another passing thought. I just wanted to enjoy the night with Alexander.

"I am wondering," I admitted. "But you don't have to explain. We're not living in the past anymore, remember?"

"You're right, angel. It's all about right now. This moment," he said and extended his arm to twirl me in a circle. When I came back to him, I looked up into his painstakingly beautiful blues.

"And this moment is perfect," I told him. He met my gaze and held it steady before taking my chin in his hand.

"Move in with me."

I slowed my pace until I was almost at a standstill, shocked by his suggestion.

"What?"

"You heard me. I said move in with me," he repeated.

I can't move in with you! I have a life, I have a... What do I have?

I was so confused, his proposition totally throwing me off balance. I couldn't think of one single particular reason for why I shouldn't move in with him, I only knew I couldn't.

"Alex, I can't move in with you."

"Why not?"

"Why should I?" I questioned back, baffled as to what brought this on.

"You should because you belong there. At the penthouse. With me. I don't like it when you're away from me."

He pulled me tight against him, forcing me back into the gentle rhythm we had a few moments before.

"Alex, we've barely established we're a couple. I'm not

saying I would never consider it, but I think it's too much too fast."

"So, don't give up your apartment. We can do a trial run and see how it goes," he pushed.

"But, Alex..."

"I need you, Krystina. I don't want a part time relationship anymore. You promised me no more nights alone, but that has yet to happen. I want to wake up every morning with you beside me. I want to come home with you in the evening. Everyday needs to begin and end with you," he said huskily as his eyes seared into mine. I looked away, unable to withstand the intensity of them.

I rested my head against his shoulder, thinking about what it would be like to wake up in the same arms I had been lost in the night before. It was a real struggle to fight off the urge to give in to his request.

"Alex, it sounds appealing, but I can't. Not yet."

What he suggested was more than just appealing – the idea of waking up with him each day caused elated butterflies to dance around in my stomach. But I had to be sensible about it. If I moved in with him, I knew it wouldn't be long before I started to envision the white picket fence. That was dangerous, and it was just something I couldn't afford to do.

The first song finally ended, and the lead singer made an announcement to invite all remaining guests out to the dance floor. The band kicked it up a notch and began playing a more upbeat Peggy Lee classic, but I still couldn't think past Alexander's suggestion to move in.

I need a minute to think.

Using the change of song pace to get away from the

pressure I was suddenly feeling, I took a step back from Alexander. I intended to make an excuse about having to use the restroom but was prevented from doing so when he took hold of my arm.

"Where are you running to, angel?" he asked. There was a twinkle in his eye as he snapped his fingers in time to the music. Grabbing me around the waist, he sent me into a full three-sixty spin before bringing me back to crush his hips against me.

"Oh!" I squeaked out in surprise after having almost lost my footing during the unexpected twirl.

"We need to work on your dancing skills, my lady," he laughed.

"Hey! I can hold my own just fine. You caught me off guard!"

"Oh, yeah? Let's see how well you can keep up, angel," he challenged.

He extended his arm to spin me again, before leading into a smooth rock on the downbeat. I didn't know the steps, but Alexander's lead made it easy to keep up.

Mirroring his movements, I stepped back with my right foot before shifting my weight to the left. Before long, I learned the dance was pretty basic, following a six-count step. But just when I thought I had it figured out, Alexander threw me off center with a tuck double underarm turn.

"Where did you learn to dance like this?" I asked, feeling slightly out of breath. I was completely in awe over his flawless moves.

"East Coast Swing, baby. My grandmother was the best."

"She taught you?"

"Everything she knew."

Another loop around and I began to notice the guests were watching us.

"Alex, everyone is staring," I whispered, feeling extremely self-conscious. Alexander was so fluid in his movements, I was sure to look like I had two left feet by comparison.

"Probably because they've never seen me dance before. I'm not one to engage in frivolities at these types of events. But who cares?" Another double spin before he brought me tight to his chest. "Let them stare, angel. I want them all to know you're my girl."

"Your girl?" I laughed. "Are you adding to the list of ways you can introduce me?"

He gave me a rueful smile and my heart fluttered.

"Not at all, angel. I'm just stating a fact." He gazed down at me in a stare so powerful, it penetrated through to my soul. "Make no mistake – you are mine."

The music slowed down to a smooth, yet powerful stream of guitar strings being strummed. Feeling short of breath, I melded against Alexander's chest as he pulled me into another slow dance. Settling into a rhythm, I hummed along to the band's rendition of "Wicked Game".

When Alexander began to sing the lyrics to the song, I was stunned silent by the emotional tenor of his voice. Not only did he have stellar dance moves, but he had an amazing voice as well. As he sang about not wanting to fall in love, I pulled back and looked into his sapphire blue eyes.

All at once, a moment of perfect clarity came forth. He had me completely taken. Emotion squeezed at my heart until I felt it might burst.

I'm falling for him.

The realization crashed over me like a tidal wave, crushing me upon impact. At first, I was momentarily flooded with happiness. But then reality swept me away in a fierce undertow.

I can't fall in love with him. He'll never love me back.

Alexander had been very clear on his position. And so was I. We both agreed there would be no strings attached.

It's the song. It's just the song.

I tried to shake off the overwhelming feelings, thinking it was just the music and Alexander's singing messing with my head. Up until fifteen minutes ago, I didn't even know he could dance *or* sing. I barely knew him. I could not possibly be in love with him. The idea was ludicrous.

The music began to transition once again, but I was barely hearing it as Alexander leaned down to place a soft kiss on my lips. My throat tightened and my eyes began to burn, threatening tears I couldn't afford to shed. They were tears of sadness, for I knew loving Alexander would ultimately destroy me.

"Angel..." he said, his voice heavy with emotion. The term of endearment almost broke me. My heart began to hammer in my chest.

Don't. Please don't.

Just one more word from him and the geyser would break open.

Out of the corner of my eye, I saw Justine walking toward us. I pulled slightly away, stopping whatever he was about to say to me. I focused my attention on Justine. She appeared to be troubled about something.

I looked back up at Alexander.

"Justine is headed this way," I told him.

"I need to cut in," she said rather curtly once she reached us.

"No, Justine. I'm dancing with Krystina right now," Alexander tried to shrug her off, never tearing his eyes away from mine. They were blazing so intense, I had to blink and look away.

"Alex, I don't want to dance with you! I need to talk. Right now," Justine said in a panic. He turned to face her, and his expression changed instantly. He looked alarmed.

"Justine, what is it?"

"I think Charlie is here."

Alexander paled. I didn't know who Charlie was, but it was the second time his name was mentioned over the course of the night.

"Who is Charlie?" I asked, but Alexander waved me off. I bristled at the way he brushed me to the side.

What the hell?

"Not now, Krystina," he dismissed before turning back to Justine. "Where do you think you saw him?"

"Going into the kitchen. I'm pretty sure it was him. He was dressed like a member of the kitchen staff. I tried to find Hale, but he hasn't come back from bringing Suzanne home yet."

"Dammit!" Alexander swore and his eyes flashed with anger. "Krystina, I need to handle this. Justine, take Krystina to the table. I want both of you to stay put until I say so. Do you hear me?"

"Yes," Justine responded without skipping a beat. "Krystina, come with me."

Having little choice because I hadn't a clue about what

was happening, I followed Justine to our table. Once we were there, I looked pointedly at Justine.

"For the second time, who is Charlie?"

"Charlie is my ex-husband," she told me, looking about the room nervously.

"So?"

"He's a problem. A big one."

"You're not giving me much here. Elusiveness must run in your family," I said sarcastically, feeling very annoyed over how rudely I was being dismissed. And not just by her, but by Alexander as well.

"It's a complicated story. If Alex wants to tell you, he will."

By the way her eyes continued to dart around distractedly to various people in the room, it was obvious she wasn't going to give me any more information. I sat down in a chair, trying to access what I knew about Alexander and his sister so I could piece together some sort of explanation on my own.

Why does her ex-husband pose such a threat?

Before I could come to any conclusion, Alexander was back. He was flushed and looked thoroughly rattled.

"I'm not sure if it was him, but I spotted someone who could have been him slipping out the kitchen's back door. I only saw the back of his head, so I can't be sure," he told us. "This may be nothing, Justine. Are you sure it was him?"

Justine suddenly looked doubtful.

"I don't know, Alex. Sometimes I feel like I see him everywhere. But I could swear..." she trailed off and shook her head. Her panicked look returned, and Alexander placed his hand on her shoulder.

"It's okay. Just relax. Let me get a hold of Hale."

Alexander grabbed his suit jacket that was slung over the back of one of the table chairs. He reached into his pocket and frowned.

"What's wrong?" Justine asked.

"My phone. I would swear I left it in the breast pocket."

We all glanced around the top of the table and under it to see if we could locate it.

"I don't see it, Alex," I said. "Ally loses her phone all the time. We usually find it by calling it. Do you want me to try?"

I reached for my purse to pull out my cell, but Alexander stopped me.

"Don't bother. I turned the ringer off when I was giving my speech."

"I'll check with the wait staff later," Justine offered. "Maybe someone picked it up accidentally when they were clearing the table. Just use my phone to call Hale."

"Fine. Give it to me." Alexander took Justine's phone and hastily punched in the numbers. "Hale, what's your ETA?"

While Alexander was talking to Hale, Justine leaned in to whisper to me.

"This place is crawling with security," she said. "But Hale is the best. I should have had someone else drive Suzanne home. I wasn't thinking."

I didn't comment, as I was too bewildered over the situation to say much of anything. I looked back at Alexander with the hope he would clarify something soon but saw there was very real alarm written on his face.

"What? That can't be right. Circle around to make sure. I'll wait on the line," Alexander instructed Hale.

"What is he saying?" Justine demanded. "Circle around where?"

"I'm here," Alexander said into the receiver, rather than answer Justine's demands. He became quiet again as he listened to whatever Hale was saying. He had that angry tick to his jaw, so I knew whatever it was couldn't be good.

"Alex!" Justine hissed, but he held up his finger to silence her. When he spoke again, there seemed to be real panic in his voice.

"I don't know why the fuck they would be together. Have your men follow them," he said and looked to me. There was conflict in his eyes. "In the meantime, I want you to take Krystina back to the penthouse. Justine will stay with me until we can make a more inconspicuous exit. I'll take care of making sure she gets home safe."

Now it was my turn to ask questions.

"Alex, what's going on?"

"You're both leaving," he said after he ended the call with Hale.

"Why?" Justine and I both exclaimed at the same time.

"Justine, you weren't mistaken. Charlie was definitely here. I shouldn't have to explain why it's important for you to leave."

All the color drained from her face.

"You're right," she whispered. In the blink of an eye, it was if a switch flipped. Justine's stricken look was replaced with a professional air. "Yes. I'll go start making my round of goodbyes."

Turning away, she went off to mingle with the last remaining guests. I shook my head, amazed at how quickly she was able to change gears, before rounding on Alexander.

"I'm glad Justine knows what the hell is going on. Are you going to explain it to *me*?"

"Krystina, you have to understand. Charlie is a dangerous man. He is very much like my father was, if you can catch my meaning. He's not supposed to be here. His presence is a violation of the restraining order Justine has on him. Combined with..." he trailed off and shook his head. "It doesn't matter. What matters is getting you both away from here."

"Alex –," I started.

"This is not up for debate! You will not argue and just do what I say!" he hissed.

I blanched at his menacing tone. I only wanted to ask why I had to leave too. I didn't understand why Justine's ex-husband would pose any sort of threat to me. He couldn't possibly even know who I was. But then again, maybe he did for all I knew. I was reminded of how unforthcoming Alexander could be with information.

This is bullshit.

"You know what? I think I'll find my own way home," I told him.

He grabbed hold of my arm.

"Krystina," he pleaded in a softer tone. "Please, just trust me on this."

I wanted to yank my arm from his grasp, but there was something in his eyes that gave me reason to pause. He looked visibly afraid.

"What is it?"

"Charlie has been threatening to expose the past. Given the speech I gave tonight, it won't be difficult to add credibility to what he might say."

Once again, I still didn't understand why it was such a big secret, but it was a losing battle with him. Nevertheless, I was getting the impression Alexander wasn't quite telling me everything.

"There's more to it, Alex. It's written all over your face. What else is going on?"

He shook his head, looked to the ceiling, and took a deep breath. When he brought his gaze back to meet mine, his expression was full of trepidation.

"He just knows too much, angel. None of it can come out."

I could see his pain over the idea of having the past brought to light. It was as if he lived with a looming black cloud over his head. Tonight should have been perfect, yet it ended up being ruined because of Alexander's fear of exposure. It wasn't fair for so many reasons.

Reluctantly, I conceded to leaving. But as I exited the building with Hale, I felt overwhelmed with the need for answers. What had happened to Alexander was tragic. I could empathize with that. But, in my opinion, he was obsessing over keeping his past hidden. Nobody would find fault with him over what happened. He was his own worst enemy in this situation.

Perhaps if he knew the truth, things would be different. Because of that, my resolve to find the truth about the murder of Alexander's father was now stronger than ever.

24

Alexander

The penthouse was quiet when I walked in. Assuming Krystina had already gone to bed, I made my way down the hallway to the bedroom. My eyes roamed over the décor as I went, noting how much of a stark contrast it was to Krystina's apartment. It suddenly didn't matter that I'd spent a small fortune on the interior design. To me, it was beginning to feel cold and lifeless. The penthouse lacked the little feminine touches only Krystina would be able to bring to it.

When I entered the bedroom, I saw she was fast asleep. Her dress from the evening was tossed neatly over a chair in the corner, and her feathered headpiece was sitting on the dresser.

I walked over to her and ran my hand lightly down her arm. She stirred but didn't wake. I noticed her skin felt cool to the touch, so I pulled the comforter further up and over her shoulder.

Stay sleeping, angel.

I didn't want to have to answer the barrage of questions she was sure to have, but I also knew I couldn't keep the truth from her for too long. She was right when she said there was more to it. It wasn't just about Charlie. It was more, so much more. Her uncanny ability to read through me was startling, but I couldn't tell her at that moment.

I didn't have it in me to tell her Trevor Hamilton was lurking just outside the venue doors, and he was seen walking away with Charlie Andrews.

I could still picture her face on the night I took her to Club O – so pale and horrorstricken. I may not have known Hamilton was the reason for it at the time, but I knew I never wanted to see that look on her face again.

I left Krystina to sleep and went into my office. I sat down behind the computer and rubbed my hands over my face. For the life of me, I couldn't figure out why Hamilton was with Charlie Andrews in the first place.

How do they know each other?

Together, they had put me into an impossible situation, forcing me to choose between the safety and well-being of the two most important women in my life – Justine and Krystina. There had to be an explanation, but none of it made any sense.

Hale's crew, who had been tailing the two men, lost them in a mob of people filling Times Square. As it stood, we had no idea of their whereabouts. Because of this, leaving the charity gala had been nerve wracking. Justine was constantly looking over her shoulder, paranoid Charlie would pop up. She didn't know about Trevor Hamilton, and I knew adding him to her list of concerns would send her into a downward spiral. She had been shaking like a leaf by the time we left the venue, all of her energies spent on keeping up the proper façade in front of the guests.

I leaned forward to turn on the computer monitor. My inbox was already open and waiting. I scrolled through the emails to find the one Hale had sent me just that morning, the report of his findings on Trevor Hamilton. Had I known Hamilton would be a potential threat tonight, I would have made reading it a priority before now.

TO: Alexander Stone
FROM: Hale Fulton
SUBJECT: Trevor Hamilton Background Info

Mr. Stone,
Attached is the information you requested regarding Trevor Hamilton. If you would like me to dig further into any particular area, just let me know.

Hale

I clicked on the attachment.

FULL NAME: Trevor Joseph Hamilton
DOB: December 19, 1992
PLACE OF BIRTH: Westlake, OH (St. John Medical Center)
PHYSICAL DESCRIPTION:

Height: 5 feet 11 inches

Weight: 185 lbs.

Hair: brown

Eyes: hazel

ADDRESS:

Current address: unlisted/unknown

Previous address: Greenwich Residence Hall, 636 Greenwich St, New York, NY 10014

PHONE: (440) 239-5001

PARENTS:

Joseph P. Hamilton, Jr. (father, born March 1, 1960)

Sandra L. Marx-Hamilton (mother, born July 2, 1961)

Gross annual income: $1,329,000.00

SIBLINGS:

Jessica Ann Hamilton (infant sister, born premature November 23, 1989, deceased November 24, 1989 due to complications at birth)

EDUCATION:

Dover Elementary School (gr. K-4)

Dover Intermediate School (gr. 5-6)

Lee Burneson Middle School (gr. 7-8)

Westlake High School (gr. 9-12)

New York University, Stern School of Business (un-enrolled March 2015 by school administrators, re: charges of harassment and sexual assault by Lisa O'Hara and Angela Draper)

OCCUPATION: No job history found

RECREATION:

High school football (receiver)

Lakewood Country Club (lifetime member)

Club O (joined February 2015, unlimited access granted
January 2016, membership revoked October 2016)
SOCIAL MEDIA PLATFORMS: Facebook, Twitter,
Snapchat, Tinder, How About We
CRIMINAL BACKGROUND
Constructive Possession of Narcotics (cocaine), January 2015,
fined $2500, charges were reduced to a misdemeanor
Sexual Assault, April 2015, plaintiff: Lisa O'Hara, charges
dropped October 2015, case settled out of court
Sexual Assault, May 2015, plaintiff: Angela Draper, charges
dropped December 2015, case settled out of court
Sexual Assault, July 2016, plaintiff: Sarah Mayall, case
pending trial
BANK INFORMATION:
Bank of America
Current balance: $497.26, Average daily balance: $12,384.00
Last deposit amount: $5500.00 on August 30, 2016 (JP
Morgan Chase incoming wire transfer)
90-day history shows frequent withdrawals from Aqueduct
Casino, Club O, The Playhouse Gentlemen's Club, and Starlets

I SAT BACK in my chair and read the information over again. I
was pleased at how extremely thorough Hale had been with
his research, but I should not have expected anything less.
Hale had a wealth of contacts at his disposal for this sort of
thing. Whenever I asked him for a full background check, he
never failed to deliver.

I was disgusted by what I read. Based on Hamilton's

sexual assault charges and removal from the University, the man was quite obviously a predator. It amazed me that he got through Club O's rigorous vetting system.

The bank withdrawals from the strip clubs came as no surprise. However, the casino withdrawals gave me reason to pause. They might explain how Hamilton and Charlie knew each other.

But that still doesn't tell me why they were seen leaving the charity gala together. What was their purpose?

I could only assume what Charlie was up to, but Trevor Hamilton was another story. After wracking my brain for a solid thirty minutes, trying to come up with an explanation, my eyes began to feel heavy. I looked at the clock. It was nearing two o'clock in the morning.

I need sleep.

Hoping I'd have a clearer head in the morning, I powered down the computer and went back to the bedroom.

I looked down at Krystina's sleeping form. She looked so peaceful. Innocent. I dreaded having to tell her about Hamilton, but I knew I had to for her own protection.

Tomorrow. I'll tell her tomorrow.

I climbed into bed next to her and the bed dipped under my weight. Krystina's eyes fluttered open.

"Alex," she murmured.

"Shh, angel. Go back to sleep," I told her. I ran my hand soothingly over her head and watched her eyes close once again.

I moved in closer and draped my arm over her waist. I shuddered when I thought of how afraid I was to ask Hale to take her home. It wasn't that I didn't trust him – I trusted him with my life. I just couldn't bear the thought of Krystina being away from me while her abuser was so near.

As I settled into her warmth, I thought about the answers I didn't have, and about the whys of what went down tonight. But, if there was one thing certain, Krystina would not leave my sight until I figured out what was going on.

25

Krystina

I awoke early the next morning. Alexander was still sleeping when I slipped quietly out of the penthouse. I left him a note, stating I had some errands to run and I'd come back to his place later. Now, here I was back in my own apartment, feeling a twinge of guilt for sneaking out while he slept.

I had a ton of questions to ask him in regard to what happened last night, and I was sure he had things of his own to say. However, I knew if I started a conversation with him about it first thing in the morning, my plans to research the murder of Alexander's father at the library would most likely be delayed for another day.

If Mr. Roberts hadn't kept me so long yesterday, I may have gotten something accomplished.

Between the long workday and the party last night, I was exhausted. My body screamed for caffeine. I slipped on a pair of sneakers and grabbed my laptop bag. It was just past nine. The library opened at ten o'clock and I wanted to be among the first to walk through the doors. If I hurried, I would have just enough time to stop by La Biga for a quick cappuccino beforehand.

Allyson came stumbling out of her bedroom just as I was getting ready to leave. She looked like a wreck.

"Hey, sleepy head," I joked.

"Morning," she mumbled.

"Late night?"

"You can say that again," she whined and made her way into the kitchen. "I was out with some people from work. One drink led to another...you know how it goes. You should have come. It was a fun time."

"I had the gala last night," I reminded her.

"That's right. I forgot," she said as she reached up into the cupboard for a mug. "Coffee?"

"No thanks. I was actually just leaving. I'm going to stop at La Biga while I'm out."

"Don't leave yet. I want to hear about last night."

"As much as I'd love to fill you in, I don't have time right now. How does later sound?" I suggested. "I don't have plans for this evening, so we can have our girl's night if you're free. Murphy's maybe? We haven't been there in a while."

"Not Murphy's. I'll do whatever else you want as long as there's no alcohol involved."

"Okay. I'll think of something else," I laughed. "I'll text you later and let you know what time I'll be home."

I left Allyson to nurse her hangover and headed out the door. Once outside, I braced against the cold wind biting at my cheeks and crossed Bleecker Street to make my way towards the Redline that would take me to La Biga on West 57th. It was a short ride, but anticipation over enjoying one of my favorite indulgences had my mouth watering. I hadn't been to my favorite coffee shop since I stopped working at Wally's and I was long overdue for one of Angelo's famous cappuccinos.

As usual, I smelled the coffee shop before I stepped through the doors, a delicious aroma of fresh ground coffee beans and pastries. The familiar chime of bells that rang overhead as I entered made me smile.

I need to make sure to come here more often.

I looked around and saw they were just as busy as I expected them to be. However, I was surprised to see Maria working behind the espresso bar and not Angelo.

"Morning, Maria."

"Ah, *buongiorno*! There's my favorite girl! Cappuccino?" she assumed.

"You got it. Did Angelo take the day off?" I inquired.

"No, no. He isn't feeling well. Stomach upsets," she told me. She frowned and shook her head.

"Oh, I hope he feels better!"

She leaned over the counter and lowered her voice.

"He's nothing but a big faker I think!" she said, her Italian accent becoming more prevalent as she whispered. "Our daughter and her husband are working here today. He just didn't want to hear any more of their ideas about modernizing the café. *Che palle!* Left me alone to deal with it instead!"

I laughed at her accusation of conspiracy while she began to prepare my drink.

"I'm not touching that one!" I joked.

"Just like I said to you before. Men. Can't live without them, but we still need them. How is your handsome gentleman caller by the way?"

I grinned at her old-fashioned term.

"He's good," I admitted, knowing this would spark an entirely new line of conversation about the day when Alexander stalked me to La Biga.

"Aha! I knew it!"

"Yeah, you might have called that one right," I agreed with a smile.

Topping off the cappuccino with a good solid dollop of foam, she handed it to me and shook her head. She looked thoughtful for a minute before motioning to one of her employees. A cute girl of about sixteen made her way over.

"Giovanna, take over. I'll be right back," she told the girl. Maria stepped out from behind the counter and turned to me. "Come this way, honey. We'll talk."

Here we go.

I was in a hurry, but inwardly I was smiling. I couldn't wait to hear Maria's new words of wisdom. We went over to a vacant table and sat down. She watched me strangely for a moment but didn't speak.

"What is it Maria?" I finally asked. I took the first sip of my favorite drink, licked the foam from the top of my lip, and waited patiently for her to answer.

"Krystina, you have been coming here for quite a few years now. Yes?"

"It's been at least four," I told her, not sure where she was headed with this.

"I've seen you happy, I've seen you sad. Sometimes you look lost. When your gentleman came to see you here a few weeks ago, I saw a fire in you that I have never seen before."

I recalled how angry I had been that day. It was no wonder why she thought that.

"Alexander can bring out the worst in me sometimes. Sorry about that," I said sheepishly.

"No, no! You misunderstand me, honey. When I say fire, I don't mean anger. Your fire was passion. A good thing. But your generation, women, they tend to practice..." she trailed off. "What's the word I'm looking for? For a proud woman? Thinks she is equal a man?"

"A feminist?" I suggested.

"Yes, yes. Your generation of women takes pride in being a feminist. That's okay in the working world, but privately it's another matter. Men need certain things, Krystina. Don't be so busy perfecting your feminist side that you don't pay attention to the heart."

I wasn't sure what she was trying to say exactly. If I wasn't mistaken, it seemed like Maria was telling me to roll over for Alexander. Considering the many exchanges that I'd witnessed between her and Angelo in the past, I found it hard to believe. Maria was nothing short of a spitfire.

"Maria, you are as independent as they come. And me, I am who I am. I'm not going to change for Alexander or any man."

"You misunderstand again, honey. What you see is not always as it seems. Yes, I am bossy. But I give in when Angelo needs it. That's why I've never had to count husbands," she joked before turning serious again. "Angelo has always been the one for me, but we have had our challenges. Love is about give and take. There's only so much room for stubbornness. Our fate was always to be together, but it did not come without compromise."

"I don't believe in fate," I told her truthfully. "I'm the only one who can control my destiny."

She looked at me sadly.

"*Bella ragazza.* Your destiny, your fate. You do not decide it. It has already been written in the stars."

Alexander

I ROLLED ONTO MY SIDE, the light from the bedroom windows disturbing my slumber. It took me a minute to register how bright it was. I sat up and looked at the clock on the dresser. It read nine-thirty in the morning.

I never sleep that late.

I glanced over to Krystina's side of the bed. She wasn't there, but there was a note propped up on her pillow.

Went out to run a few errands. Be back this afternoon.

Krystina

Dammit! Figures. The one time I sleep in past six...

I reached over to the nightstand for my phone, but my grasp came up empty. The phone wasn't there.

That's when I remembered I misplaced it the night before. In all the chaos, neither Justine nor I remembered to see if a member of the wait staff had accidentally grabbed it.

I jumped out of bed, irritated over my predicament, and went straight to my office to power on the computer. While I waited for the desktop to load, I dialed Krystina's cell from the landline phone in my office.

She needs to get her ass back here where it belongs.

It went straight to voicemail.

I slammed down the receiver and a feeling of unease began to set in. I didn't want her out on her own and unprotected until I found out what Hamilton was up to.

Once the computer was up and running, I opened my inbox clicked on the button to compose a new message to my lead computer technician.

TO: Gavin Alden
CC: Hale Fulton
FROM: Alexander Stone
SUBJECT: Immediate Response Needed!

Gavin,
My phone went missing last night. I need you to put a trace on its location. I also need you to trace the location of Krystina Cole's phone. I'll be on standby waiting for your response.

Alexander Stone
CEO, Stone Enterprise

I flagged the email as urgent and hit send, praying he would see it on a Saturday morning. Gavin was a Monday through Friday, hourly employee. However, he worked from home and usually came through in a pinch. I hoped today was one of those days.

Thankfully, it was. My email pinged back with a response no less than three minutes later.

TO: Alexander Stone
CC: Hale Fulton
FROM: Gavin Alden
SUBJECT: Re: Immediate Response Needed!

Mr. Stone,
I was able to locate both phones on E 42nd Street near Madison. The exact location is odd. The phones appear to be between two buildings. Please advise on how you would like me to proceed.

Gavin

Both phones? Why would both phones be in the same location?

At first, I thought perhaps Krystina found it before she left the charity gala and just forgot to tell me. But then another possibility came to mind, one I didn't want to consider because it made me doubt her trustworthiness.

No. She would not have taken it deliberately. Or would she have?

TO: Gavin Alden
CC: Hale Fulton
FROM: Alexander Stone
SUBJECT: Re: Immediate Response Needed!

Are you sure both phones are in the same location?

Alexander Stone
CEO, Stone Enterprise

I thought about everything that happened last night, then about her absence this morning.

What errands did she have to run?

She never once mentioned she had anything to do today.

TO: Alexander Stone
CC: Hale Fulton
FROM: Gavin Alden
SUBJECT: Re: Immediate Response Needed!

Mr. Stone,
I'm positive. They are about five feet apart to be exact, in between a bank and a deli, but not inside either establishment. If you suspect they may be stolen, I suggest you have me deactivate them.

Gavin

I wasn't sure if I wanted to do that just yet, as I may need to track the location again if I couldn't find Krystina.

TO: Gavin Alden
CC: Hale Fulton
FROM: Alexander Stone
SUBJECT: Re: Immediate Response Needed!

Not yet. I'll be in touch.

Alexander Stone
CEO, Stone Enterprise

I hit send and immediately dialed Hale. The uneasy feeling that I was experiencing began to intensify. Call it gut instinct, but I knew something wasn't right.

"Hale, did you see the email thread?" I asked after he picked up.

"I did, sir."

"Are you in the area?"

"Yes, Mr. Stone. I'm about a block away from the penthouse."

"Good. Bring the car around. We need to take a ride over to E 42nd and Madison."

"I understand, sir."

I was sure he did too. Something was up, and I was about to find out.

26

Krystina

Cappuccino in hand, I exited Grand Central Terminal and made my way up East 42nd. Much to my dismay, I ran into a large tourist group taking a walking tour of New York City. They were moving at a snail's pace as their guide pointed out landmarks just up ahead.

"Our next stop is The Stephen A. Schwartzman Building, part of the New York City Library system, which is the second largest in the country," the guide told them.

Yeah, yeah. That's where I'm trying to go. Of all the dumb luck.

Rather than fight the crowd, I cut through an alleyway that would take me over to 41st. That quickly proved to be a bad idea, as I had to pinch my nose to block out the smell of urine permeating in the air.

I should have just hailed a cab in Greenwich instead of detouring to La Biga.

As I neared the end of the smelly passageway, a man stepped in front of me and blocked my path. His clothes were filthy, and he had stringy blond hair that looked like it hadn't been washed in weeks.

Ugh. This is what I get for trying to take a short cut.

I tried to side step him, assuming he was a homeless person looking for a handout. Normally, I would have sympathized with his situation, but this man made me uneasy for some reason.

"Hello, Krystina," he said, catching me by surprise. I looked at him again. He looked oddly familiar, but I couldn't quite place him.

"I'm sorry, but do I know you?"

"No, I don't believe you do. But I know very much about you," he leered.

Okay, now I'm getting creeped out.

I nervously looked around.

"I think you're mistaking me for someone else. If you'll excuse me, I have someplace I need to be," I told him. I tried to sound polite so as not to upset this could be lunatic.

"Oh, no sweet thing. Not yet. Not until you see what I need to show you."

Casually, I reached down into my purse and felt around for the can of pepper spray I always had on me. My hand closed around the metal can.

"I'm sorry, but –" I stopped short when he grabbed hold of my arm and squeezed tight. "Let go of me!"

As I tried to shrug out of his grasp, the can of pepper spray went clinging to the ground.

"Pepper spray? I was warned you might try something

stupid," he sneered. He squeezed my arm tighter and thrust a cell phone in my face. "Look at this."

I focused my vision on the cell phone screen he held in front of me. It was a black and white video of some sort.

"Please, mister. I don't know what that is. You –"

"Yes, you do! Don't play stupid! Look again!"

His eyes were wild, manic almost. I looked around in search of other people who may have entered the alleyway short cut.

This is New York! Why isn't anyone around?

There wasn't another soul in sight. And now, having lost the protection of the pepper spray, I thought it best to just do as he asked. I could only hope he would go away after I complied. Moving as slowly as possible, I took the phone from his hands and began to watch.

The video was of a crowd of people. Some appeared to be dancing while others mingled and sipped on drinks.

"It looks like a nightclub," I said.

"Is that what you freaks call it?" he said and laughed loudly.

"What do you mean? I think..." I trailed off as I caught a glimpse of something quite out of the ordinary for a nightclub. There was a woman bent over on a stage. And a man.

This is footage from the night I was at Club O.

I looked more closely at the cell phone in my hand. I instantly recognized it as Alexander's phone, the one that had gone missing the night before.

"Now do you see, sweetheart?"

I snapped my head up to look at him.

"Who are you? Where did you get this?"

He ripped the cell phone from my hands and shoved it into his pocket. Before I could react, he grabbed hold of me and pushed me against the brick surface of the building. He pressed his face to my ear. His breath was hot and stale on my neck. I had to fight the urge to gag.

"Does that sick bastard make you call him your Master?" he whispered as he squeezed one of my breasts. I wanted to throw up.

"Get off me!" I struggled, but felt the walls closing in. My pulse began to thud in my ears. This situation was all too familiar. I had to get away. "Someone help me!"

He slapped a clammy hand over my mouth.

"Shut up you stupid bitch!"

I scratched and clawed, but all I could think of was the people. Somebody had to see what was going on.

The tour group.

I screamed, but it was muffled against his damp hand.

"Hey!" I heard somebody yell from my right.

Oh, thank god.

I strained my head towards the voice, my savior from the crazed lunatic, but what I saw made the ground feel like it was falling out from under me.

No. Not him. Not him of all people.

"Fuck you, Trevor. Just help me get her into the car."

This can't be happening.

I struggled to free myself, straining with every muscle in my body, but was overpowered by the two men.

"Help!" I tried to scream again, but my cry earned me a harsh blow to the side of the head.

"Krystina, shut up!" Trevor hissed.

The world was spinning. My arms burned from the

struggle, but I didn't really feel it. It was as if I was numb as they dragged me, kicking and screaming, down the alley. There was a car that had been backed into the entrance I had come through, effectively blocking any passerby from seeing what was happening. The car trunk was open and waiting.

No. Please. No.

My head smashed against the rear bumper as I was tossed into the trunk. My vision blurred and I felt something warm slide down my face.

Blood.

I tried to scream again but was silenced when a strip of duct tape was slapped over my mouth. Zip ties were fashioned around my wrists, before Trevor reached down into the trunk and removed my purse that was still slung around my neck.

"No funny business," he warned.

By taking my purse, he had also taken my phone. Any hopes I may have had about calling for help vanished.

What is happening? Why is this happening?

The trunk was slammed shut and everything went dark. The car engine roared to life. I could hear the two men talking in the car. It was somewhat muffled, but not enough that I couldn't make out what they were saying.

"Is this asshole going to pay up without question?" I heard Trevor ask. "I don't want cops involved in this."

"Oh, he'll pay. No question about it. Stone goes to great lengths to protect his privacy. This will be no different. We struck gold when I found that video on his phone," he laughed in the most sinister of ways. "And here you were just hoping for a bank account number. Trust me. This is better. He won't want that released."

"I don't see why we had to nab Krystina, though. It complicates things."

"We need her. She's our insurance policy in case he tries to resist."

"Charlie, are you sure?"

"Don't be a fucking chicken shit. I was married to his sister for seven years. I know him well. He'll pay. The sucker always pays."

Charlie? Justine's ex-husband? Bank account numbers?

The car turned left, and I was slammed roughly against one side of the trunk.

Think, Cole. Think.

I tried to remember the make and model of the car they put me into, but I was coming up blank. I listened to the sounds outside the car, hoping it may help me to determine where we were. All I could make out was the sound of the tires against the pavement and the occasional horn blaring. At the very least, the sound of car horns told me we were still in the city.

"Make a right up here. We need to get on I-78 towards Newport," I heard Trevor say.

"The warehouse is safe?"

"Yeah. My father's company never uses that one anymore."

"Good. Nobody will notice her stink for a while then," Charlie said.

My stink?

Then the realization dawned on me. I knew exactly what Charlie meant by my stink.

Things like this don't happen to real people! I have to get out of here.

Feeling like I was living in a terrible B rated movie, I began to beat at the lid of the truck. I kicked against it and beat with my fists until my knuckles were raw and burning.

"What do you mean her stink?" Trevor questioned, voicing the same thought I had. I stopped thrashing to listen, hoping beyond hope my assumption was wrong.

"Her corpse, numb nuts. After a while, I don't think it will smell very pretty," Charlie laughed.

My heart was racing out of my chest as I struggled to find more air than I even needed. Panic consumed me, burying itself into the recesses of my brain until I couldn't think.

"What the fuck are you talking about? We aren't going to kill her!" Trevor exclaimed.

"We have to. She wasn't supposed to see you, remember? Our cover is blown."

"Fuck, man. She only saw me because you couldn't stick to the game plan. I told you she was a fighter. But who cares if she saw me anyway? I'll just find an alibi like I always do."

"No. You don't know Stone. He'll crack any alibi you come up with. We do this my way. The girl has to go."

"This is total bullshit, Charlie. I didn't sign up for murder. I was just looking for some extra cash."

"Yeah, must suck to be cut off from your trust fund," Charlie sarcastically commented.

"Screw the trust fund and screw you. I'm out. Pull over."

"Hell no. You ain't backing out now pretty boy. I need your connections to pull this off."

"I said pull over," Trevor asserted.

Yes, pull over!

I listened, waiting to see how Charlie would respond. My heart was racing a mile a minute as I silently pleaded Trevor would somehow talk him out of his plan. It was ironic, really. The man I hated more than anyone could potentially save me from a madman.

The car jerked suddenly to the right, then to the left. I could hear the two men yelling, but I couldn't make out their words over the squealing of the car tires.

There was a loud crunch, and the sound of crumpling metal reverberated through the car. I had barely registered that we'd crashed, when my body was slammed forward, then back. I was like a ping-pong ball, suspended in the air at times.

The car is rolling.

My arms flailed as I tried to reach for something to hang onto. My head hit the lid of the trunk. My vision blurred, then all went black.

Alexander

"You need to make a left at the next intersection," Gavin said to Hale and me through the Porsche Cayenne's PCM mobile communication system. "The GPS signal ends on 4th Avenue near 29th Street."

"Traffic is backed up. It looks like an accident up ahead," I observed. I glanced at Hale. He was craning his neck in an attempt to see around the cars lined up in front of us. The only things we could see were brake lights and the flashing lights of emergency vehicles.

Based on the location Gavin had originally given me, Hale and I tracked Krystina's phone into an alleyway. She wasn't there, but we did find the remnants of a recently spilled cappuccino from La Biga. Once I saw that, I went on high alert. I immediately knew something was very wrong. Since that moment, we had been on the line with Gavin, who was updating us on the movements of her phone.

"You're only about a thousand feet away from the signal of both phones," Gavin informed us.

On impulse, I reached for the handle of the passenger door.

"Fuck this," I said and got out of the car. I had a sinking feeling in my stomach. Call it instinct, but for some reason, I was driven to walk on ahead to see what the holdup was.

"Sir, wait," Hale interjected as he scrambled out from the driver's seat to follow me.

"I'm going to see what's going on," I called out over my shoulder. "Something isn't sitting right with me, Hale. Stay with the car."

Rather than do as I instructed, Hale followed me up the street. I didn't insist he stay back because I could see the worry written on his face. He was just as concerned as I was.

As I got closer to the accident, I could see a car was flipped up onto its side. It was a tan Chevy, and it didn't look good. Blood was splattered all over the inside of the windshield, obstructing any view of who might be inside. There was a man standing with his back to me near the wreck. A police officer appeared to be questioning him. As I approached, I realized the man's voice sounded familiar. I took a closer look at him. Instantly, the pit in my stomach plummeted.

It was Charlie.

This can't be a coincidence.

"That son of a bitch," I sneered.

"Mr. Stone, we shouldn't assume anything just yet," Hale warned, but I wasn't really hearing him.

The air seemed to buzz as my pulse pounded in my ears. Without thinking, I sprinted to close the distance between Charlie and me. When I reached him, I spun him around. His shirtfront was saturated with blood, and I couldn't tell if it was his or someone else's. There were a few sizable shards of glass embedded in his forehead, gruesomely distorting his left eyebrow. His eyes were glazed as he focused on me. When he realized I was standing before him, he looked horrified.

I gripped his shirtfront, not caring how injured he was. My gut told me he knew where Krystina was.

"Where is she, you fucking worm?" I hissed through gritted teeth.

"Sir, please!" yelled the police officer. I ignored him and tightened my hold on Charlie's shirt.

"Alex, I – I didn't. I don't – I don't know," Charlie sputtered. I reared back a fist.

"Don't lie to me! I tracked her phone to this location. Now, where is she?"

"Sir, let go of him now!" the police officer insisted as he tried to separate me from Charlie. "This man is injured, and he needs medical attention."

"Mr. Stone," Hale said from beside me as he put his hand firmly on my shoulder.

"He knows where she is!" I growled and tried to shrug off Hale's hand. Rage boiled hot and fierce, as I wanted nothing more than to slam my fist into Charlie's sniveling face.

"Alexander, please. You have to come with me now," Hale insisted. His use of my first name gave me reason to pause. Hale never called me by my first name.

I loosened my grip on Charlie, only to see his expression change to one of panic as he focused on something behind me. I released him completely and turned around to see what he was looking at. The fire department was near the back of the smashed vehicle, attempting to pry open the trunk. I could see there was someone inside. I looked at Hale. He no longer looked worried, but afraid.

I walked towards the car, feeling as if everything were moving in slow motion. As the lid of the trunk opened inch by inch, I could see what looked like a mass of chestnut brown curls.

No. It can't be her. It can't be her.

I repeated the chat over and over again as I continued to put one foot in front of the other.

When the fire department finally got the lid completely open, it was as if time momentarily stood still. Krystina, my beautiful angel, lay lifeless in the trunk. Blood covered one side of her face, matting her hair to her forehead. Zip ties were around her wrists, slicing through her tender skin.

"Angel," I whispered. Even to my own ears, my voice sounded breathless and full of fear. Grief crushed through my heart. I couldn't feel anything other than overwhelming devastation.

No. Please, no.

All at once, everything seemed to speed up, catapulting

me into a frenzy of people rushing around and shouting orders.

"We need a medic over here!" I heard somebody yell.

I found myself by Krystina's side, trying to smooth her hair away to find the source of the blood, only to be pushed away by emergency medical technicians.

"Please step aside, sir," one of the EMT's said to me.

I watched as they fastened her limp body to a long spine board. They cut the ties at her wrists and began to move her towards the ambulance. I felt helpless in the surreal turn of events.

A cold numbness spread through my veins.

I did this. This is my fault. I should have protected her.

Memories flooded through me. Krystina's expressive eyes and breathtaking smile. Her laughter that could brighten even the bleakest of moments. Her response to my touch. The memories choked me until I thought I couldn't breathe.

"Mr. Stone," Hale said quietly. "We should leave to go to the hospital now. It's going to take us a while to get through the traffic."

I looked at him, noticing how stricken he appeared. It felt as if we were living in a different reality.

I struggled to find stability and shook my head to clear it. Seeing Krystina so pale and broken had gutted me, but I would be of no use to her this way. I needed to find strength. I had to think rationally and find some measure of control within the chaos.

"No. I can't leave her. I'm going to ride in the ambulance with her. Follow me to the hospital."

"Yes, sir," he responded with a nod.

"And call Allyson Ramsey on the way. She needs to know

about this. You can get her contact info from Laura," I added as I move to climb into the back of the ambulance.

As soon as I was in, the doors slammed shut. The sound of sirens could be heard from overhead. I looked down at Krystina, so colorless and still, and I had to fight off the panic still threatening to overtake me.

She's a fighter. She'll be okay.

She had to be. Because now that she was in my life, I knew I could never survive without her.

27

Alexander

I sat by Krystina's bedside in a silent vigil, hoping beyond hope that she would wake up. Twenty-four hours had passed since the car crash, each hour bringing on a new level of anger and rage I had never before experienced. I wanted to hurt someone. Anyone.

"Krystina, please," I spoke to her still form. I pushed aside the intravenous line pumping fluid into her veins and took hold of her limp hand. The cuts and bruises around her wrists were beginning to scab over and were turning purplish red in color. I closed my eyes and tried not to think about the plastic ties ripping apart her beautiful skin when she was found.

I pressed my lips to her delicate fingers, kissing each fingertip with reverence.

"Alex," said a female voice. I looked up. Allyson was standing in the hospital room doorway.

"What?" I barked. I blinked back the water in my eyes, hating the fact I was in such a vulnerable state.

"Justine wanted me to tell you Charlie is out of surgery and he's come to. The police will be here soon to talk to him."

"Fine. Let them handle it. If I talk to that motherfucker right now, I'll kill him." I turned back to Krystina. She was the only one who mattered to me at that moment.

"Justine thought you might say something like that," she said quietly. "You should know she already spoke with him. You might want to hear what he has to say before the police do."

"I don't want to talk to him. He can tell the police anything he wants. I'm done. I'm done with it all."

Done with the lies. Done with hiding. Screw everything. This is my fault.

"Well, then you should also know Elizabeth Long is on her way up with Frank. They'll be here in about twenty minutes."

Son of a bitch.

I was sick and tired of having to deal with people. Elizabeth Long may be Krystina's mother, but to me she was just someone else interrupting my time with my angel.

"Fine," I snapped. "Anything else?"

"No, that's all," she said sadly. "I'll leave you be."

Allyson left the room and anguish over took me once more.

"I'm so sorry I didn't protect you," I whispered. "This is all my fault. If I hadn't been so hell bent on keeping secrets, none of this would have happened. Please wake up, Krystina.

I love you so much. I didn't even realize how much until now. I need you, angel. Please."

I lowered my head down to the mattress and pressed her palm to my cheek. Regret consumed me. Regret over the past. Regret over not protecting her. Regret over never telling her I loved her. She had to wake up. I needed the chance to set things right.

I looked up when I heard a commotion in the hallway. Elizabeth Long came busting into the room with her husband in her wake.

"Oh, no!" she exclaimed once she laid eyes on Krystina. "My baby girl!"

She rushed over to Krystina's bedside.

"Hello, Mr. and Mrs. Long," I said stiffly. I was annoyed by their presence, although I knew I had no right to be. Krystina was their daughter and stepdaughter. They deserved to be here, perhaps more than I did.

"Alexander," Frank Long said with a nod. "Allyson didn't have many details for us when she called. Please, tell us what happened."

"I don't know much either," I said and shook my head. "I only know there was a car accident. Krystina was found in the trunk of the car. The passengers in the car were Charlie Andrews and Trevor Hamilton."

Elizabeth Long snapped to attention at that.

"Trevor?" she repeated incredulously.

"Yes. Why Krystina was in the trunk is unknown as of right now."

"Who is this Charlie person?"

"My sister's ex-husband," I explained in a stoic tone. "I

suspect he may have been the reason for everything, but that is also unclear."

"Yes, but –," she began, but was cut off when the Krystina's neurologist entered the room.

"Dr. West," I greeted and stood to shake his hand. "This is Frank and Elizabeth Long, Krystina's stepfather and mother. Mr. and Mrs. Long, this is Dr. West, the neurologist assigned to Krystina's case after she was brought in."

Dr. West was one of the first physicians to evaluate Krystina's condition. I researched his credentials almost immediately and found he was knowledgeable and extremely thorough. That, combined with his on the hour visits to her room, gave me enough reason to believe Krystina was in highly capable hands.

"Nice to meet you," Dr. West said with a nod in their direction. "I have the results from Krystina's tests."

"What do they say?" Elizabeth hurriedly asked.

"The CAT scan and MRI do not indicate any abnormalities. Her vital signs and respiratory patterns are good. The assessment of posture and body habitus shows no signs of damage to her central nervous system. Combined, there is little reason for me believe her head trauma will incite any long-term damage."

"What do you mean by little reason to believe?" I asked, noting how he was noncommittal about Krystina's recovery.

"I can't say for sure until she wakes up. For now, she appears stable. But she could be in this state for several days to several weeks. Sometimes longer. I won't be able to give a more accurate diagnosis until she emerges from the coma."

"What happens when she does?" Elizabeth questioned.

"That depends on the individual, but she will most likely

need special attention for some time to come. We don't know what combination of physical and psychological difficulties she'll suffer from. Even the most responsive patients often need care after returning home."

"Oh, my," Elizabeth choked out. She brought her hand to her heart and her eyes glistened with tears.

"I have rounds to make right now," Dr. West informed us. "But if you notice any changes, call the nurses station immediately and they'll get in touch with me."

"Will do, Doctor. Thank you," I told him.

"Frank, get with Ally," Elizabeth said after the doctor had left. "We need to talk to her about packing up Krystina's things. After all of this, she'll need us. The best thing for her is to move home."

Over my fucking dead body.

"No," I stated firmly.

"What do you mean?" Elizabeth asked, obviously taken aback by the authoritative tone of my voice.

"I mean exactly that. No," I reaffirmed. "Krystina will not be moving back to Albany. She will stay right here in New York. This is her home now. When she wakes up, and she will wake up, she will come home with me. I will take charge of any care she might need."

Elizabeth laughed as if what I had said what the most absurd thing she had ever heard.

"With you?" she spat out bitterly. "She barely knows you. I don't think so."

"Elizabeth," Frank interjected. "I think you're putting the cart before the horse here. We don't need to decide anything right now."

"Actually, this is not up for debate," I told them both.

"Not now. Not ever. Krystina will be staying with me. And I don't mean temporarily. She will be there permanently."

Krystina

I COULD HEAR TALKING, *voices echoing quietly in the distance.*

Alexander. My mother. Frank.

They were arguing.

I heard my mother shouting at Alexander, and Frank trying to calm her down.

"You don't know what that man put her through!" my mother raged. "She was like an empty shell of a person for a full solid year! And now here she is, barely back on her feet, then you come along. Now look at her! Look at her! I'm sure this all has something to do with you! Do you honestly think I would let you destroy everything she's worked to overcome?"

Her voice seemed far away, like she was yelling through a fog.

Why is she yelling?

Who are they talking about?

"Elizabeth, calm down," my stepfather pleaded with her.

"No, you're wrong about that," I heard Alexander say.

His voice. I loved the sound of his voice. I felt so confused but hearing him was calming.

"Don't you dare try to pretend you know what I'm talking about!"

"But I do. I know exactly what he put her through. In fact, it's possible I know more than you do. But I am not Trevor."

Trevor.

No.

Why did Alexander say that name? His name?

Just hearing his name brought back a firestorm of memories. The shame and denial, my confusion and pain – the emotional onslaught ripped at my heart and brought me back to a dark time filled with so much uncertainty; to a time when I was overwhelmed with self-doubt, terrified nobody would believe me if I told the truth about the rape.

It was a time I had worked so hard to forget.

I had a vague recollection of seeing him again. In an alley.

Why was he there?

He shouldn't have been there?

Why was I there?

I wished Alexander and my mother would stop talking about him. I didn't want to remember.

I wanted to forget it all. To not think. About him. About everything.

I allowed the darkness to take me once again, effectively tuning out any further mention of the memories I wanted to leave buried.

28

Alexander

It was day nineteen, four hundred fifty-six hours since Krystina was brought to the hospital. She hadn't changed, but was still as lifeless as she was on the day she was brought in. If it weren't for the heart monitor quietly beeping in the background, I would feel the need to check her pulse every sixty seconds.

I tried to ignore the paleness of her skin and the frailty of her frame. Each day, she seems to shrink smaller and smaller in the oversized hospital bed. I felt like she was slipping further and further away from me with each passing minute, but there was nothing I could do to stop it.

"Knock, knock."

I looked up at the sound of Matteo Donati's voice. My friend, along with Allyson, had become regular company during my watch over Krystina. They brought food and offered words of encouragement and were a sharp contrast to Krystina's mother. She was full of what-if's and negativity, always focused on the worst possible outcome – an outcome I couldn't bear to think about.

Because of that, Elizabeth Long and I had many heated arguments during Krystina's first few days in the hospital. Thankfully, the nurses stepped in and advised everyone who was present to focus on positive conversation. If they hadn't, there was a good chance I would have resorted to drastic measures in order to keep her barred from the room.

Since then, Matteo, Allyson, and I did exactly that, choosing to spend our time in the hospital talking about good things and funny memories in the off-chance Krystina could hear us. Elizabeth Long, however, had chosen to limit her presence to just thirty minutes a day going forward. It was fine by me. The less that woman was around, the better.

"Hey, Matt," I said absently.

"How is the princess today?" he asked, using the nickname he adapted for her after I told him about Krystina's email that she'd signed 'Princess from Alderaan'.

"Same."

"I brought leftover turkey from my mother's house. Sorry it isn't more," he apologized as he set a bag of plastic containers down on the table in the corner. "I would have brought you a proper dinner, but my contractor ripped out the old ovens at the restaurant a few days ago. The new ones won't be installed until Monday."

"Whatever you brought will be fine. It's food. How are things coming along?" I asked, although I didn't really give a rat's ass. I only posed the question to help pass the time.

"Good, good. I've settled on the menu layout and I placed the order for the street signage."

"Oh, really? Have you finally decided on a name for the restaurant?" I asked, feeling genuinely curious and interested in a discussion for the first time in weeks. The name of Matteo's restaurant had been a point of frustration for him for quite some time.

"I have," he began and looked to Krystina. "Do you remember the night you brought Krystina to the restaurant?"

"Of course, I do."

"I joked with you that night about naming it after her. Well, I've been watching you over these past few weeks, my friend. I've listened to your stories about her. And I see the way you look at her. I know your heart is breaking."

"Matt," I said in a warning tone.

"Hear me out. You know I believe Krystina will come around."

"And she will," I said vehemently. "We've all concluded she's just being stubborn. Krystina never does anything until she's good and ready."

"True words, my friend. True words," he agreed and laughed. "She is stubborn. I don't know how she's put up with you for this long."

I pursed my lips in annoyance.

"Matt, where are you going with this? We were talking about the name of your restaurant," I reminded him.

"*Sì, sì*. We were. I want you to know that, no matter what the outcome is for you and your princess, you've inspired me. You both have. Because of that, I decided to name my restaurant Krystina's Place."

I picked up Krystina's hand and brushed my thumb over the top of it, thinking of our first date. Even though I didn't think of it as a date at the time, that night would always be important to me. It was the first time I was able to get a feel for who she really was. Her spunk and liveliness drove me mad, yet it drew me to her at the same time. I now realized it was the night I first started to fall for her.

"Krystina's Place," I said quietly. "I think she'd like that. Thanks, Matt."

"So, I ah…" he trailed off in hesitation.

I looked up at him and saw his brow was furrowed, as if he were trying to find the right words for what he wanted to say.

"What?" I asked.

"I just spoke to Justine."

I closed my eyes, not wanting to think about my sister at that moment, or about how absent she had been since the car accident.

"What did she say?"

"She's in panic mode right now. The press is still digging for answers," he informed me. "Between your speech, the accident, and Charlie's ramblings at the scene of the crash, they are putting two and two together. You were front-page headlines again today, but it's still just speculation. Justine's afraid they will uncover the truth."

"They won't find anything. I made sure of that years ago. I just need to make sure Charlie keeps his mouth shut."

"The judge refused to set bail for him."

"Good. Let the asshole rot," I spat out.

"There's more."

I shook my head.

"There's always more. Just lay it out, Matt. My patience is slim to none right now."

He looked at me sympathetically before continuing.

"He's talking about a plea deal."

"That's bullshit!" I shouted angrily. "He's a gambling degenerate who should be jailed for blackmail, extortion, intent to embezzle, and kidnapping. Top it off with vehicular manslaughter, and he should be going away for a long time."

"That's just it," Matteo explained. "Charlie's story is that Hamilton took the wheel and caused the wreck. Charlie doesn't want to do time for manslaughter. He's more willing to plead guilty for the other stuff because the sentencing isn't as long. If he took the wrap for everything, he'd be looking at a minimum of twenty-five years."

"I'll make some calls. He's not going to get off that easy."

"Honestly, I don't think you should be worrying about any of that right now. Your focus should only be on Krystina."

Instantly, my temper flared.

"Don't you think I fucking know that? She's been my only focus, Matt! I've been here, with her every day, for almost three goddamn weeks!"

He held up his hands in surrender.

"I know, man. You don't need to justify anything to me. I've seen you. It's been rough."

"I'm sorry," I said and backed off. "I know you understand how difficult things have been. I didn't mean to snap, but I just can't stop thinking about how I might have been able to change things. If I had warned Krystina that Charlie and Hamilton were up to something on the night of the gala, if she had even the slightest heads up, maybe this could have all been avoided."

"You can't change it. Even if you did tell her, you know how she is. She never would have listened to you."

"I wish I knew what she was doing in that alley in the first place," I said and shook my head. "I don't know. I should have put her on a fucking leash."

"Well, figuratively speaking my friend, I'm sure you have one."

I choked out a laugh, but not one of amusement. It was bitter.

"Only you would say –," I stopped short and looked down at Krystina's hand. It was still resting in my palm and could have sworn I felt her finger twitch.

"Leashes are for dogs, Alex."

I slowly brought my gaze up to meet her face, thinking I was just imagining the voice I had been waiting to hear for three long weeks. The voice that called to me in my sleep. The voice that fueled my veins and set my world on fire.

Krystina peered at me through sleepy eyes, her mouth tilted up in a small smile.

"*Grazie a Dio!*" Matteo exclaimed. "I'll get the doctor."

Krystina

I LOOKED at Alexander through heavy eyes. It was a true effort to keep my lids open.

"Krystina," Alexander choked out.

He seemed visibly shaken, and his exhaustion was apparent. Stubble shaded his jaw line and his eyes were blood shot. He appeared haggard and completely strung out, as if he hadn't slept in days.

"Hi," I whispered. My throat was so dry. "I'm thirsty."

"You're thirsty," he repeated, his voice clogged with emotion. His eyes were filled with worry and relief. "Oh, angel. I don't think I've ever heard sweeter words. I was so worried."

He closed his eyes and took a deep breath. To my astonishment, I saw a tear begin to slide down his cheek. This man, a force of nature, his powerful self-possession so magnetic it put all those around him in his shadow. Yet here he was, brought to his knees because of me. It was a humbling sort of feeling.

"I'm sorry," I said hoarsely. "I didn't mean for you to worry."

He quickly wiped away the moisture under his eye and brought a finger up to my lips to silence my apology.

"Shh. No, don't. Don't apologize for anything. I'm just so glad you're awake. How are you feeling?"

I tried to focus on how I felt but found it was difficult to concentrate.

"Groggy," I told him honestly.

He pressed a kiss to my forehead, and I could feel him trembling against my skin. It was as if he were desperately trying to maintain his composure. I tried to reach up to touch his face, but the sheer effort it took to move my arm made me want to go back to sleep.

"Rest, angel. Don't try to move."

Why do I feel so weak?

The minute the question popped into my head, the memories of what happened came flooding back. They were blurred at first, almost as if it had been a dream. But then all at once, everything seemed to erupt with clarity.

The alley. Charlie. His hand on my breast. Trevor. The car. Tires screeching on pavement.

Then... nothing.

What happened?

I remembered being in the trunk of a car but didn't recall anything after that point. Possibilities of what may have transpired began to fill my head in an overwhelming onslaught to my senses.

Taken against my will. Two men. Both with a history of abuse towards women.

I didn't know much about Charlie, but the other was my rapist. Instinct directed my attention south, to the intimate parts of my body that may have been violated.

No pain. Everything feels like it's in order.

Relief flooded through me, but nausea still threatened to overtake me. I began to panic as hysteria rose up to my throat. I didn't want to know what happened, but I knew I had to find out.

"Tell me what happened, Alex," I begged, my voice hitching up an octave.

"Not now. There is plenty of time to talk. Right now, we need to wait for the doctor to come in and get you checked out."

I tried to move to a sitting position, but the room began to tilt. I rested my head back against the pillow, fighting to keep my eyes focused.

Stay alert. I have to stay alert.

"Please, Alex. I don't have the strength to argue. Just tell me."

His eyes were full of anguish and sadness before he dropped his head into his hands. When he looked up at me again, he looked conflicted.

"A lot has happened. I don't want to overwhelm you. We should wait for the doctor."

"No. I can handle it," I vehemently croaked out.

I had no choice but to handle it. I needed the reassurance that history did not repeat itself, or worse.

"Well, look who decided to join us." I turned my head towards the door just as a gray-haired man in a white coat entered the room. He smiled at me with kind eyes as he came over to my bedside. "Krystina, I am Dr. West."

"Hello," I said with a small smile. Even smiling seemed to be an effort.

"She said she's thirsty," Alexander told him.

"I'll bet she is. I think we can get her some ice chips for now until I can arrange for something more substantial," Dr. West said. He began to look over the machines keeping track of my vital signs. Leaning over me, he flashed a light in my eyes. I blinked from the shock of the brightness. "Looks like you may be out of the woods, kid. How do you feel?"

"Kind of fuzzy. Tired too, but I don't want to fall back asleep," I told him.

"It's normal to be tired. Most likely, you'll only be awake for short spans of time over the next few days. Don't worry about sleeping or frequent naps. Your body is going to need it for a while."

"Krystina was just asking me to tell her what happened," Alexander said. "I told her I wanted to check with you first."

"Only she knows how she feels," he said to Alexander before turning back to me. "Krystina, I don't want you to push yourself too much. Take it one step at a time. If you're tired, rest. Don't fight it. I'm confident you will have many opportunities to become apprised of the situation in the coming days."

"I won't overdo it," I promised.

"Good. Now, Mr. Stone. Your friend Matteo asked me to tell you that he is making the necessary phone calls to friends and family. His exact words were 'enjoy some peace and quiet with your princess'. That being said, I'll check back in an hour or so. Please let me or the nurses know if you need anything in the meantime."

"Thank you, doctor," Alexander said with a nod of appreciation.

When the doctor left the room, I turned to Alexander.

"Is Matteo a good friend of yours?" I asked. It occurred to me that I didn't know how close he and Alexander were to each other. I didn't know him all that well, but I had a vague sort of recollection of hearing his Italian accent often while I slept. Although I couldn't recall the specifics of what he had been saying, I thought he might have been in this room quite a bit.

"He is a very good friend," Alexander confirmed. "I've known him since we were kids. He's come up every single day to see you. Allyson has also been here every day."

Alexander ran his hand over the top of my head softly. The action was soothing, making it difficult to fight my exhausted state.

"Hmm, that's nice of them," I said sleepily. It was good to know Alexander had people here to keep him company while I was out.

"You've had quite a few visitors. Your mother has been

here, too. She's been staying at your apartment and usually visits in the mornings."

I noticed how he stiffened when he mentioned my mother. I didn't know what the reason was, but I would worry about it later. I was so tired. I just needed to stay awake for a little while longer.

"My mother. She wants you to come with me back home. For Thanksgiving."

Alexander chuckled.

"I'm pretty sure that won't be happening."

"Why not?"

He took my hand and placed it over his heart.

"Because today is Thanksgiving. And let me tell you, angel. I've never been more thankful for anything else in my life. Your heartbeat. Your breathing. The sound of your voice," he said, his words cracking slightly. "I'll never take those things for granted again."

Today is Thanksgiving?

Barely registering the fact I had been out for weeks, my eyes closed. Unable to fight the heaviness of my lids anymore, I surrendered myself over to sleep.

29

Krystina

There was a faint beeping noise in the distance, sounding over and over again until I was dragged away from my peaceful slumber. It took me a minute to remember I was in a hospital. I opened my eyes and saw Alexander sitting in the chair beside me.

"Hello, sleeping beauty," he said to me.

"Hey." I gave him a sleepy smile.

"How are you feeling?"

"Better. A little more with it," I told him. I thought about what Dr. West had said about needing sleep. He couldn't have been more correct. My thoughts weren't nearly as clouded anymore, and I felt remarkably refreshed.

"Are you hungry? Thirsty? Dr. West has given you clearance to eat something more substantial. I can order anything you want."

"I'm not really very hungry right now."

"You need to eat, Krystina," he pointed out.

"I know. And I will. I just want to talk first."

"Whatever you want, angel," he agreed, although somewhat hesitantly. "What do you want to talk about?"

About everything. About what happened. About what Trevor and Charlie may or may not have done to me.

"I want you to tell me about everything. I need to know what happened."

"Krystina, the doctor said you shouldn't push yourself," he warned.

"I'm okay, Alex. If I get tired, I'll let you know. I just need answers," I implored. "Please, tell me."

He leaned back in his chair and looked at me thoughtfully. His brow furrowed from internal conflict and I could sense his uncertainty.

"You're not going to let this go, are you?"

"No, I'm not," I told him with a slight shake of my head.

"I figured," he said with a frown. He raked a hand through his gorgeous dark waves and sighed. "Charlie, Justine's ex-husband, has been blackmailing her for a couple of years now. I thought I took care of the situation for her, but I was wrong. He has a gambling problem and is completely driven by his addiction. I should have never underestimated how powerful that addiction could be."

"Why me though? And why was Charlie with –" I stopped short, unable to speak Trevor's name aloud because of my fear of a very possible truth.

"Why was Charlie with Hamilton?" Alexander assumed. Bitterness crept into his voice. "The two met over a dice table. Hamilton was bitching about losing his membership to an exclusive nightclub, Charlie was complaining about his ex-wife's brother. They began to talk to one another, and eventually discovered a very loose mutual connection. Me."

I tried to comprehend what he was saying. Even though my thought process was clearer, I was still feeling a bit sluggish and I had to fight to keep up.

"I'm trying to connect the dots here, Alex. What does any of that have to do with me?"

He stood up and began to pace the room.

"How you got dragged into it is complicated. As it turns out, Hamilton was recently cut off from his trust fund. Apparently, his parents were tired of bailing him out of trouble. Sexual assault. Possession of cocaine. You name it, and he seemed to be into it. Charlie is a different matter. He's nothing but a gambling degenerate, but he was also piss broke. He knew his well had run dry with Justine and me. He had to come up with something more creative to increase his cash flow. Once he found out that Hamilton had a slew of computer hackers at his disposal, the solution to their money problems was simple. Or, at least they thought it was," he added acidly.

"What was their solution?"

"They came up with an artless plan to steal my phone, obtain bank information, and bleed me dry," he said with a sneer.

I thought back to the time I was dating Trevor, and about his circle of friends. They were always up to something or another on a computer, but I had dismissed them as just boys and their video games. I never thought they could possibly be doing something illegal.

"Did they?" I asked incredulously.

"Hell no. Little did the assholes know, I don't keep

anything like that on my mobile device. It was a bold move, and an extremely stupid one. They never would have gotten very far."

The memory of Alexander's phone being shoved into my face flashed in my mind.

"No. It wasn't just bank account numbers," I said and shook my head. "There was a video. Of us at Club O. It was on your phone."

"I know, angel. I'm so sorry for that. If only I could go back in time. If I had just deleted the damn thing..." he trailed off. He rubbed his temples, then looked to the ceiling. "If they were able to obtain the bank information they were looking for, they could have attempted to go through with their original plan. Since they didn't, Charlie got desperate. That's when he stumbled across the video in my inbox. They put together a last-minute change of plan, one poorly thought out, based on the assumption I would pay big to get the video back. That's where you come in. You were their insurance policy in the event I didn't."

Insurance policy.

I remembered Charlie and Trevor saying that while I was bouncing around in the trunk. I also remembered Charlie plotting my murder. Tears stung my eyes, burning until they began to fall.

"They were going to kill me, Alex," I sobbed.

"Shh, no. No, angel. It wouldn't have gotten to that point," he said and brushed away a tear from my cheek. "I would have found you. I was tracking your phone. That never would have happened."

I hiccupped through another sob, feeling annoyed that I was falling apart. I took a deep breath and looked at

Alexander. His face was twisted in pain and I knew he hated to see me this way. I had to stay strong, for him just as much as myself. But the sudden burst of tears had left me feeling incredibly drained. I wanted to go back to sleep, but I still had more questions that needed answering.

"Why was the video from Club O on your phone in the first place?" I asked.

"I had it because I was trying to find out who the man was who confronted you as we were leaving Club O. Once I found out it was Trevor, I began looking into his background. I never wanted him to hurt you again," Alexander said sadly. "He was there with Charlie the night of the charity gala, angel. I knew it and should have told you. I'm sorry I failed you. That I didn't protect you. I never should have let you out of my sight."

I knew there was more to it on that night.

"It's okay. You're here now," I said sleepily.

"Krystina, I have to ask. Why were you in that alley?"

"I was on my way to the library. I wanted to help you."

"With what?"

"Your parents. I wanted to see if I could find answers about your parents."

"Of course, that's what you were doing," he broke off in a garbled laugh. "Always so many questions, Miss Cole. Never satisfied until you have an answer."

My eyes burned from both tears and exhaustion. I wanted to desperately close them and I was starting to get a headache. My exhaustion was frustrating, as I had barely been awake for twenty minutes. But no matter how tired I was feeling, there was still one more thing I had to find out.

"Alex, tell me how this ends. Where are they now?"

"There was a car crash. Trevor was killed upon impact. Charlie is sitting in a cell as we speak."

A crash. He's dead. Trevor is dead.

"So, they didn't – Trevor didn't..." I sputtered, unable to speak the words. I picked up my head to glance down in the direction of my thighs.

Realization dawned on Alexander's face.

"No, angel! No! Nothing like that happened!"

Reassurance surged through my veins after hearing his words. They gave me a sweet and heady sort of feeling. The weight that had been pressing down on me lifted and I felt like could finally breathe again.

Nothing happened. I wasn't raped again.

My eyes welled once more with tears, but this time they were tears of relief. I looked to Alexander, the man who had sat by my bedside for weeks on end. For the first time in a long time, I was filled with hope for the future.

I'm okay. Everything will be okay.

"Thank you. Thank you for being here with me," I whispered.

"Oh, angel. There's no other place I'd rather be."

I closed my eyes and smiled when he decided to crawl into the bed beside me. We barely fit together in the narrow bed, but the warmth of his body was a welcoming comfort.

"Are you going to stay the night here with me?"

"Yes, angel. Just like I have for the past three weeks," he said. He positioned his arm under my head, tucked me in close, and planted a soft kiss on my cheek.

"Where do we go from here, Alex?"

"Oh, Miss Cole, we can go many places. But you need to

get better. Once I bust you out of this place, the first place you'll be going is home with me. As in, you're moving in."

Perhaps it was exhaustion taking over. Or perhaps I hit my head harder than I thought. But Alexander's words had a pleasant sort of appeal to them, as if moving in with him would set everything right in the world.

"I suppose I could do that," I murmured sleepily. "I'll need to pack my things."

He placed his hand to the side of my face and chuckled. I leaned in but didn't have the energy to open my eyes.

"Go to sleep, angel. I'll take care of everything."

Alexander

I LAY next to Krystina for a long while, just staring at her beautiful face. She looked peaceful, but I was still worried about her. When she spoke, she sounded incredibly weak, as if it took every ounce of her energy to just say a few words. It was difficult to hear her this way. She was normally so energetic and full of life. I missed her spunk.

She'll be okay. She just needs time. And care.

Care was one thing I was absolutely set on giving her. I would do everything within my power to make sure she was restored to her normal self once again.

Satisfied she was sound asleep, I carefully untangled myself from her limbs and climbed out of the bed. I had a call to make to Allyson, and it could go one of two ways. Either Allyson would agree with what I had to say, or she'd fight with me over it. But no matter what happened, I didn't want my conversation to disturb Krystina's rest.

I stepped out into the hallway and closed the door. Walking by the nurse's station, I ignored the ogling from the two young female interns and made my way to the waiting room.

I frowned when I saw the room was full of people. They all varied in age and appeared to be related. They were all arguing an opinion on the medical treatment of someone who I could only assume to be a fellow family member.

And they were loud.

So much for hushed hospital voices. This will never do.

Heading back to the nurse's station, I hoped someone there could point me to someplace quieter.

"Excuse me," I said to the woman behind the desk.

She looked up and all conversations around her stopped. She looked behind her, as if I wasn't the one addressing her, only to find the two interns staring wide-eyed at me. I fought the urge to roll my eyes.

The gawking from the interns was getting old. One would think they'd be used to seeing me here by now, as well as understand the fact I was quite unavailable.

The woman shifted her attention away from them and back to me.

"Um, ye – yes," she stammered and turned ten shades of red.

Christ, get it together woman.

I looked down at her nametag. It read Michelle Fogarty, RN Unit Coordinator. I hadn't seen her around before, and half wondered if she was new. She seemed to lack the air of authority needed for someone in her position.

"Michelle, I'm in need of a quiet place to make a telephone call," I informed her. "The waiting room is a bit too noisy."

"Oh, um. Of course," she said and scrambled to get up from her seat. I held up my hand to stop her.

"It's okay. You don't have to get up. Just point me in the right direction."

"The nurses lounge is empty," one of the female interns offered. She flashed me a toothy grin. "I would be more than happy to show you the way."

Intern number two made a strangled choking sound.

Unbelievable.

I ignored them both and kept my attention on the Unit Coordinator, who looked momentarily shocked at the brazenness of the intern who stood behind her. However, she covered it up quickly enough.

"Yes. The nurse's lounge will be fine for you to use, sir. It's just down the hall, third door on the left. And I'll make sure you are given privacy," she assured and turned to glare at the interns. They shrunk under her icy gaze.

Perhaps she's more capable than I thought.

I nodded my thanks and made my way down the hall. Grateful to find the lounge empty, I pulled out my cell and dialed Allyson.

"Alex, how is she?" she immediately asked upon answering.

"Good. Tired, but good."

"I was so happy when Matt called me!" she gushed with relief. "But he said we should give you some time alone with her. I've been anxiously waiting for you to give me the go ahead to come up."

"Krystina is sleeping now. She's only managed to stay awake for short periods of time, so there's no rush."

"Even if she's sleeping, I still want to see her. It is Thanksgiving after all," she added. "Did Matt give you the Thanksgiving dinner leftovers I packaged up for you?"

I frowned.

"He did, but I thought they were from his mother?"

"Oh, well..." she trailed off in hesitation. "They were technically from her. I just packaged them up after we finished eating."

Well, now isn't that interesting.

I noticed how often Allyson and Matteo had their heads together in whispered conversation, but I just assumed they were talking about either Krystina or me. Perhaps there was more to the furtive glances they tossed at one another.

"You're free to come up whenever you want, but I'm actually calling because I have a favor to ask of you," I told her.

"What is it?"

I was careful with the selection of my words. In the weeks I had spent in the hospital talking to Allyson, I learned about the bond she and Krystina shared. They had been inseparable for most of their lives. I had to handle Allyson carefully, so Krystina didn't have a reason to change her mind.

"You and I have discussed the care Krystina might need once she's released. I spoke to her about it and she's agreed to move in with me."

She was quiet on the other end of the line for a moment. When she spoke again, her tone was flat.

"I get the feeling she won't be staying with you for just a few weeks."

"No, Allyson. The move will be permanent."

"I'm surprised she agreed to it," she said somewhat testily.

"Don't be upset," I said calmly. "This would have happened eventually anyways."

"Maybe, but..." she paused and sighed. "Krys and I have always been together. It will be weird not having her around."

"You're not losing her as a friend. She'll only be a few miles away."

"But things will be different."

"Change isn't a bad thing. Think about her and think about who I am. You've gotten to know me pretty well over these past few weeks. In fact, you know me better than most now. You know I will be good to her."

"I do know that, which is why this is hard. You're not just another boyfriend, Alex. You're the real deal."

"I love her. This is as real as it gets," I said honestly.

"Have you told her yet?"

"Told her what?"

"That you love her," she clarified.

"Not yet, but I will. I'm heeding your advice. You once told me I would have to tread carefully on the stepping stones to Krystina's heart. That's exactly what I am doing."

"Elizabeth Long will be furious," she commented.

"I know she will be, but I'll handle her."

"Alright, then. You said you needed a favor. What do you need me to do?"

"This move has to go as smoothly as possible for

Krystina," I said adamantly. "I don't want her to be stressed about anything. I'll need you to pack up her personal belongings. Hale will be at your disposal to assist with anything you need."

"Packing is the easy part. It's the unpacking that is a royal pain in the rear," she pointed out.

"Very true," I acknowledged. "I'll take care of doing that. Just let me know when you have it all ready to go."

She agreed to do as I asked, albeit somewhat reluctantly, and I ended the call. I took a seat in one of the chairs and leaned forward to rest my chin on my fist. I contemplated all the boxes full of Krystina's belongings that would be arriving at the penthouse in just a few days' time. Between the books, CD's, and various trinkets highlighting Krystina's personality, I was having a hard time picturing her things in the lifeless space in which I lived.

Where should I put it all?

The spare bedroom I had would be ideal. Not much was in the room, other than basic furniture. I tried to picture Krystina's things in there, but it didn't feel right. I didn't want the essence of her to be confined to just one room. I wanted her to have more space and freedom to make it feel like her home.

I could leave everything packed and let her decide. Or maybe....

Another idea came to mind and suddenly everything was very clear.

That's it!

I pulled out my phone again and dialed Laura.

"Hello, sir," she greeted.

"Laura, where do things stand with the Westchester deal?"

"Everything it set, but with everything you've had going on, I've delayed the closing until further notice."

"Perfect. I need to change some things."

"Sir?"

"I need you to write down everything I say, then get with Stephen. He's going to try to argue about what I want him to do, so you'll need to reiterate I am resolute about this. He must make all the necessary modifications I am going to lay out for you."

"Yes, Mr. Stone. I have a pen and paper in front of me as we speak. I'm ready when you are," she told me.

I quickly outlined my plan. Laura probably thought I was out of my damn mind. Stephen would most likely rupture an artery over it. But it didn't matter.

I had never been more sure of anything else in my life.

30

Krystina

Two weeks later, I lay sprawled on Alexander's couch with him curled up behind me. I still viewed the couch as his, just like I saw everything else in the penthouse as his. He insisted I should view everything as 'ours', but it was a hard notion to grasp.

After my release from the hospital two days prior, I came here to find all of my clothes from my apartment in Greenwich had been brought over and hung neatly in his enormous walk-in closet. My toiletries and makeup lined the shelves of his bathroom and my books were added to his office library. I knew he did it all to make me feel more comfortable, but I was still struggling with the concept that this was now my new home. It was a surreal sort of feeling.

His housekeeper, Vivian, had just left. The idea that I had a housekeeper may very well be something I never get used to. She arrived daily to clean, do laundry, and bring groceries. Today's groceries included Christmas cookies from a local bakery, reminding me of the fact Christmas was just over two weeks away. I had nearly forgotten, as there wasn't one bit of holiday cheer to be seen in the penthouse.

"You're quiet. Are you feeling okay?" Alexander asked.

"I'm okay. Do you want to put on some Christmas music?"

"Sure, angel," he agreed. He reached over my head to grab the stereo remote from the end table. A moment later, a soulful a cappella by Pentatonix filled my ears. I smiled to myself, appreciating the soothing effect their breathy vocals had.

"Alex, I was just wondering. Why don't you have a Christmas tree?"

"Honestly, I've never had one. I didn't think about it," he said as he lazily twirled a piece of my hair around his finger. "Would you like to get a tree?"

"You've never had a Christmas tree?" I asked in complete astonishment.

"Not since I lived with my grandparents, no. Holidays have always just been another day to me," he shrugged off.

I sat up and turned to face him.

"Christmas is not just another day! We're not talking about some random Hallmark holiday here! I mean, you live in New York for crying out loud! How can you be immune to Christmas? It's my favorite time of year in this city. It's not just the decorations either. Everyone just seems a little bit nicer, a little bit kinder. It's magical!"

He laughed.

"Lay back down, angel. You're not supposed to be over exerting yourself."

"Oh, hell no. I'm perfectly fine. You are not going to use the 'you need your rest' excuse to get out of this one. First thing tomorrow, we are going to get a Christmas tree."

He held his hands up in surrender.

"Okay, okay! If it means that much to you, then that's what we'll do. But why wait? Let's go out tonight to get one. Maybe we can even walk around the city afterward and you can show me a bit of that magic," he joked.

I reached up and tousled his hair.

"You're teasing me."

"I would never," he said with a wicked smile. He lightly traced the line of my collarbone with his fingertip. I loved when we shared moments like this, and we had quite of few of them when I was in the hospital. The fun, flirty, and lighthearted exchanges gave me a glimpse into the future and what could be between us. My heart swelled.

I love him. I really do love him.

I fretted over how to tell him exactly that, unsure of how he would take to hearing those words. I needed to find the right setting. The right time and place. I wanted it to be special when I told him for the first time.

Rockefeller Center. Next to the Christmas tree. No. That might be too cliché.

"Are you serious about walking around the city tonight?" I asked.

"Maybe," he murmured and leaned in to nibble along the line of my jaw. "I could call Hale to pull the car up right now if you want."

His hand skimmed up my waist and brushed past the side of my breast. We were fully clothed, but even without the flesh on flesh contact, I was turned on in an instant.

Shivers raced down my spine and heat crashed between my legs. The immediate arousal was all consuming, as Alexander and I had not been together physically since before the car accident.

"We don't have to go right now," I breathed.

His hand moved down to slip under the waistband of my sweatpants, scorching a path over my skin. I sharply sucked in a gulp of air when he made gentle contact with my already moist folds. It had been too long since I last surrendered to his touch. I arched under him and moaned.

"Easy, angel," he warned. "I don't want you to push yourself."

I did as I was told and settled my hips back down on to the couch cushions. He was right. I shouldn't push it, as I was still feeling exhausted more often than not. But that didn't mean I didn't want this – that I didn't want him. To say it had been a rough month would be a gross understatement. I needed that physical connection with him, even if it was only a little, just so I could feel normal again.

"How do you want me, Alex? I need this," I pleaded. "I'll do whatever you want me to do."

"Oh, baby. You don't know how those words thrill me. So submissive," he said in a voice heavy with desire. "Just relax and let me do the work."

Slowly pushing my T-shirt up, he palmed the weight of my breasts and circled each nipple with the pads of his thumbs. I gasped when he latched on with his teeth, slowly suckling each one and coaxing them to an aching, straining peak. He worked me into a desperate frenzy before moving a hand back south.

His lips moved up to meld with mine. I kissed him

desperately, our tongues sliding deep, clashing, then tasting. My passion grew at a fevered pace, too quick after being so long without him. I needed to feel him, the other half of two souls that were on fire.

He worked his finger gently through my swollen flesh and teased my clit, his repeated flicking motions causing me to squirm. He pushed a finger in to the knuckle, flexing it against the heated walls just inside my entrance. My hands flew up to grip at his hair, the buildup to my orgasm coming swift and sweet.

"Oh, god," I moaned and began to convulse around his fingers. Our time apart worked against any sort of self-control I may have once had. I stiffened beneath his merciless hand and came quickly and unexpectedly.

My body took over and I went off like a rocket. Fireworks exploded before my eyes. I quivered around him as he gently worked me back down from the explosive release. And after so many weeks of being lost, I finally felt like I was home again. Where I belonged.

Alexander

I COULD SENSE Krystina's desire, her longing for more, as she squeezed my bicep and rode out the rest of her orgasm. My cock ached, as I wanted nothing more than to claim her hard and fast.

But not today.

No matter how long it had been, no matter how impatient I felt, she needed delicate handling. Today was not the day for dominance and submission. There would be no kinks, no exploration of limits. We had plenty of days ahead for that.

Fate, the fickle bitch, had finally decided to smile down on me. I had been given a second chance and I didn't want to fuck it up. Krystina was here, alive and well, and I'd be damned if I would allow Fate to get the last laugh.

Krystina purred beneath me as I slowly worked her pants down her legs. I left a trail of kisses down each thigh as I went, down her calves, ankles, and toes. I tossed her sweats to the side and stood to remove my own. After I shed my T-shirt, I moved back to the sofa. Positioning her ankle over one of my shoulders, I continued where I left off. She gripped at my hair as I made my way back up, provoking a fierce desire to surge through my veins.

My lips trailed up her body, over her hips and across her smooth stomach.

Perfection. She is nothing short of perfection. And she's mine.

I closed my eyes and inhaled the scent of her skin, needing her more and more with every breath I took.

She placed her hand on my chest and over my heart as I looked into her rich chocolate eyes. So expressive. So unguarded and exquisitely tender.

"Take me, Alex," she whispered. "I need you."

Her words almost broke me, and my heart began to hammer in my chest.

I took her hand in mine. I kissed each of her fingertips as she scissored her legs around my hips and pulled me closer. The weight of my cock pressed against her warm and velvety heat. Blood surged from the desperate need to possess her.

"Be still, angel. It's been a while and I don't want to come the minute I get inside you. I want us to come together."

Her eyes glowed sultry and provocative, but she nodded her consent and remained still as I slowly slid in. I pushed all the way to the hilt, instantly lost in her all-consuming heat.

Oh, fuck.

I watched as her eyes rolled and head tilted back in unabashed pleasure.

Yeah, baby. I feel it too.

It was as if I were feeling her for the first time, and I was overcome with complete and total bliss. Her tissues constricted around me to adjust to my girth, each pulse threatening to send me over the edge.

Not yet.

I began to move, slowly and deliberately, fighting with every shred of my being to hold on. To wait for her. She just felt so damn good.

I continued to drive into her, absorbing every sensation and savoring her every reaction. I loved that she was so responsive. I was so close, but I knew she wasn't there yet. Knowing what she needed, I changed the pace and increased my thrusts. I could only hope beyond hope she would get there soon.

I saw when she closed her eyes and her face reflected the pleasure that was imminent.

"Oh, Alex," she said in between panting breaths. "I missed you. I missed this. It's been too long."

Her words were enough to launch me over the edge.

"Angel, I hope you're there. I can't hold back much longer."

"I'm there. Come with me, Alex."

I withdrew once more, then pushed forward. Then again and again. Her fingernails raked down my back and I felt her stiffen beneath me. Our gazes locked and I hurled us both to the brink of ultimate pleasure.

At her shattered cry, my orgasm burst forth in an explosive surge that was both agony and ecstasy. I choked out a strangled cry, pouring myself inside her. It was a moment of earthshattering intensity, a perfect union of heart and mind.

I collapsed down on top of her, careful to balance my weight on my elbows so I didn't crush her. My cock twitched as she quivered around me, still giving up the last remnants of our release.

Once our breathing returned to a more normal rhythm, I reluctantly withdrew from the heated clutches of her body. She whimpered in protest.

"I'll be right back," I told her and kissed her softly on the lips.

"Where are you going?"

"Just to get a washcloth before we make a mess. I'm rather fond of this sofa and I don't think Vivian will take kindly to having to clean it," I said with a light laugh. There were some lines my housekeeper would simply not cross.

After retrieving the washcloth from the master bathroom, I returned to Krystina and began to wipe the evidence of our lovemaking from between her legs.

"I can do that," she protested and tried to sit up.

"Lay back down. Let me take care of you," I scolded. "How are you feeling?"

"I'm fine, Alex. You don't have to baby me. I'm not helpless you know."

I folded up the washcloth, placed it on the coffee table, and looked pointedly at her.

"I'm not babying you. I'm asking for a specific reason," I told her as I slipped back into my jeans.

"Oh? And what reason would that be?"

"Because I wasn't planning on this little impromptu reunion we just had. I'm not sure where your energy level is. If you're still up to it, I thought I would call Hale about taking us to get the Christmas tree you want."

She beamed instantly, her grin splitting from ear to ear.

"I'm definitely up for that! Then afterwards, we can do as you suggested and walk around the city. I can show you all of my favorite things. We should probably start at Bloomingdale's for all of the window displays first. Then maybe head over to Rockefeller Center. I know it will be crowded, but there's no avoiding that. Oh, and we should go to Little Italy to eat!"

I raised my eyebrows, startled by her zealous display of enthusiasm. I already had a plan in motion, none of which included any of the things she was saying. She was talking rapidly and making my head spin.

"Whoa, whoa! Easy tiger," I laughed. "One thing at a time. Remember, you can't overdo it. Let's just go get a tree first, then we can see what you feel up to doing afterwards."

She frowned.

"I'm just tired of sitting around and doing nothing," she complained. "All those weeks in the hospital, now here. I don't know. I feel restless."

"That's because you're starting to get your energy back.

Trust me when I say, nobody is happier to see that than I am. But you're still tiring easily. Remember the doctor's orders?" I reminded her.

"Yeah, I know. I know. Rest when I need to," she waved off.

"I know you're excited to get out, but let's see how much you can handle before we go full out on Christmas in the city," I said and reached down to take her hand. I pulled her up into a standing position, noting she no longer seemed to be embarrassed over being naked in front of me.

"You're right," she conceded.

"I know I'm right, angel. Now, go get dressed while I call Hale."

She made her way to the bedroom and I went to the foyer closet to see about winter gear. It was cold outside, the temperature just below freezing. I wanted to make sure Krystina had something suitable to help keep her warm, as I didn't know how long we would spend out of doors.

Pleased to find she had a down jacket and thermal gloves, I pulled a matching scarf and hat from the top shelf and brought everything to the dining room.

Once I had everything laid out, I took my phone from my pocket and dialed Hale. I was surprised to find my hand shaking slightly. Not overly so, but enough, and I had a hard time selecting the buttons for speed dial.

It was irritating. I was not the nervous type. But then again, so much hung on the balance of what I was about to do. I shook off the feeling of trepidation and made the call. Hale answered on the first ring.

"Bring the car around. It's time," I told him, emphasizing the last word.

"Time for what?" Krystina asked from behind me.

I spun around, surprised to see her there. She dressed quicker than I anticipated. Without saying another word to Hale, I hit end on the screen and pocketed the phone.

"Time to get a Christmas tree, of course. Come on, angel. Let's go for a ride."

31

Krystina

"Where are we going?" I asked Alexander. We had long since left the hustle and bustle of the city and were traveling northbound on the I-87.

"You said you wanted a Christmas tree, right?"

"Yes, but we don't have to drive to Timbuktu to get one. I'm sure there are plenty of places within the city where we could have gotten one."

"I'm sure there are," he said absently. "But there's a place in Westchester that has what I want."

I tried to picture us driving all the way home from Westchester with a Christmas tree strapped to the roof of the Porsche Cayenne. The idea was almost comical.

"Westchester? You really have no limits, do you? When you get an idea in your head..." I trailed off and shook my head.

Alexander didn't comment, but simply took my hand in

his and stared out the car window. He had been acting strange ever since we left the penthouse nearly thirty minutes ago. I couldn't figure it out, but he seemed uncharacteristically nervous.

Fifteen minutes later, Hale pulled the car over to the side of the road. I looked out the window, expecting to see a lot full of Christmas trees, but saw only a snow-covered hill. We appeared to be in the middle of nowhere, as the nearest lights I could see looked to be about a half mile away.

I looked to Alexander questioningly. He flashed me a devilish smile and shook his head.

"No questions, angel. Just come with me."

Hale came around to open the door for us.

"Everything is all set, sir," he told Alexander once we stepped out of the SUV. Then he turned to me and winked.

What the hell is going on?

I looked around for a clue but found nothing that would give me an inkling of knowledge.

Alexander took my hand once more and led me up the hill. Snow crunched under our feet as we walked the incline. After a few moments, I started to become short of breath. It wasn't that the hill was terribly steep; it was more due to my weeks of extremely limited physical activity.

I kept looking around, waiting to see a tree farm of some sorts come into view, but there wasn't anything ahead. Alexander had been so concerned about me not overexerting myself and I found it hard to believe he would have me walking all this way for nothing.

"How much further?" I asked, noting the increase in my heartbeat. I could see my breath in the cold night air, puffs coming out in rapid succession.

"Almost there. It's just up this way," he said and glanced down at me. "Are you okay?"

"I'm alright for now. But I will say, as soon as I get clearance, I'm getting back to the gym," I laughed in between pants.

Alexander stopped walking and, before I could process what was happening, he bent to scoop me up behind the knees. Cradling me in his arms, he pressed a kiss to my cold cheek.

"I don't want you to become worn out," he said with a wink.

"I won't argue, just as long as you watch your footing. The last thing we need is for both of us to go toppling down the hill," I said with a laugh.

"I've got you, angel. I've always got you."

He kissed me again, this time softly on the lips, before continuing the trek up the hill.

Once we reached the top, we came upon a lonely pine tree standing about twenty feet away.

"There it is," he announced proudly and set me back on my feet. I shook my head in bewilderment.

All this way for that?

I thought it was rather large for a family room Christmas tree. The sheer size of the tree would make it impossible to strap to the roof of the SUV. Not to mention the fact neither one of us had an ax or a saw to cut it down in the first place.

"This is the tree you want?" I asked, trying not to sound too judgmental. After all, Alexander told me he never bought a Christmas tree for himself before. His lack of experience was quite obvious.

"Stay here," he ordered instead of answering.

He left my side and walked over to the tree. Once he reached it, I saw him bend over and start fiddling with something, but I couldn't quite see what it was due to the darkness of the night.

A moment later, light temporarily blinded me. I blinked in surprise as thousands of lights lit up the tree. Red, green, yellow, and blue – each bulb casting its own magical twinkle. An angel was perched at the top, her golden halo reflecting far across the white snow-covered ground. I had never seen a more beautifully lit Christmas tree.

"Oh!" I gasped in awe.

"Come here, Krystina."

I slowly walked towards him, curious about what he might have up his sleeve next.

"Alex, what is all of this?"

"I have a confession to make. I lied when I said I didn't think about getting a Christmas tree. I knew you would want one."

"So, you decided on setting one up here? In the middle of nowhere rather than inside the penthouse?" I laughed.

"This isn't the middle of nowhere, Krystina. I put an offer on this piece of land a couple of months ago. The papers have been drawn up. The bank is just waiting on our signatures."

"Ours?"

"Yes, ours. I want to build a house on this land. Together with you."

What?!

I had barely gotten used to the idea of living with him at the penthouse, and now here he was proposing we build a home together.

"Alex, I –" I began to protest.

"No, hear me out," he interrupted. "The day you were in that car crash, I was there when they pulled you from the wreck."

"You were?"

"Yes. And when I saw you, I –," he stopped for a moment, his voice thick with emotion. "When I saw you, I thought the worst. I thought you were dead. It was as if my heart had been ripped from my chest. But when I found out you would be okay, everything became clear to me. Nothing matters now except you."

"Alex, so much has happened in such a short period of time," I said, shaking my head in disbelief.

"It has. We've stared hell right in the eye and survived it. Through it all, you've changed me in ways I never thought possible. Things haven't always been easy between us, and I know there are more obstacles still ahead. I can't erase the past. I still have issues with who and what I am. I worry every day that I'll turn out like my father. I won't deny that it's not a concern for me. I can't promise everything will always be perfect. But I can promise I will try. I believe in us, Krystina. And I know you do too."

He plucked one solitary ornament off the Christmas tree and placed it in my palm. I looked down at the silver ball in my hand. The top was adorned with a green satin bow, while its glittered surface swirled into the triskelion symbol.

"A triskelion," I observed aloud.

"Do you remember how I told you the symbol carried many meanings?"

"Yes."

"The Celtic belief is that everything happens in threes.

The triskele can be a representation of past, present, and future. Angel, you are my past because I feel like I've been searching my whole life to find you. You are my present because you are here with me now. You are my future because I can't envision anyone else by my side."

He reached for the ornament in my hand and untied the ribbon. The ornament split open to reveal a round cut diamond ring, featuring two shield-cut sapphires, nestled in a bed of green satin.

I gasped and felt like the ground had quite literally fallen out from beneath my feet. Nervous butterflies danced in my stomach as I stared down at the diamond in front of me.

"Oh my –"

He brought a finger to my lips to silence me.

"I love you, Krystina Cole. I ache when I'm not with you. I want you to be with me, always and forever. I want you to be my wife."

32

Krystina

His wife.

Alexander was a man who lived nearly his entire life in solitary, yet he was able to accept me into it so completely. I wanted us to be together in every way we could be. However, he was envisioning a life I was terrified to imagine. I had doubts about whether or not we were ready to take that plunge.

The rational part of me was airing on the side of caution. There were so many things we had yet to learn about each other. Too many unknowns. But at the same time, a lifetime with Alexander just *felt* right. It was if it was the way things were meant to be.

I stared down at the intricate design of the glittering diamond and sapphire ring. It was reflecting all the colors of the lights from the Christmas tree, a rainbow kaleidoscope that matched the emotions in my heart.

As I continued to stare, my vision became blurry from tears. I tried to blink them away and looked up into the night sky. The stars sparkled against the black, reminding me of what a wise Italian woman had said to me not so long ago.

"Your destiny is already written in the stars."

Hot tears continued to well until they spilled down my cheeks.

I looked back to Alexander. His gaze was fixed solidly on me, practically begging me with his eyes.

"I already warned you once," I reminded him. "I told you I'd be too much trouble for you."

"And I told you I wasn't any good for you."

"We are a nuclear combination."

"And baby, I can't wait to make fireworks," he said with that crooked smile I loved so much. To my astonishment, he got down on one knee, seeming oblivious to the frozen snow beneath him. "Say you'll marry me, angel. Say you'll share forever with me."

I gazed down into his beautiful sapphire blues, so vibrant and full of love, that I couldn't possibly mistake it for anything else.

Trust it. Trust him.

I took a deep breath to steady myself before speaking.

"Alexander, there are a million and one thoughts swirling in my head right now. You are controlling, arrogant, and assuming. Your bossiness drives me insane. You keep secrets and you hold things back. I am hot tempered and untrusting more often than not. I'm a pain in the ass. I question everything, and I probably always will. We both have demons in our pasts that have interfered with our ability to be content and happy. While I think we've made a bit of progress, we still have so much further to go," I paused for a moment and took another deep breath. "There are so many things that need to be worked out. You don't know who killed your father, and you still don't know if your mother is alive or not. The trial for Charlie Andrews is pending, and I know it means your carefully guarded life is about to be blown wide open. We have a rough road ahead of us."

"What are you saying?" he asked, his voice full of uncertainty. He looked so vulnerable there on his knees, and I knew it wouldn't be fair of me to make him wait any longer. I had been searching for the right moment to tell him I loved him, and I couldn't have picked a better time.

"I'm saying that I'm not going to listen to my head. For the first time in my life, I'm going to listen to my heart. I'm saying I want to work through our issues together. And I'm saying I love you, Alexander. I want the white picket fence. I want forever with you."

He stood up and grasped my shoulders. Pulling me tight against him, he began to rain kisses on my cheeks, forehead and nose. Tears leaked down my face as I fiercely clung to him. I was truly a blubbering mess.

"Oh, Krystina. I love you so damn much it hurts," he said, his voice raw with so much emotion.

I reached up to trace the lines of his face with my finger. His strong jaw, chiseled cheekbones, and flawlessly sculpted lips. He was perfection, and he was mine. All mine.

"I love you too. But I'm scared, Alex."

"Don't be afraid, angel."

"We have a lot of issues that can't be ignored. I think we should maybe consider counseling," I suggested tentatively.

"I've never been a big fan of shrinks, but I have to admit, I think we would both benefit from it. I need to work out the dreams I have. I don't ever want to be in a position where I may hurt you. So, if that's what it takes, that's what we'll do."

"One more thing. I would also like to get more involved with the Stone's Hope women's shelter. I had some time to think when I was in the hospital, and I think there are a lot of women who would benefit from hearing about my rape experience. I could help them – teach them they're not alone."

"Angel, I think that's a great idea," he said and pulled me closer to press a kiss to my forehead.

Snow began to fall around us in big white flakes that melted on our faces. I smiled and stuck out my tongue to catch one, just like I did during my childhood.

"Have you ever made a snow angel?" I asked impulsively.

"No," he laughed. "I can't say I have."

"I don't know, maybe it's the idea that I'm going to be Mrs. Alexander Stone, but I'm suddenly feeling incredibly silly. Humor me. Make a snow angel with me," I said and sat down on the ground.

"Right now? Together?" he asked incredulously. His sapphire eyes were bright with humor as he stared down at where I sat on the frozen earth.

"Yes," I said in all seriousness and tugged on his hand. "Together. Always together."

And I meant exactly that.

Together.

It wasn't that the unknown didn't scare me, or that I wasn't afraid of the future – I was terrified. But despite it all, somehow, I knew as long as Alexander was by my side, we would weather anything thrown our way.

Always together.

And as we lay down in the freshly fallen snow, I realized how right he was about the past, present, and the future. He was all of those things to me, and so much more.

To be continued...

SET IN STONE

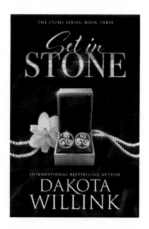

Thank you for reading *Stepping Stone*! Will Alexander solve the mystery of his parents? The heart-wrenching and seductive story of Alexander and Krystina continues with *Set In Stone*, the powerfully moving third book in *The Stone Series*.

One-click SET IN STONE now!

Two declarations of love, and a past that won't set them free...

Alexander

I had rules. Krystina broke them. That's just the way things were. But that didn't mean I didn't want to make her my wife. She exemplified the triskelion, representing my past, my present, and my future. Without her, I am nothing.

But then the past returns to rear its ugly head. As it turns out, I wasn't the only one with a secret. Everything I believed is nothing but a lie.

The strangling grip of chaos squeezes until I can't breathe. I don't know who I am anymore. The only thing I can do is go back to being the man I once was—to the only place where I once knew control.

Krystina

Alexander was the glue holding my shattered soul together. It should've been one of the happiest times in my life, but the darkness still looms.

I thought I knew the man I committed myself to, but more questions continue to arise. I don't know if Alexander is who he says he is. Everything we fought so hard to overcome is threatened in the blink of an eye. Now I'm faced with a terrible decision: go against Alexander to save him or sit idly by and watch as his world crumbles around him.

No matter my choice, it could destroy the very thing in which our relationship is built—trust.

If you loved the first two books in *The Stone Series*, check out a some of the other books in my catalogue!

The Sound of Silence

Meet Gianna and Derek in this an emotionally gripping, dark romantic thriller that is guaranteed to keep you on the edge of your seat! This book is not for the faint-hearted. Plus, Krystina Cole has a cameo appearance!

Fade Into You Series

What's your favorite trope? Second chance, secret baby, suspense, enemies to lovers, sports romance? *Untouched*, *Defined*, *Endurance* will give you all that and more! Prepare to be left breathless!

MUSIC PLAYLIST

Thank you to the musical talents who influenced and inspired *Stepping Stone*. Their creativity helped me bring Krystina and Alexander to life.

Listen on Spotify!

"The Gates" by Young Empires *(The Gates)*
"That's Life" by Frank Sinatra *(Nothing But The Best)*
"Unsteady" by X Ambassadors *(VHS)*
"Smoke and Mirrors" by Imagine Dragons *(Smoke + Mirrors)*
"Ex's & Oh's" by Elle King *(Love Stuff)*
"Still Breathing" by Green Day *(Revolution Radio)*
"Erotica" by Madonna *(Erotica)*
"You and I" by PVARIS *(White Noise)*
"Until We Go Down" by Ruelle *(Up in Flames)*
"Numb" by Linkin Park *(Meteora)*
Mozart: Symphony No. 41 'Jupiter' by London Philharmonic Orchestra & Alfred Scholz
(111 Classical Masterpieces)
"Alone" by Patricia Kaas *(Kabaret)*
"Dream a Little Dream of Me" by Ella Fitzgerald and Louis Armstrong
(Ella & Louis for Lovers)
"Fever" by Peggy Lee *(The Best of Peggy Lee)*
"Wicked Game" by Ursine Vulpine feat. Annaca *(Single)*

"Save You" by Turin Breaks *(Lost Property)*
"Hallelujah" by Pentatonix *(A Pentatonix Christmas)*

BOOKS & BOXED WINE CONFESSIONS

Want fun stuff and sneak peek excerpts from Dakota? Join Books & Boxed Wine Confessions and get the inside scoop! Fans in this interactive reader Facebook group are the first to know the latest news! JOIN HERE: https://www.facebook.com/groups/1635080436793794

OFFICIAL WEBSITE
www.dakotawillink.com

NEWSLETTER
Never miss a new release, update, or sale!
Subscribe to Dakota's newsletter!

SOCIALS

ABOUT THE AUTHOR

 Dakota Willink is an Award-Winning and International Bestselling Author. She loves writing about damaged heroes who fall in love with sassy and independent females. Her books are character-driven, emotional, and sexy, yet written with a flare that keeps them real. With a wide range of published books, a magazine publication, and the *Leave Me Breathless World* under her belt, Dakota's imagination is constantly spinning new ideas.

The Stone Series is Dakota's first published book series. It has been recognized for various awards, including the *Readers' Favorite* 2017 Gold Medal in Romance, and has since been translated into multiple languages internationally. The *Fade Into You* series (formally known as the *Cadence* duet) was a finalist in the *HEAR Now Festival Independent Audiobook Awards*. In addition, Dakota has written under the alternate pen name, Marie Christy. Under this name, she has written and published a children's book for charity titled, *And I Smile*. Also writing as Marie Christy, she was a contributor to the Blunder Woman Productions project, *Nevertheless We Persisted: Me Too*, a 2019 *Audie Award* Finalist and *Earphones Awards* Winner. This project inspired Dakota to write *The Sound of Silence*, a dark romantic suspense novel that tackles the realities of domestic abuse.

Dakota often says she survived her first publishing with coffee and wine. She's an unabashed *Star Wars* fanatic and still dreams of one day getting her letter from Hogwarts. She enjoys traveling and spending time with her husband, her two witty kids, and her spoiled rotten cavaliers. During the summer months, she can often be found taking pictures of random things or soaking up the sun on the Great Lakes with her family.

ACKNOWLEDGMENTS

This has been quite a journey. From the day I hit the scary "publish" button on Amazon for *Heart of Stone* up until now, I have learned and experienced so much. Most importantly, I learned how generous the network of independent authors is. While there are too many individuals to list by name, you know who you are. You are amazing and I am so proud to be a part of this community.

To *Readers' Favorite* – thank you for giving recognition to *Heart of Stone*. I am appreciative of the opportunities you have opened up for me and I hope to see you next year!

To my readers – you have made this experience so much fun! You remind me of the reasons for doing what I do each and every day. From Facebook comments to helping me pick out an outfit when I'm in a panic – I love our interactions! I look forward to many more in the future. You are priceless.

To my beta readers – Audra, Jenny, Katherine, Beckie, Sasha, Lori, and Amanda. I couldn't have done this without you. Your feedback on *Stepping Stone* was immeasurable and I will forever be grateful for your contributions.

And last, but never least, to my husband – thank you for allowing me to pursue my dream. I love you so very much.